I0612602

A SPOILER OF MEN

OTHER VALANCOURT BOOKS TITLES OF INTEREST:

By Richard Marsh

THE DATCHET DIAMONDS
THE JOSS: A REVERSION
PHILIP BENNION'S DEATH
THE SEEN AND THE UNSEEN
CURIOS: SOME STRANGE ADVENTURES OF TWO BACHELORS
BOTH SIDES OF THE VEIL
BETWEEN THE DARK AND THE DAYLIGHT *(forthcoming)*
THE GODDESS: A DEMON *(forthcoming)*

By Bram Stoker

THE SNAKE'S PASS
LADY ATHLYNE
THE MYSTERY OF THE SEA
MISS BETTY *(forthcoming)*
THE LADY OF THE SHROUD *(forthcoming)*

By Bertram Mitford

THE WEIRD OF DEADLY HOLLOW
RENSHAW FANNING'S QUEST
THE SIGN OF THE SPIDER
THE KING'S ASSEGAI
THE INDUNA'S WIFE
THE WHITE SHIELD

VALANCOURT CLASSICS

A SPOILER OF MEN

BY

RICHARD MARSH

AUTHOR OF "THE BEETLE: A MYSTERY," "THE JOSS: A REVERSION," "THE
SEEN AND THE UNSEEN," "BOTH SIDES OF THE VEIL," &C.

Edited with an introduction and notes by
Johan Höglund

𝕶𝖆𝖓𝖘𝖆𝖘 𝕮𝖎𝖙𝖞:
VALANCOURT BOOKS
2010

A Spoiler of Men by Richard Marsh
First published by Chatto & Windus in 1905
First Valancourt Books edition 2010

Introduction and notes © 2010 by Johan Höglund
This edition © 2010 by Valancourt Books

All rights reserved. The use of any part of this publication
reproduced, transmitted in any form or by any means, electronic,
mechanical, photocopying, recording, or otherwise, or stored in
a retrieval system, without prior written consent of the publisher,
constitutes an infringement of the copyright law.

ISBN 978-1-934555-07-1

Composition by James D. Jenkins
Published by Valancourt Books
Kansas City, Missouri
http://www.valancourtbooks.com

CONTENTS

INTRODUCTION

RICHARD MARSH made his literary fame with the publication of *The Beetle* in 1897 in the weekly magazine *Answers*. For the next couple of decades, this novel, wrongly assumed to be a palimpsest of *Dracula*, outsold Stoker's novel, and if it had not been for *Dracula*'s successful transition from literature to film, through F. W. Murnau's *Nosferatu: A Symphony of Horror* in 1922, Stoker's reputation as the grandfather of late-Victorian gothic might be disputed today.[1]

Since *The Beetle* is the only novel by Marsh that remained in print during the twentieth century, Marsh is routinely assumed to be primarily a gothic writer. However, while Marsh's gothic imagination did spawn some of the most interesting horror stories of the late nineteenth century, Marsh is as much a writer of crime and detective fiction as of gothic novels. In fact, his prolific and very regular production, averaging more than three novels per year, contains far more crime stories than gothic fiction.[2] Until recently, these stories have lived a secluded life, seeing the occasional reprint in anthologies of crime fiction, but receiving very little critical or scholarly attention. This is regrettable because Marsh's turn-of-the-century crime writing is some of the most interesting to come out of the period and it deserves, for many reasons, to be read alongside that of Conan Doyle, Agatha Christie, and Arthur Morrison. In particular, Marsh's early crime fiction fuses the strange and entertaining Victorian broodings of De Quincey, Wilkie Collins, and Dickens with the latent fears and

---

1 The filming of *The Beetle* predates the filming of *Dracula*, as the serialisation of *The Beetle* in the penny weekly *Answers* predates the publication of *Dracula* in 1897, but the film did not have the success of Murnau's version of *Dracula*, and today it appears to be lost.

2 Minna Vuohelainen, "Introduction" in Richard Marsh, *The Beetle*. Kansas City: Valancourt Books (2008).

desires of English fin-de-siècle culture as expressed by Doyle and Arthur Machen.

Fortunately, Marsh has begun to earn some of the attention he deserves both as a writer of gothic stories and of crime fiction. During the last few years, a number of Marsh's novels have been reprinted, and more are on their way. Furthermore, two scholarly editions of *The Beetle* have appeared, the most recent by Minna Vuohelainen, published by Valancourt Books. Vuohelainen is also the author of the very thorough doctoral thesis *The Popular Fiction of Richard Marsh: Literary Production, Genre, Audience* (2007). As the first full-length study of Marsh's writing and literary career, this is essential reading for anyone researching the more than 70 novels and innumerable short stories produced by the author. Before Vuohelainen, Marsh has been given consideration in works by Kelly Hurley, Rhys Garnett, and Roger Luckhurst.[1]

As the reader of Vuohelainen's dissertation soon discovers, there is little information to be had on the life of Richard Marsh. To all appearances, he lived a secluded life and left no letters, diaries or autobiographical writings behind. He also gave few interviews, and there are only a couple of photographs of his person. In fact, Richard Marsh was born Bernard Heldmann and it was under this name that he began his literary career. As Bernard Heldmann, he produced a series of morally uplifting adventure tales for boys under the tutelage of the prolific writer of juvenile literature for boys, George A. Henty.

William Baker has suggested that the change of names was due to Heldmann sounding too German in an increasingly xenophobic London while Richard Dalby has argued that there might have

---

1 Kelly Hurley, '"The Inner Chambers of All Nameless Sin": Richard Marsh's *The Beetle*', in *The Gothic Body: Sexuality, Materialism, and Degeneration at the Fin de Siècle* (Cambridge: Cambridge University Press, 1996), Rhys Garnett, "*Dracula* and *The Beetle*: Imperial and Sexual Guilt and Fear in Late Victorian Fantasy", in *Science Fiction Roots and Branches: Contemporary Critical Approaches*, edited by Rhys Garnett and R.J. Ellis (Houndmills: Macmillan, 1990); Roger Luckhurst, "Trance-Gothic, 1882-1897", in *Victorian Gothic: Literary and Cultural Manifestations in the Nineteenth Century*, edited by Ruth Robbins and Julian Wolfreys (Basingstoke: Palgrave, 2000), 148-167.

been a scandal of some sort in the background.[1] Both suggestions are, in fact, quite plausible, but the case may also have been that Marsh wanted to wrest himself free of the Heldmann literary heritage; the two gothic novels that mark Marsh/Heldmann's return to novel writing have little in common with the juvenile, often religious fiction of Heldmann. However, for the time being the actual reason for the change in names will remain a mystery that, perhaps, the new interest in Marsh can help resolve.

Popular anxieties

As a popular writer, Richard Marsh rarely strayed far from the topics of the day. With both the instincts and the training of a journalist, he incorporated many of the concerns of his period into his writing, even when dealing with gothic horror as in *The Beetle*. As Roger Luckhurst has argued in his lucid "Trance-Gothic", *The Beetle* can be perceived as an "exemplary tex[t] not so much of the gothic revival as the fin de siècle *itself*."[2] The novel's popularity can no doubt be attributed partly to Marsh's ability to, in the words of Vuohelainen, accurately gauge "the mood and tastes of the fin-de-siècle public".[3]

This is true also for *A Spoiler of Men*. Like *The Beetle*, it traces a number of contemporary concerns and issues. The end of the nineteenth century and the beginning of the twentieth are often described as periods racked by a series of crises concerning empire, politics, medicine, gender, and domestic reform.[4] Indeed, during the first years of the twentieth century, Britain's worldwide and seemingly indestructible empire suddenly appeared weak after the hard-won victory of the Boer War and the German willingness to compete for maritime supremacy. Meanwhile, political unrest

---

1 William Baker, "Introduction" in Richard Marsh, *The Beetle*, edited by William Baker (Stroud: Alan Sutton/University of Luton, 1994), pp. vii-x; Richard Dalby, "Richard Marsh: Novelist Extraordinaire" in *Book and Magazine Collector*, 163 (October 1997), 76-89.

2 Luckhurst, 11.

3 Vuohelainen, "Introduction" xi.

4 See, for example, Elaine Showalter's classic study *Sexual Anarchy: Gender and Culture at the Fin de Siècle*. (New York: Viking, 1990).

in Russia, increased organisation among the working classes in Britain, and occasional anarchist violence made the once so self-assured British Empire seem brittle as evidenced by a wealth of pamphlets and novels that described the imminent fall of the empire into the hands of the Socialists, the Germans, the Chinese or, as narrated by H. G. Wells in *War of the Worlds* (1898), the Martians.

To this came the pseudoscientific concerns of the Eugenicists. Inspired, rather than educated, by Darwin's evolutionary thesis, the Eugenicists feared that the absence of the struggle for survival in Britain and Western Europe was causing the Anglo Saxon "race" to degenerate. In fact, the rise of the "New Woman" was sometimes perceived as evidence that men had begun resigning their power to women, which provided additional proof that the Anglo Saxon had indeed degenerated to a lower stage on the evolutionary ladder.[1] Meanwhile, on the European continent the criminologist Cesare Lombroso—inspired by and inspiring early Eugenics—claimed that moral degeneracy in general and criminality in particular manifested itself in the form of crooked nooses, large jaws, long arms and fleshy lips so that latent criminality was revealed through a monstrous physiognomy.

To further add to the sense of turn-of-the-century unease, the view of the human being as essentially stable and in control, as long as he or she kept within the confines of his or her own class, was further challenged by early psychological theories launched by Freud and his associates. These theories suggested that the human mind might be far more complex, far more brutal, and far more susceptible to outside influence than was ever assumed by high Victorian medical and psychological science.

Indeed, this was a time when men could be spoilt in uncountable ways: through the allures of new forms of sexuality and alternative gender roles, through social, mental, and physical deterioration, through a host of apocalyptic and arguably perverse political theories and through the dismantling and dismemberment of the very Empire that the Victorian era had left as its legacy, an empire

---

1 See Donald Childs's *Modernism and Eugenics: Woolf, Eliot, Yeats and the Culture of Degeneration*. (Cambridge: Cambridge University Press, 2001), 2.

that until recently had seemed indestructible, fit to challenge both Greece and Rome by its presumed longevity.

As research into the period has shown, these fears were the concern of much fiction published at the turn of the century. For example, in William Le Queux's now largely forgotten but once immensely popular *The Invasion of 1910*, London is ground to dust under the boots of alien invaders while in Stoker's *Dracula* and in several of Conan Doyle's stories, an insidious, colonial presence infects the British capital, threatening collapse from the inside. Finally, in Rider Haggard's *She* (1887) a terribly powerful female presence threatens moral, sexual and political apocalypse.

A Spoiler of Men

Marsh's writing tracks the same currents as these classic novels, but does so in ways that are sometimes pleasingly different to the modern reader. Interestingly, Marsh's heroines are significantly stronger than most of the female characters created by his contemporaries. *A Spoiler of Men* is no exception to this and the powerful heroine who propels this novel forward is likely to baffle a modern audience as much as she confounds the villains she is set upon to destroy. Unhampered by Victorian societal rules, Marsh's heroine is active, cunning, scheming, and remarkably strong, physically as well as mentally. Unlike the hero of the novel, she possesses the ability to understand the criminal mind with which she is confronted.

Furthermore, while *The Beetle* is arguably Marsh's most successful attempt at frightening his late-Victorian readers by tapping into the undercurrents of imperial anxiety, sexual deviance, class differences, and medical confusion, *A Spoiler of Men* also manages to explore a number of late-Victorian concerns through its story of greed, hypnosis, and drug-induced mind control. First published in 1905, the novel is a thoroughly entertaining combination of the literary styles and concerns of fin-de-siècle culture, fusing the gothic landscape and sinister ambiance of Victorian London as explored by Doyle and Stoker with the nefarious wit of Oscar Wilde. The novel takes the reader on a journey through the geography of late-Victorian London, from fashionable Chelsea and Hyde Park to the slums lining the docks in Lambeth. It would seem that Marsh knew the class anatomy of the city very well, and while avoiding the realist descriptions of squalor and decay of writers such as Thomas Hardy and George Gissing, the reader is left with the sense that Marsh knew the poor sections of London as well as he knew the well-to-do. The trip through the various classes of London society is further complemented by a journey comprising the far reaches of the British Empire and to a Germany that smells distinctly of the alchemical substances first encountered in Mary Shelley's *Frankenstein*.

The centre of attention is the sinister and unscrupulous Jack the Chemist and his helper, the wicked and pathologically tall hypnotist Professor Fentiman. As the reader soon discovers, Marsh likes his villains and generally gives them much more room than most of his fellow crime writers who were, as a rule, more interested in charting the detective's hunt for and ultimate capture of the criminal. The two villains of *A Spoiler of Men* share two traits: They pursue their selfish goals with a determination so fierce that it appears to be innate, and they further their causes with the help of different mind-controlling techniques. In this way, the novel aligns itself with a number of gothic narratives from this period that also explore the notion of mind control and the pliability of the human consciousness. Thus, in the novel, the minds of the central characters are controlled through both mesmeric practices and early psychopharmacological drugs, making them either the unwitting tools of the mesmeriser or turning them into what can in fact be described as the first example of the zombie character in English fiction.

Animal Magnetism

Hypnosis, mesmerism, or animal magnetism, as it was also referred to, was a much debated and often highly controversial issue during the late nineteenth and early twentieth centuries. It acquired one of its names from Franz Anton Mesmer in the late eighteenth century. Mesmer was convinced that he had discovered a force as real and as invisible as that of regular or mineral magnetism. He speculated that the universe was alive with a universal fluid and that this fluid also permeated the human body. The role of the magnetiser was to ensure that this fluid moved unobstructed through the body, and his treatment of his patient involved inducing various hypnotic states that would allow him to control the fluid.[1] While Mesmer appears to have had some success in treating various ailments at the time, he was unable to acquire either funding or legitimacy for his practice and it remained a pseudoscience during the first half of the nineteenth century. It was not until the 1840s that it slowly began to acquire a limited scientific legitimacy. This transformation can largely be attributed to the Scottish physician James Braid who re-theorised the phenomenon of mesmeric magnetism into that of hypnosis, arguing that the mesmeric sleep was a perfectly natural psychophysiological occurrence. The rationalization of mesmerism was continued by the French neurologists Jean-Martin Charcot and Hippolyte Berheim. Although championing different views of how hypnotism should be understood and employed in the service of medicine, both contributed to the changed status of the practice and both also influenced the most important of all early twentieth century hypnotists: Sigmund Freud.

As hypnosis became more widely accepted by the medical establishment, it began to receive a much wider popularity and became associated with a number of other late-Victorian practices such as spiritualism and occultism. In late-Victorian society, mesmerism, hypnotism, and spiritualism were often performed publicly before an interested, sometimes sceptical, but generally paying audience. When practiced as entertainment or when connected with occultism and spiritualism, the practice often retained both the name mesmerism and the supernatural dimension ascribed to it by Anton Mesmer. As the practice spread, there was also a concern that mesmerism could be used for things other than entertainment or medical treatment. In an anonymous article entitled "Unconscious Consciousness", published in the popular weekly *All the Year Round* in 1892, the possible dangers

---

1 See David Edwards and Michael Jacobs, *Conscious and Unconscious: The Latent, the Disowned, the Dissociated and the Unknown.* (Maidenhead: Open University Press, 2003), 23.

of the practice are discussed at great length. According to the French school of mesmerism, the author argues, the free will of "a hypnotic subject . . . can be so obliterated that the most moral may become vitiated, and the most high-minded perverted, under the influence of the magnetiser". To an early nineteenth century audience, then, the possibility that a man (or, even more likely, a woman) might be stripped of his or her faculties, to become the helpless pawn of a more powerful and sinister mind, was no doubt both frightening and perfectly plausible, and in A Spoiler of Men Marsh explores this anxiety in ways that are both terrifying and entertaining.

Furthermore, the separation of the conscious from the unconscious through hypnosis also had a decidedly gendered aspect at the time. When hypnosis acquired status as a medical practice, this happened in conjunction with the exploration and treatment of the supposedly most female of maladies: hysteria. As Elaine Showalter and David Trotter both observe, psychoanalysis began with hysteria.[1] Charcot used hypnosis most famously to induce a state of hysteria in his (primarily female) patients. Similarly, Charcot's disciple Freud also hypnotised women in order to explore how women responded to, primarily, the cultural pressures of late-nineteenth century middle class society. Thus, hysteria, perceived as a predominantly female affliction, became intimately tied to hypnosis, and all over Europe (self-proclaimed) physicians attempted to regain control of the hysterical female through this practice. Interestingly, precisely what hysteria was remained largely unaccounted for, allowing this affliction to be associated with a number of different behaviours and imprecise ailments, from mild depression to neurasthenia. Interestingly, hysteria was often tied to the appearance and political programme of the New Woman so that an increasingly pressurized and self-conscious patriarchy was perfectly happy to diagnose the endeavour by the New Women establish a less unjust society as essentially hysteric.[2] Thus, their desire for political, economic and

---

1 Showalter 40-41; David Trotter, The English Novel in History 1895-1920, (London: Routledge, 1993), 140.
2 Showalter, 40.

sexual equality could be construed as a pathology that required medical treatment (preferably in the form of hypnosis) rather than serious consideration.

Not surprisingly, fin de siècle literature features a number of confused, sometimes dangerous, and often sleepwalking women, sometimes under the charge of a powerful male hypnotiser. Apart from Marsh's own novels, the most obvious examples are Stoker's *Dracula* where the count bites and infects only women, turning them into hysterical somnambulists suspended between life and death, and George du Maurier's *Trilby*, where the Jewish hypnotist Svengali masters the mind and body of the beautiful Trilby O'Ferrall. Interestingly, and to Marsh's credit perhaps, the hypnotist of *The Beetle* is a hermaphroditic Egyptian sorceress/ sorcerer who is as happy to mesmerise men as he/she is to take advantage of women.

The zombie

A Spoiler of Men explores mind control not only from the perspective of hypnotism, but also from the point of view of modern and ancient chemistry. As the reader soon discovers, poison is used to induce a state of absolute, passionless obedience in a number of characters, forcing the victims to do the bidding of the novel's sinister villain. That chemical substances may have the ability to transform the mind and the body of the Victorian subject had been dramatised by several writers of the period already, most notably perhaps in Stevenson's *Strange Case of Dr Jekyll and Mr Hyde* (1886) and in Stoker's *Dracula* which both describe how respectable and trustworthy men and women lose self-control and succumb to the base desires and uncontrollable appetites of their unconscious that lurk underneath their reliable veneers. In the case of *Dr. Jekyll and Mr. Hyde*, the separation of the personality is, of course, induced by drugs and it is fair to assume that Marsh was, to some extent, inspired by this successful novel. Similarly, the infectious bite of Dracula also creates an insatiable individual, willing to feed on the blood of small children. In *A Spoiler of Men*, however, the dangerous characters remain fully conscious, fuelled by personal ambition and a moral decrepitude rather than by drugs or the tainted blood of the undead. In *A Spoiler of Men*, drugs instead induce different states of pliability, producing an essentially harmless and perfectly controllable personality; as is the case in many Marsh novels, the villain needs no pharmaceutical or supernatural encouragement to commit his heinous crimes.

In this way, *A Spoiler of Men* is different from its more illustrious predecessors. This does not suggest that Marsh invented the notion of mind-controlling or life-arresting poisons by himself. Marsh often (mis)quotes Shakespeare in his novels, and it may safely be presumed that he was familiar with Shakespeare's *Romeo and Juliet* in which Juliet drinks a mixture which gives her the "borrow'd likeness of shrunk death".[1] In addition to this literary inspiration, the late nineteenth century saw the publication of C. J. S. Thompson's often reprinted *Poison Romance and Poison Mystery* (1899) which discusses love potions as well as the use of poisoned rings, both of which are featured in *A Spoiler of Men*.[2] Thompson expanded his first edition in 1902 and 1904 and added modern poisoning cases, including one taking place in Lambeth in 1891-92.

In addition to this, a few years before *A Spoiler of Men* was published, Imperial Britain had recently been shocked by Hesketh Prichard's *Where Black Rules White: A Journey Across and About Hayti* (1900). This widely popular travelogue predictably describes the recently formed Haitian republic as a nation characterised by political chaos, physical ruin, cannibalism, and pagan worship. For the British, as for most European nations at the time, the idea of black self-rule was frightening in many respects and the idea that a black population might rule over white people seemed, even if disregarding the rumours of cannibalism, positively gothic to many, a fact to which contemporary reviews of the book testify.

From the perspective of *A Spoiler of Men*, the most interesting aspect of the book is, however, its description of Voodoo or "Vaudoux" as it is termed in *Where Black Rules White*. Prichard devotes an entire chapter to this phenomenon and gives particular

---

1 William Shakespeare, *Romeo and Juliet*, (IV. i. 105).

2 C. J. S. Thompson, *Poison Romance and Poison Mystery*, (London: Scientific Press, 1899).

attention to the "Papaloi" or the Voodoo priest (more commonly referred to as Houngan today) and their use of poison to frighten and control the Haitian population. According to Prichard, this "Borgia in poisons"[1] is able not only to induce terrible pains or death, he can also "produce a sleep that is death's twin brother", so that the human body can be buried, dug up and then "brought to consciousness".[2] This state of arrested life no doubt made both strange and terrible sense to the contemporary audience already familiar with the concept through both Shakespeare and Stoker.

More importantly, Prichard's account is perhaps the first description of the zombie figure in English writing. While Prichard never uses this particular word, the reference to this phenomenon is clear. Furthermore, there is no suggestion in either Prichard or Marsh that this re-awakened body should be in any way aggressive. In fact, the image of the zombie as a violent and flesh-eating creature was not widely popularized until 1968 with Romero's *Night of the Living Dead*. Before this, the zombie was perceived as a frightening but pitiful creature often forced to do the bidding of some form of master, as seen in the 1933 film *White Zombie*. Here, members of the Haitian population and a couple of young Americans are turned into zombies with the help of a potion delivered by the local witch doctor. These zombies become the hapless slaves of the doctor in question.

While there is no evidence that Marsh was familiar with Prichard's book, or with the zombie figure in general, it is interesting to view *A Spoiler of Men* from this perspective. Whether based on Haitian mythology or not, Marsh's novel portrays the transformation, through the use of drugs, of normal human beings into soulless zombies, forced to ceaselessly do the bidding of their master. In this way it may be argued that *A Spoiler of Men* does, in fact, feature that first instance of the zombie character in British fiction.

To the avid reader of either the Victorian gothic or the crime genre, this may be reason enough to pick up the novel. However, it is certainly not the only reason. In tracing so many of the late

1 Prichard, 101.
2 Ibid., 93.

nineteenth century concerns and anxieties, in exploring a number of contemporary social strata and in taking the audience on a ride through a London as brightly lit and as darkly sinister as ever found in a novel by Doyle, the novel will reward its reader with a better understanding of late-Victorian life in the metropolis. In addition to this, the novel truly deserves the much worn epithet of roller-coaster ride for its blend of horror, crime, and humour, making it a novel in which, as a contemporary reviewer observes, Marsh "has brought into play his customary constructive talent and florid imagination, the result being a tale that is pre-eminently readable."

JOHAN HÖGLUND

March 10, 2009

ABOUT THE EDITOR

JOHAN HÖGLUND is Senior Lecturer in English Literature at Linnaeus University in Sweden. He holds degrees from Brown University and Uppsala University and his doctoral thesis *Mobilizing the Novel: The Literature of Imperialism and the First World War* (1997) concerns the invasion novel popular in Britain during the late nineteenth and early twentieth centuries. His research interests today comprise both the late-Victorian novel and more modern imperialist narratives produced primarily in the United States after 9/11. He has published extensively on the relationship between imperialism and popular culture in its various forms, most recently "Le gaming néo-colonial: géographie virtuelle et politique de l'espace dans *Call of Duty 4*" in the French journal *POLI: Politique de l'Image*. He is currently working on a study that discusses the relationship between Richard Marsh's novels *Mrs. Musgrave – And Her Husband*, *The Beetle* and *The Joss* and the notion that criminality is at the same time inherent and physically apparent on the body, as suggested by the influential criminologist Cesare Lombroso during the late-nineteenth century.

A SPOILER OF MEN

CHAPTER I

THE LADY

As Mr. Cyril Wentworth opened the door of his flat and stepped into the little hall on the other side, he paused. It was past midnight. He had not been home since the morning. There was no one else upon the premises; everything requisite was done for him by his laundress, who left shortly after breakfast for the day. He expected, therefore, to find everything in darkness. The flat consisted of five rooms: kitchen, bedroom, bath-room, living-room, and a tiny, nondescript apartment which he called his study. In front of him, as he entered, was the door of his living-room. That it did not fit quite closely was shown by the fact that a pencil of light gleamed along the bottom.

"Who the deuce is in there?" asked Mr. Wentworth of himself, since this pencil of light suggested that some one was. "And how have they got in? If it's Fentiman, and he has got a pass-key which admits him to my chambers——"

He did not finish his unspoken sentence. With quick steps he crossed the little hall. Gripping the handle, he flung the door wide open; he strode forward—to pause with a sensation of even greater surprise than he had felt at first. Whatever—whoever—he had expected to find within he alone could tell; certainly his expectations were not realized.

The room was of fair size, being the only good room the flat contained. It was well furnished, as was befitting in the case of a man of means and taste. Against the wall, on the further side, was a handsome writing-table. At this table sat a lady—a young lady, a well-dressed young lady. She wore no hat. An evening cloak, thrown open in front, only partially covered a costume which suggested either a ball or the opera. She looked as if she had just alighted from her carriage; yet Cyril Wentworth had noticed no vehicle in the street without.

So entirely at home did she appear to be, that she did not even look up from the paper she was examining as he came in. On his part, Mr. Wentworth was so taken by surprise that for some moments he was speechless. He stared at as much of her as could be seen from the back, in order to ascertain who his visitor might be, she all the time calmly continuing her occupation. When he decided that, so far as he was able to judge, she was a stranger, his surprise increased.

"Who are you?" he demanded. "And to what am I indebted for the pleasure of your presence here?"

As he spoke, the lady turned coolly, leisurely, as if it were really too much trouble to pay any attention to him at all. In her left hand she held a pair of long white gloves, which she began to draw through the fingers of her right hand. She regarded him with a mixture of amusement and indifference, her eyes seeming only half open, her lips parted by a smile, as if he were some impertinent intruder, in whom she felt but a languid curiosity. But she answered nothing.

Her beauty, her air of tranquillity, almost of contempt, her silence, puzzled the owner of the flat. He hinted at a possible solution of what, under the circumstances, seemed to be the mystery of her easy bearing.

"I fancy, madam, that you have made some mistake."

She smiled openly. She flicked her right hand with the fingers of her gloves softly, looking at him with something in her eyes and on her face which did not suggest appreciation. There was a perceptible interval before she spoke; then it was with a gentle, lazy drawl, which was rather insolent than friendly.

"Oh dear, no. It is not I who have made a mistake; it is you."

He stared at her still more keenly, feeling that there must be some clue to her manner if he could only find it.

"How can that be, since these rooms are mine, the hour is late, you are here uninvited, and I have not the pleasure of your acquaintance?"

"I know who you are; for me that is enough."

"Who am I?"

"You are the person who was once known as Jack the Chemist."

Wentworth started. The premonition which he had when opening the door that something disagreeable was close at hand had a fair chance to be realized. He was a great believer in his own premonitions. On the other hand, in a life such as he had lived, and still was living, there were so many opportunities for the disagreeable that it did not require much foresight to perceive one coming. But this was a disagreeable of a distinctly unexpected— five minutes ago he would have said of an impossible—kind. The period during which he had been known as Jack the Chemist was so long ago, the scene on which Jack the Chemist had figured so far distant, the circumstances were so peculiar, that for years he had taken it for granted that if there still were two or three persons living who were aware of the fact that he once had borne that cognomen, they were negligible quantities. That this lovely stranger should let that ill-omened nickname drop from her pretty lips with so matter-of-fact an air, had on him the effect of a shell fired from a gun whose very existence he had never suspected.

He stared at her for a second or two, open-eyed and open-mouthed. Then his muscles stiffened, his fists involuntarily clenched themselves, his breath came quicker. That this woman should know him by that name meant danger. When he was conscious that there was danger to be faced, he was always ready. He still held the door open in his hand. Now he closed it. He eyed her steadily, searching her features for some clue which would tell him who she was, and found none. Yet he prided himself on his memory for faces; and surely this was a woman who once seen could never be forgotten. Before he put to her another question he had almost convinced himself that he had never seen her before; certainly not—not where he had been known as Jack the Chemist.

"Who are you?"

"I am The Unknown. Every line on your face shows that."

"Why did you call me by that name?"

"To make it sufficiently clear that although you don't know me I do know you."

"How did you get in here?"

"Through the door. It has a keyhole. Nothing could be simpler."

"You mean that you have committed burglary?" A slight movement which she made with her gloves might signify anything; it was her only answer. He put to her another question. "What do you want now that you are here?"

Again there was that little movement with her gloves. She seemed to be considering. She almost entirely closed her eyes; presently partly re-opening them, as if it were too great a labour to open them wide.

"Now I don't know that I want anything. I've seen—and done—everything I want; at least, I think so."

"What do you mean by saying that you've seen and done everything you want?"

Once more she moved her gloves, as if she intended by the gesture to call his attention to the condition of the room.

"I came, Mr.—I understand that, at present, you call yourself Cyril Wentworth; quite a euphonious name——"

"My name is Cyril Wentworth."

"Precisely, for the moment; though I do not think that you will care to deny—to me—that you have had others. Shall I remind you of some of them?"

"Tell me why you came here?"

"I came to examine your papers, particularly your more private papers, in search of certain information of which I stood in need; and—I have obtained it."

Throughout he had been conscious that the apartment was in a state of disorder; now he realized to what a degree the disorder went. Every drawer in the writing-table stood wide open; the contents had apparently been turned out anyhow upon the floor. Almost at her feet was a box whose presence he recognized with a sensation which was distinctly the reverse of pleasant. In it he kept not only certain memoranda, which had for him a peculiar interest, but also other articles which possessed not only an esoteric interest, but also a very obvious value—jewels which were worth large sums of money had he cared—or dared—to sell them. He perceived that some of them were lying on the table at her side. He strode towards her with a feeling that at last he had something tangible with which to deal. He pointed to the jewels.

"So it is a case of common theft!"

"Do you wish me to believe that you think I intended to steal them, as you did?" The arrow went so near the mark that he actually quivered. "You know better. The story they tell to you, and have told to others, is not so comfortable a one that I should wish them to tell it to me. Besides, there are certain details about these trifles which make them dangerous things to steal, especially supposing ignorance in the thief. For instance, this pretty lady's ring, with the pretty opal, that unlucky stone. Was ever a prettier opal seen? or was ever a sillier superstition?* And yet I fancy that the lady who would wear this opal would find there is something in the superstition now and then. Was there never a lady who wore this ring once, and once for all, and since then has never worn another? Think, Jack the Chemist."

He snatched the ring out of the speaker's hand.

"What devil has sent you here?"

"The devil who walks always at your heels, and who, one day, will trip you up, for ever."

Bending down, he leant towards her. Although only a few inches divided them, not a muscle of her face quivered, nor did she make the least attempt to avoid his scrutiny.

"Have I ever seen you before?"

"Have you?"

Such a light blazed in his eyes that the wonder was it did not scorch her cheeks.

"Don't you think that you can play the fool with me because you're a woman and pretty."

"Women have learnt that to their cost before to-night; haven't they, Jack the Chemist?"

It seemed for a moment as if Mr. Wentworth's feelings would find vent in language of a vigorous kind. But he was a man who was accustomed to keep himself in hand. The look of anger was exchanged for a smile; not altogether an agreeable smile, but still a smile. He spoke in a tone which was almost unpleasantly suave.

"Might I ask you, as a favour, not to address me by that name.

How you come to be aware that certain persons once associated me with that nickname, I do not know; but—it is long ago, and here in England I am known only by my own name, Cyril Wentworth."

She returned his smile with interest; hers was a pleasanter smile than his was.

"You see, to me you will always be known as Jack the Chemist."

"Why?"

"Because!"

"Tell me who you are; why you have favoured me with this unceremonious visit; by what right you have been searching among my papers."

"I shall tell you nothing, nothing."

"Won't you? Do you imagine that I shall allow you to leave this room—a free woman—unless you give me a satisfactory explanation? And you pretend to know something of my character."

"It is because I know your character—and history—well that I say I shall go when and how I please."

She made as if to rise. He laid the fingers of his right hand on her bare shoulder.

"Sit still."

"Remove your hand." Instead of complying with her request he increased the pressure. With a quick movement she slipped away from under his hand and rose to her feet. "Do you imagine that I will suffer you to touch me—you?" She drew her cloak closer about her with what might have been a little shiver of repulsion.

"If necessary I shall do a great deal more than touch you. One does not use ceremony with burglars, whether male or female."

"I am going, Jack the Chemist."

Turning her back upon him she seemed to be about to suit the action to the word. Springing forward, he once more confronted her.

"If you try that I'll tie you to a chair while I fetch a constable, and he shall deal with you."

She smiled in his face.

"A constable! You talk of constables? There'll come a day, and it's not far distant, when every constable in England will be looking for you. I promise you they shall not look in vain. Stand aside, Jack the Chemist. I have found what I came for. Now I am going."

For answer he stepped towards her, and she fell back, whipping out a revolver from underneath her cloak, which she pointed directly at him. He recognized it as one which he kept in a drawer in the writing-table.

"You have even stolen my revolver, and you have the audacity to threaten me with my own gun."

"If you attempt to touch me, or to intercept my passage, I shall fire. Be well advised. I have no fear of what will follow."

Neither, apparently, had he. She scarcely ceased to speak when, springing forward, he gripped the wrist which held the revolver. As he did so a bell sounded; some one was ringing at the outer door. The sound appeared to take him by surprise. He turned with a start, and gave a jerk to the girl's wrist which fired the revolver. There was a report; an exclamation like a drawn-out "Oh-h-h!" The girl was lying on the floor at his feet, while by some accident, which was beyond his comprehension, the weapon itself was in his hand.

CHAPTER II

PROFESSOR FENTIMAN

For the second time there was a ring at the outer door; this time a continuous ringing, as if the ringer had but a limited stock of patience. He frowned as he listened.

"I suppose that's Fentiman, at this moment of all moments. Confound the man!" He leant over the prostrate girl. "What's the matter? Has the bullet grazed you anywhere? Are you hurt?"

She was still, uncomfortably still. He did not like the huddled-up way in which she was lying, the look which was upon her face. He had seen before that night people who had been killed by pistol-shots. He touched her. She showed no sign of resentment, as she surely would have done had she been conscious of his touch. He drew her cloak aside, looking for some sign of a wound. The bullet was of such small calibre that, at that range, it was quite possible for it to kill, and yet leave, to superficial observation, no mark upon the clothing. It was obvious that she did not breathe. He watched eagerly for some trace of pulsation. There was none. She lay motionless, lifeless. And all the while the bell at the outer door kept ringing. Accustomed though he was to delicate situations, here was one which puzzled him.

"What on earth am I to do? I can't show her to Fentiman. He'd want all sorts of explanations, which I can't give, and which he wouldn't understand—or believe—if I did. Damn that bell!"

It was, perhaps, the persistent ringing of the bell which compelled him to a sudden resolution. Lifting the girl bodily, he bore her through the adjoining study into the sleeping-room beyond, where he placed her on his own bed. The way in which she had lain, as if fibreless, boneless, sapless, in his arms, had been pregnant with eloquence to him. Shutting the bedroom door, he left her there alone.

Crossing the miniature hall, he opened to the ringer, addressing him in tones of remonstrance—

"Why do you keep on ringing in that ridiculous way? You might have guessed that I was engaged, and have given me time to come to you."

The remonstrance was scarcely well received. The gentleman without—it was a gentleman—crossed his arms upon his breast and glared. He replied in a voice which was more raised than it need have been.

"I may be your bravo,* Mr. Wentworth, but I am not your slave, to hang upon your pleasure. When I condescend to ring at your door I expect it—instantly—to be opened."

Mr. Wentworth glanced at the speaker. Without another word he ushered him into the sitting-room. When he was in he spoke to him again.

"You've been drinking, Fentiman."

The accusation seemed in no way to abash the stranger. In his right hand he carried a malacca cane. He brought the ferrule sharply against the floor, extending, at the same time, his left arm at right angles to his body, as if it were a semaphore.

"Yes, sir, I have been drinking; I am glad to say it. I have arrived at that condition in which I frequently find that drink—strong drink—is the thing most to be desired. When I have been drinking, I defy my conscience; when I have not been drinking, my conscience defies me, and I suffer. Yes, sir, I suffer."

This was a singular looking person. Mr. Wentworth was tall, but Mr. Fentiman was taller, probably six feet three or four. Though his shoulders were broad, his person was thin almost to the point of emaciation. His face, which was long, thin, and cadaverous, was rendered remarkable by the size of his mouth and eyes. Not only was his mouth of unusual size, but the lips were thick and protrusive enough to be negroid. His eyes were huge—great black orbs set in a sea of white.* They had that peculiar quality of distention which a cat has. At one moment you would be struck by the fact that they were all white, with but the speck of a pupil in the centre. Then, suddenly, the pupil would begin to enlarge, the iris would appear, and the two together would increase and expand until, practically, there was no white left. A very uncanny effect the performance of that trick had upon the spectator who saw it for the first time. Indeed, there were persons—and they, probably, were in the majority—who never could look at Mr. Fentiman's eyes with comfort. Nor was the eerie sensation with which they inspired many beholders lessened by the fact that, to a large extent, the changes seemed involuntary. So soon as he became excited, his eyes, as if afflicted by a sort of St. Vitus' dance,* seemed to grow larger and smaller, distend and decrease, as if in some weird physical sympathy with their owner's moods.

There were individuals who would have gone a very long way to avoid meeting Mr. Fentiman's eyes; but, plainly, Mr. Wentworth was not one of them. He stood a little in front of his visitor, not only returning him glance for glance, but coolly searching his countenance with his own shrewd grey ones, as he had searched a woman's face a few minutes before.

"If you persist in using strong drink to enable you, as you put it, to defy your conscience, you'll soon lose your power; that will be one result among others."

"My power? Which power? You speak as if I had only one."

"So you have, worth anything; and that is not what it was."

"Isn't it? No, you are right; it isn't. It is greater than it ever was. Sometimes its greatness startles even me. One day I may be able to prove how great it is upon your own vile body."

Mr. Wentworth laughed.

"You've tried your hand at that already, and you've failed."

"That's because the conditions were not favourable. Let the conditions suit me, as one day they may, and it's possible that you will become as wax in my hands. What have you been firing at?"

Mr. Wentworth had moved towards the fireplace. As the other's question gave a sudden twist to the conversation, he turned to the speaker with something very like a start.

"Firing at? What do you mean?"

"What I say. As I stood outside I heard the report of a revolver."

"What nonsense are you talking?"

"My good Mr. Wentworth, do you imagine that you can hoodwink me as you try to hoodwink all the world? Do you take me for an utter fool? I know the sound of a revolver as well as any man, and I tell you one was fired; and here, possibly, is the very weapon." Stooping, he picked up off the floor what, in plain truth, was the actual weapon. In the first shock of his surprise it had probably fallen from Mr. Wentworth's startled hand, unnoticed. Some papers had partially covered it. He had carried the girl's body into the other room, and had then gone to open to his visitor, oblivious of its presence on the floor. Mr. Fentiman turned it over in his huge hand. "One chamber discharged; I should say this was the weapon."

Mr. Wentworth, as always, was ready.

"It went off in my hand."

"In your hand?"

"In mine; whose else's?"

"Haven't you had a visitor?"

"I only came in just before you arrived; I brought no one with me, I assure you."

Mr. Fentiman was glancing round the room.

"It looks as if you had had a visitor, and one who had been taking liberties. You would hardly throw your own property about the room like this, unless you were in a very curious frame of mind, and you seem to be sane, or leave those pretty baubles lying upon the table there. What are they? I have a constitutional fondness for pretty things."

Mr. Fentiman moved towards the table, only to be anticipated by the other, who unceremoniously bundled into a drawer the jewels which still lay on it. His tone was dry.

"I believe, Fentiman, that you have come here on certain business; if you don't mind, we'll stick to it. How goes it with your brother professor, my reverend uncle, the scholarly Dr. Hurle?"

Mr. Fentiman was a second or two before he answered. He looked at the place where the jewels had been, at the revolver he was holding, at the papers littered about the room.

"Was I approaching a disagreeable subject? Is there a mystery about the firing of this revolver? about your visitor? about all this, you man of mystery?"

Mr. Wentworth replied to the inquiry with another.

"I was asking you about my uncle. Professor Fentiman, when did you last see Professor Hurle?"

Mr. Fentiman looked at the speaker as if to make sure of his mood. With a distortion of his thick lips, which was, perhaps, intended for a smile, he tossed the revolver on to the writing-table.

"That was a dangerous thing to do," commented Mr. Wentworth. "You might have discharged another barrel."

"Was that how you discharged the first?"

Mr. Wentworth only smiled.

"I ask you, for the third time, when did you see my uncle last?"

This time Mr. Fentiman condescended to give the required information.

"This afternoon."

"With what success?"

"With every success—every possible success. Professor Fentiman found in Professor Hurle, as usual, an ideal subject."

"You put him under influence?"

"At once, with the greatest ease."

"To what extent?"

"That should answer your question better than any words of mine."

Mr. Fentiman took from an inner pocket of his coat some printed papers, which he passed to Wentworth, who glanced at them with an apparently non-understanding eye.

"What are these?"

"They are a sufficient demonstration, if one were needed, that my power is greater than it ever was, and an illustration of the various uses to which it may be applied."

"No doubt. I asked you what they are."

"They are the Greek papers which are to be given to the candidates for honours in the forthcoming examination for 'Greats.'"

"Do you mean that they are examination papers?"

"They are. And there are young gentlemen at present in residence at the university who would give a good round sum for a sight of them. Worth money, those papers are."

"Nice brutes the young gentlemen you refer to must be; and it's a pretty fine compliment you pay to the university!"

"You don't imagine that it is men of ripe years like you who monopolize the taste for dirty tricks. Some young folks like them, too. I shouldn't be surprised if you yourself began quite early."

"That tongue of yours, Fentiman, has got you into trouble before to-day; it will again. All men are not so patient as I am. How did these papers come into your possession?"

"Quite simply; simplicity always marks the artist. I was aware that Professor Hurle was to be the examiner in Greek. I asked him if the papers were ready; he said they were. I invited him to give me a set, and he did."

"Under influence?"

"Of course."

"Then he must be madder even than I thought."

"I doubt if he is mad; indeed, I am sure he is not. But I admit that he is eccentric."

"Or he would not know you?"

"Precisely; or, to put it more correctly, I should not be on those terms with him which I at present am. Professor Hurle's little eccentricities are known to the whole wide world, particularly his partiality for dabbling in what he calls the occult sciences. Occult! Bear evidence to how occult they really are, you witnesses from the unseen." Professor Fentiman held out his hands and hunched his shoulders as if in the enjoyment of some private joke. "For instance, in his time he has studied spiritualism, esoteric Buddhism, Christian science, telepathic transmission of thought—I have heard him, with much enjoyment, tell how, seated in his college rooms, he once, for days together, endeavoured to place himself in telepathic communication with a gentleman of similar mind who happened, at the moment, to be in Melbourne University.

The experiment, I fear, was something of a failure—and now, since his researches in all these faiths have been crowned with but little satisfaction, he is devoting his attention, almost as a last resource, to certain abstruse sides of that great mystery of mind transference which is commonly known as hypnotism."

"Poor devil!"

"I should not describe him myself as exactly a wise man, in spite of his scholarship."

"But that he should have put himself in your hands—you of all men!—and at your mercy!"

"We have one thing in common—we're both of us professors."

"Yes! You are a professor of the three-card trick; he is, at least, an honest man."

"Is it to address to me remarks of that kind that you have brought me here at this hour of the night, or, rather, morning? Or do you yourself wish to pose as an honest man?"

"Not I; I have no wish to pose as anything. Only I have had rather a worried day."

"And a troubled night; witness the discharged revolver."

Mr. Wentworth went on unheeding. "And the consequence is I'm tired, and your platitudinous hypocrisies stick a little in my gorge. Come, to business, Fentiman. Do you think you can do it?"

"Do what? Explain exactly what it is you wish me to do. So far you've dropped more or less vague hints; but this is a matter in which no loophole ought to be left for misunderstanding."

"I'll be plain enough. I want you to get from him a will—in proper form, and properly witnessed—in which he leaves to me absolutely everything of which he dies possessed. If what you have told me is true, you ought to be able to get such a document from him while he is under influence."

"Nothing can be simpler. Only—what I want to know is—where do I come in?"

"Hand me such a will, and I will hand you a discharge in full—as full as you can possibly desire—for you know what."

"Together with certain papers?"

"Together with certain papers; but with this proviso, that when you have once got from him that will you are never to go near him again."

"Being afraid that, having got one will out of him for you, I might get another for myself?"

"Never mind of what I am afraid. That condition will be attached to the discharge; if it is broken, it will render it invalid."

For the first time Professor Fentiman removed the wide-brimmed felt hat he had been wearing. He placed it and his malacca cane on a small chair, and himself in an easy chair. Leaning back, he clasped his huge hands in front of him, extending his long legs to their fullest length. Ensconced in that position of vantage, keeping his strange eyes fixed upon his host, he spent some moments in what seemed private cogitation, presently delivering himself of what possibly were the fruits of his thought.

"Your terms will suit me; on them I have no comment to make; only—I don't understand what it is you're at, or what it is you think you're at, and in delicate matters of this sort I do like to understand my principal. I doubt even if you understand yourself what you are at. Don't speak; let me first explain, then your turn will come. I take it that you're aware that, as matters stand at present, everything your uncle has is left by will to his niece—your cousin—Miss Mason."

"I know—Letty, white-faced cat. She's as cold-blooded as a fish, infernal little prig."

"Is she? All that? Your uncle appears to hold a higher opinion of her than you do."

"My uncle? Go on; what are you driving at? Only let me warn you in advance to be careful how you interfere with what is not your business."

"Thanks very much for the warning; that sort of thing is always friendly; one does like to know when to be careful. As you evidently are well aware, everything is left to Miss Mason; but what I wonder if you are aware of is this, that your uncle has nothing to leave."

"What do you mean by nothing?"

"Practically nothing. I happen to know, my dear Mr. Wentworth, that you are a much richer man than you wish the world to think. I know your weaknesses, that they are many; but I believe that the love of money is the greatest of them all. You have carts-full of money hidden away, out of which you get no enjoyment of any sort or kind. Your uncle has nothing compared to what you have; and even with your love of money you'll account what he has as nothing. The income which he derives from his college and university—such as it is; it is not a very large one, anyhow—dies with him. Beyond that his possessions consist of certain articles which he esteems valuable, but which a dealer would consider worthless. When his estate has been administered, I doubt if there will be a thousand pounds for any one. What is that to you? Yet you are going to give me much more than the equivalent of that sum for a document which will be worth—to any one—very little more than the paper on which it is written."

"How did you come to know all that?"

"When the erudite Professor Hurle is under influence he tells me everything—everything!"

"Poor devil!"

"You have said that already; but I don't see how, in this particular case, it applies. No harm comes to him from acquainting me with certain facts. What I should like to know is, are you as well posted in the state of affairs as I am?"

"I prefer, Fentiman, not to discuss my uncle's affairs with you. He evidently gives himself sufficiently away without any assistance from me. Have the goodness to procure for me the document I have prescribed, and, in return, I will do as I have said."

"Then it is as I—thought."

"What do you mean by it's as you thought?"

"It's of no consequence. If you wish to keep your own counsel I will keep mine." Mr. Fentiman ascended out of the armchair, by instalments, as it were. "I think, Mr. Wentworth, that I can get for you the document which you require by to-morrow about this time."

"So soon?"

"I know of nothing which is to be gained by delay. Professor Hurle is very amenable just now, and I have again an appointment with him to-morrow afternoon. You have no idea what extremely interesting interviews I have with him. So, if I bring you the document about this time to-morrow, you will have the discharge ready for me?"

"I will."

"Then, Mr. Wentworth, in the words of the song, I think I will say au revoir, but not good-bye."

"Let me show you out."

Mr. Wentworth escorted his guest to the entrance. Just as his host was about to shut the outer door after him, something occurred to the professor.

"By the way, those examination papers; where are they? You didn't give me them back."

Mr. Wentworth reflected. "Didn't I? What did I do with them? I fancy I put them on the mantel."

They returned to look for them. If he had put them on the mantel they were not there then. But, he admitted, he might have laid them down anywhere. On the subject of what he had done with them his mind was practically a blank. He remembered having them in his hands, but he had been so engrossed in conversation that what had become of them afterwards he had not a notion. Professor Fentiman's ideas were equally vague. Apparently, unnoticed by either men, the examination papers had slipped on to the floor, and had become confused with the litter which reigned there. They rummaged among the confusion in search of them. But that litter consisted of documents which Mr. Wentworth was particularly anxious to keep private. He quickly perceived that the professor was inclined to show more interest in some of these than in the objects of their search. So he cut the hunt short.

"That'll do, Fentiman; put those down. What you're looking at has nothing to do with those things you stole. I shall be putting the place to rights directly you have gone, then I shall be sure to light on them; they've only hidden themselves away for the moment. I'll either send them on to you, or I'll give them you when you come to-morrow. Anyhow, they'll be safe with me. I'm not likely to make an improper use of them."

The professor regarded him a little curiously.

"I don't suppose you are; yet it's odd what has become of them. Still, I'll chance it. I take it that you're not going up for the examination yourself, and that you have no dear friend, for whom you would like to do a good turn, who is."

"You're right, I haven't."

"Then give me them when I come to-morrow."

On that understanding the two men parted, Mr. Wentworth again ushering his visitor off the premises. The instant he was gone, and the door was shut behind him, he came rushing back into the room, all eagerness, where before he had feigned indifference.

"What has become of those examination papers? I'll swear I put them on the mantel, just here." He touched the spot with his hand. "I have not the faintest doubt about it; I remember it distinctly. I even believe I noticed them there when I left the room with Fentiman; I am almost sure I did. They must have vanished during the minute in which I was seeing him off. If so, I wonder——"

As rapidly as he had entered the room he left it, crossing the study towards his bedroom. When he reached it he stood in the doorway and stared. The bed was empty. The dead woman whom he had left on it had vanished. He searched for her in every possible corner; in a good many impossible ones as well. There was not a trace of her to be seen.

CHAPTER III

ON THE STAIRCASE

TAKING it all in all, St. Clement's is probably the pleasantest college in the university of Camford.* Every man esteems his own college as the best, or ought to; but it is not improbable that to St. Clement's would be awarded the palm by an impartial observer. It is very old. Every college ought to begin with two centuries of history; there are many more than two centuries behind St. Clement's. It has architectural features which, hallowed as they are by the passage of the uncounted years, are not despicable. It is not too large, nor too small, but of a most reasonable size. It has a pleasant quad, and an ancient and most beautiful walled-in garden. The garden is, perhaps, the greatest of its glories. The rooms which look out on it are much to be desired. They are not many, but for the most part, as regards size and convenience of arrangement, they are good rooms in themselves; and then to have, as near friend and neighbour, that exquisite pleasaunce, the heritage of long generations of sainted gardeners!

As was befitting, the finest set was in the occupation of a famous scholar—a scholar so famous, that his mere presence within those time-worn walls lent to the college an added lustre. All the world knows—that part of it which knows about such things—that Professor Hammond Hurle was one of the greatest Greek scholars living. There was only one other man who could at all compare with him, and he was a German; and they were both so erudite that it was difficult even for an expert to distinguish between the merits of two men who, from the point of view of scholarship, were as much alike as Tweedledum and Tweedledee. Professor Hurle spoke in Greek and wrote in Greek, and was even supposed to think in Greek; which, in some respects, was a pity, because had he devoted a little more attention to the world in which Greek is not, he might have been a wiser man. It is an unfortunate truth that scholarship does not necessarily go with wisdom. In the case of Professor Hurle this axiom was illustrated to an almost painful degree. Where Greek was concerned he was regarded as a nearly infallible authority; where everything else was concerned he was looked upon by only too many persons as a simple-minded and extremely foolish old gentleman.

On the day after our introduction to a professor of quite another sort, the point of view of the undergraduates of his own college was demonstrated in a somewhat striking fashion. The professor in question—Professor Fentiman—was ascending the stone steps which led to Dr. Hurle's rooms on the first floor. He had been a pretty frequent visitor to St. Clement's of late, and his constant presence within the college precincts was regarded by the undergraduates by no means with favour. There was a certain young gentleman, Dick Sharratt, who claimed to have encountered the professor in another place, under circumstances which were scarcely to his credit. The first time he encountered the professor he said nothing—to him; but when the professor returned again and again, and seemed likely to continue to return, Dick Sharratt took advantage of an opportunity which offered to recall to his mind certain occurrences which he would probably rather have forgotten.

Dick happened to be returning from the river—he was No. 3 in the 'Varsity boat. Two other men from the boat were with him—the stroke, Miles, and Gifford, who was bow. Dick roomed immediately above Dr. Hurle. Professor Fentiman reached the foot of the staircase just as Dick and his friends were about to ascend. At sight of him Dick stopped dead.

"You're the chap who gave what you called an 'Exposition of the Marvels of Hypnotism' at the Oldfield County Hall, and who got chucked out when the whole thing was shown to be false, and who was only saved by the police from being thrown into the river."

The manner and matter of Dick's address were so unceremonious and so unexpected, that it was not strange that Professor Fentiman not only started and stared, but, for the moment, was without words with which to answer. Dick placed a somewhat unfair interpretation on what, under the circumstances, was the professor's not inexcusable silence.

"I don't wonder that you turn green at the thought. Cæsar's ghost, how you did pelt down the High Street! Until you reached the friendly shelter of a copper's arms, I don't think I ever saw a chap sprint like it. I only wanted you to understand that there's some one in the place who knows you. That's all."

With sublime insolence Dick strode past the professor as if he was not there, and, followed by his two friends, went up the stairs. It was not until the trio were already some distance up that the professor awoke to a full realization of the young gentleman's impertinence; and then—he said nothing. There had been many occasions in the course of his chequered career on which he had found that silence was golden; he decided, on the spur of the moment, that this was another. He went his way, if not in peace, then in silence; while Dick—with his friends—went his.

The incident had occurred some time ago. Since then, although Dick had had various distant glimpses of the professor, they had never actually met, possibly owing to the professor's generalship— he was used to taking precautions—until the afternoon on which, as has been said, Professor Fentiman was ascending the stone steps which led to Dr. Hurle's rooms. As it happened, Dick Sharratt, with a friend, was just then coming down. The staircase was a winding one; so narrow that one person had to draw close to one side to let another pass. Professor Fentiman was already half-way up to the first floor when he heard footsteps descending from above. He was well aware that Sharratt was the name of the young person who had treated him with such incredible insolence, and that his quarters were immediately over those of his venerable friend; it was therefore at least possible that the footsteps which he heard descending were those of that ill-bred young man. He desired nothing less than an encounter. Rather than run the risk of one he would have willingly retreated—had he been able to think of a place to which to retreat. On the other hand, if he was quick he ought to gain the sanctuary of Dr. Hurle's rooms before the other had reached the first floor; so he began to mount three steps with one hasty stride. But he did not bargain for the really disreputable fashion which Dick Sharratt had of descending his own staircase— when disposed. He used to declare himself ready to accept a wager to any amount that he would get down it quicker than any other man of his acquaintance. No one was ever so foolish as to engage with him in so desperate a contest. While Professor Fentiman supposed himself to be doing well in mounting three steps at a time, Dick Sharratt thought nothing of coming down half a dozen at a single bound, and at a rate which was as dangerous as it was undignified. The consequence was that just as the professor but needed to take another stride to find himself in safety, it was only by a miracle of dexterity that Dick kept himself from dashing into him.

Dick drew back with an apology on his lips, which was only half formed when he perceived who it was he had almost cannoned into. That apology never attained to complete formation. Instead of drawing further back Dick came forward, in such a way that it was impossible for the professor to pass. The professor, always prudent, drew himself against the wall so as to enable Dick to pass him. But Dick evinced no desire to take advantage of his courtesy. On the contrary, planting himself in the middle of the step, so that there was practically no room on either side of him, he addressed the other with distinct incivility.

"So it's you, you blackguard, is it! What do you mean by coming up this staircase when I am coming down?"

Considering how peculiar the question was, Mr. Fentiman's reply was almost unnaturally mild.

"I was not aware that it was your private property."

This proved not to be a case of the soft answer which turns away wrath. Dick's manners were worse than ever.

"Don't speak to me, you brute! And don't flatter yourself that we don't know what games you are up to with the Early-bird." The "Early-bird" was one of the nicknames by which Professor Hurle was known to the young gentlemen of his college and to others. "We've got an eye on you, and we're going to keep an eye on you, and if you're not jolly careful it'll soon be another case of sprinting down the street if you wish to keep yourself from getting wet. Do you hear what I say?"

"I'm not deaf, Mr. Sharratt."

"Don't talk to me, I tell you. Take yourself down to the bottom of these steps so that I can come down them."

"There is plenty of room for you to pass; or, if you will move a little back, in two seconds you shall have the entire staircase to yourself."

"Do you think that I'll pass you, or that I'll make way for you? Look here, Mr. Professor Fentiman—which I hear is what you call yourself, though I rather fancy 'Mr. Area Sneak' is your proper name—if you don't take yourself down to the bottom of these steps in half a brace of shakes, I'll pitch you down. Now, quick! Which is it to be?"

Professor Fentiman said nothing. Answering never a word, he turned right about face, and descended to the foot of the staircase, so that the arrogant Dick Sharratt and his friend might have the sole and exclusive use of it. It was not exactly that the professor was a coward; he had courage enough, of a kind, when nothing else but courage would serve. He was certainly not physically afraid of either Dick Sharratt or his friend. It is extremely possible that if Dick had endeavoured to put his threat into execution he might have found himself engaged in a task which was beyond his powers. The professor gave way simply because long and varied experience had taught him that it was frequently better to accede to unreasonable and even monstrous demands rather than attract an undue amount of public attention to himself and his proceedings by refusing to comply. Dick Sharratt and his friend came down and passed, the professor withdrawing himself into a corner of the outer hall to allow them to do so. As they went Dick said something else to the professor which was scarcely civil. When they had gone, Professor Fentiman reascended the stone steps, and knocked at the door of Dr. Hurle's quarters as calmly as if no disagreeable little incident had occurred to ruffle his tranquillity.

CHAPTER IV

THE TWO PROFESSORS

THE door was opened by a grey-headed individual, who regarded the professor with what were hardly glances of affection. But it was an axiom with Mr. Fentiman always, if the thing was even remotely possible, to take it for granted that every one everywhere was glad to see him. He smiled—the odd expression on his countenance was intended for a smile—as if the grey-headed man was smiling at him.

"Well, Tompkins, always bright and brisk? I can't think how you manage to do it. Do you know that you look younger every time I see you? I believe you've dropped a couple of years since I saw you yesterday. You'll be a boy in no time if you go on at this rate. Is the professor in? But, of course he's in; as he has no doubt told you—I believe he tells you everything—I've an appointment with him. See here, Tompkins, I want you to do me a little service." Mr. Fentiman held out a coin; Tompkins held out his hand, not as if he wished to hold it out, but as if it constrained him to hold it out. His fingers closed upon the coin. "There's a sovereign for you. I want you to leave me alone with the professor for a little while."

"You always want me to do that."

"Quite true, quite true! You see, Tompkins, the professor and I are engaged in some little experiments together which, for complete success, require uninterrupted privacy."

"I know, silly old fool! If I was him, I'd as soon trust myself alone with an adder in the room as I would with you."

"Now that's unkind, Tompkins—unkind. What I particularly want you to do this afternoon is not only to ensure our privacy, but not to go too far off—say, no farther off than the porter's lodge.

Then, if you can find a friend, you might beguile half an hour or so with him in conversation; at the end of which time it is possible that I, or rather the professor, may require your services and your friend's, in which case I am sure that he will see that both of you are adequately rewarded."

"I am not afraid of not being adequately rewarded by the professor for anything I may do for him, thank you, Mr. Fentiman. And as it happens, I don't ever go farther off than the porter's lodge while you're in here; I've always a sort of feeling that there's no telling when I may be wanted. Shall I tell him you are here, or will you tell him yourself."

"I'm obliged to you, Tompkins, I'll tell him myself."

Tompkins went down the stairs, and Mr. Fentiman passed into the professor's rooms, drawing the door to behind him as he did so, and turning the key gently, as if he desired the operation to be as little noticed as possible.

As it happened, Dr. Hurle was not in the outer room. It was a pleasant apartment, long and fairly lofty. Four large windows looked out upon the college garden. When Mr. Fentiman came in they were all wide open to admit the fresh air and the sunshine, and the voices of the birds, and the rustling of the breeze among the trees. The first thing he did was to close them; one could never tell who might be listening, or what might be overheard. The window frames were leaded. In the centre of each frame, in stained glass, were the college arms; the sun shining through them sometimes threw long splashes of many colours almost from wall to wall. Three sides of the room were lined with books, some of them so old as to be nearly the first products of the printing press. There were two doors, beside the one through which Mr. Fentiman had entered. The one at the end led into the professor's bed and dressing rooms; the other, at the side, almost fronting one of the windows, opened into a smaller chamber which, as Mr. Fentiman was aware, was used as a sort of lumber-room for the professor's superfluous books and papers. Beyond this was the scout's room, where, under Tompkins' guardianship, were kept the professor's private store of provisions and other things. The furniture was good, and old, and solid; the college crest was on the backs of most of the chairs; indeed, the college crest seemed everywhere.

There were no less than three tables. Judging from the papers which strewed it, on which apparently some one had recently been engaged, the large one in the centre was the one which was most in use. Mr. Fentiman, moving to it, picked up paper after paper, quickly glancing at each one to see what it was. He had just put one down when the door at the end opened, and the tenant of the rooms came in.

The impression which Dr. Hurle conveyed to every one who saw him first was that he was a very little man. There were those who insinuated that if he had not been physically so small a man, he would never have become so great a scholar. As young gentlemen of the type of Mr. Sharratt put it, he had always been such a "mere atom" that there was never anything for him to do but "swot." His size, or, rather, want of it, shut him out from the ordinary amusements of the undergraduate; it was hardly likely that he could ever have been any real good at games. Since he had probably never scaled seven stone in his life, the position for which he was fitted was cox;* but rumour had it that nothing could ever induce him to go on to the water of his own free will. He was afraid of it. He had been a bookworm all his life. He had spent all his days in trying to imbue himself with the very spirit of ancient Greece; the side of Greece, that is, which had nothing to do with out-of-door life, the stadium, the arena. He had never known what it was to have, in any wide sense of the word, intercourse with his fellows. He knew nothing of women. He had never even travelled. With all his interest in Greece he had never dreamt of going there. It was credibly reported that for nearly forty years he had never journeyed more than ten miles from St. Clement's College, with the exception of a short annual visit which he made to London, during which practically the whole of his time was spent in the British Museum. The consequence was that, although he was more than seventy years of age, in all matters outside his particular line of study he was a mere infant in swaddling clothes; immeasurably younger, for instance, than Dick Sharratt overhead.

The contrast between the two professors was striking. The one so huge, so coarse, so brutal; the other so minute, so delicate, so emasculate. Dr. Hurle was more like a large doll than an ordinary man; and though he looked his age, there was that about him which was irresistibly suggestive of a child—a physically finely-fashioned child, whose growth had been prematurely arrested. Even his head was small, and was without a hair on it. His obviously short-sighted eyes were protected by unusually large steel-rimmed spectacles. He was carelessly dressed in a suit of dark grey tweed, which had seen much wear and was not particularly well fitting. As he came across the room he held one hand out in front of him, as a blind man might have done who feels his way. He walked badly, shuffling along rather than lifting his feet; as he moved he swayed a little, as if he were not certain of his foothold. Not a word was spoken until he reached the table by which Fentiman was standing. Then he paused, resting his little withered hands on the back of a chair, as if he needed its support; and, indeed, one could see that he trembled. He turned his face towards the huge man, peering up at him with his dim eyes with an eagerness which was both painful and pathetic. He spoke in a small, squeaky voice, which was exactly the sort of voice one would have expected to proceed from such a body.

"I felt you! I felt you!"

He repeated the words twice over, as if the repetition lent them emphasis. Fentiman looked down at him as at some pigmy.

"You wanted me?"

"It is not so much that I want you—though I think I do want you, in a sense—as that I want some sleep. I have had none all night, and, in consequence, my nervous system suffers. Every bone in me seems aching. A sleepless night tries me more than it used to do. I must have sleep, or, if I don't, I feel as if something will burst."

He pressed the sides of his head with both hands as if it ached.

"You want me to send you to sleep?"

"Yes, I want you to send me to sleep—now, at once. I want rest—rest."

For answer Fentiman bent his long body till his head was on a level with the little man. He looked him full in the face with a continued, persistent stare; his strange eyes, all the while, going through some curious performances; the pupil and iris coming and vanishing, enlarging and decreasing, in a fashion which might have disconcerted any one, and which evidently had on the doctor a sinister effect. The moment the performance began a change came over him. When Fentiman commenced to wave his hands in front of him in what seemed a series of calculated movements, touching him with his outstretched finger-tips (now on the temple, now on the muscles of his neck, now behind his ears), the change grew more pronounced. Something unpleasant had happened to his eyes, so that the whole eyeball seemed to turn right round in the socket. The muscles of his face grew rigid, his lips tremulous. To an ordinary observer he looked as if he were shivering on the edge of a fit. Presently, still continuing his varied processes, Fentiman asked a question.

"Are you asleep?"

After a period of what seemed painful hesitation, he answered in a voice which was, and yet was not, his—

"Yes."

As if not yet wholly satisfied, Fentiman increased rather than diminished his exertions, presently repeating his inquiry—

"Are you asleep?"

This time the response was instant, unhesitating.

"Yes?"

"Then sit upon that chair." A little awkwardly, yet readily enough, the professor did as he was told; sitting bolt upright, in an attitude so rigid as almost to suggest some variety of tetanus. Ceasing from his acrobatic contortions, drawing himself upright, Fentiman looked down at him with inquisitive eyes. "Are you resting?"

"Yes—I'm resting."

Fentiman's great mouth was distorted by what might have been an involuntary grin. He said aloud, yet as if speaking to himself, as if quite certain that the words he uttered were inaudible to the man in front of him—

"Are you? I doubt it, and I don't think you'll find yourself much rested when you come out of it. Odd; how differently this kind of thing affects different people! Some are always asleep, whether under influence or not; I fancy that, on the whole, they're the luckiest. You, little man, seem as if you can never get any sleep at all, except when you're like this; and that's the devil, because, with a man of your age and temperament, when the influence has passed, it leaves you more in want of sleep than ever. It seems to me that before very long we shall have sucked the capacity for natural sleep clean out of you; which means, that these little experiments of ours will soon arrive at a natural termination. When you came into the room just now, you looked to me as if you were a dying man. Let's feel your pulse." He lifted the other's arm, pressing his fingers on the slender wrist; the professor paying no more attention to what was taking place than if he had been a wooden image, and the arm the property of some one else. "What a pulse! scarcely visible. There could hardly be much less of it. I fancy, Professor Hurle, that you and I will soon have to wish each other a last good-bye. Personally, I shall be sorry. I have found you, in all respects, a most delightful subject." His manner altered; he addressed himself directly to the little man. "While you're resting, Professor Hurle, I should like to ask you one or two questions, and I would request you to be careful with your answers. You informed me yesterday, while you were resting, that you were not only relatively, but actually, a poor man. For instance, you said that you had only a very small balance at your banker's. Is that true?"

"Quite true."

"And that that balance, together with what is contained in these rooms, practically represents all that you possess in the world. Again, is that true?"

"Quite true."

"Is your life insured?"

"No."

"Are you certain?"

"Quite certain."

"So far, so good. I am bound to admit that certain inquiries which I have made among your own papers and elsewhere corroborate to the full all that you have stated. Now I am going to put to you some questions which I did not put to you yesterday, and I would ask you to think, to try well back in your memory, before you reply. Were you ever richer than you are now?"

The professor, as requested, seemed to consider.

"I was once."

"You were, were you? Oh! I think that now we may be coming to it."

"Coming to what?"

"That remark was not intended for you. Your noticing it, however, shows how completely our souls are in sympathy. At the same time, you will be so good as to pay no attention to remarks which you are not meant to notice. Answer this question. What was the largest sum of money you ever possessed?"

"Five thousand pounds."

"Five thousand pounds. That's a nice little nest-egg. Where did you get it from?"

"From the sale of certain copyrights."

"When was that?"

Again the professor seemed to consider.

"About three years ago."

"What became of it?"

"My nephew cheated me out of it."

"Your nephew?"

"My nephew, Cyril Wentworth."

Mr. Fentiman whistled softly.

"Now, indeed, we seem to be coming to it. How did Cyril Wentworth cheat you out of your five thousand pounds?"

"He induced me to invest them in the shares of a worthless mining company."

"Did he? Oh! Strange how thoughtless some nephews are! What unsound financial advisers! What was the name of the mine?"

Once more the professor appeared to consider.

"It was the Great—something."

"The Great what?"

"I can't for the moment remember." All at once the professor became voluble, as if it relieved him to ventilate a grievance. "It was soon after he came back from Australia. He had been there some time, so I supposed he knew something about the country. He talked as if he knew something about mines. I happened to mention to him casually that I had this money by me, and I asked him if he could recommend to me a sound investment. He recommended me this mine. I bought five thousand shares in it at a pound apiece. Almost as soon as I had bought them, I discovered that they were absolutely worthless; that the whole thing was a swindle."

"Five thousand shares at a pound a piece, and the whole thing was a swindle. That was unfortunate—for you. Where are the shares?"

"He has them. When I found out how I had been cheated, I wanted him to give me my money back again; and when he wouldn't, I told him that I refused to compound a felony by accepting his worthless rubbish in lieu of my hard-earned cash. I told him he was a thief, and so he was. I meant the money to go, when I was dead, to my niece, Lettice Mason; and he robbed her of every penny."

"Bad man! Did you ever actually see, and handle, those five thousand shares?"

"Yes, I saw them. He brought them here, and told me all sorts of lies, and wanted me to take them; but I wouldn't."

"Then am I to understand that, to the best of your knowledge and belief, he still holds them, in trust for you?"

"He can continue to hold them for all I care."

"Try to remember what, exactly, was the name of the mine."

The professor tried again, this time with more success.

"It was somewhere in Western Australia; at least, he said it was. I've got it—it was the Great Harry Mine."

"You are sure it was the Great Harry Mine?"

"Quite sure. It was such a ridiculous name that I ought to have had sense enough to know that it was no good."

Mr. Fentiman began to pace about the room, talking to himself, and not to the professor.

"The Great Harry Mine? I seem to have seen and heard something about a mine with a very similar name quite recently. By God! Where's the paper? Professor, haven't you a newspaper in the place?"

"No. I don't take one. I'm not interested in the news of the day."

"Aren't you? Then I don't wonder you're sitting there. If it is as I suspect, I begin to see my friend Wentworth's little game. What a man! and what a fool!" The opprobrious epithet was addressed to the back of the unconscious professor. Returning to the table, Fentiman set in front of Dr. Hurle a sheet of paper, a pen, and ink. He issued a peremptory command. "Look at me!" The professor looked. The process which had originally placed him in the condition in which he then was, was repeated. Mr. Fentiman repeated all his previous contortions with such energy that at the end he was moved to take a handkerchief out of his pocket to wipe the perspiration off his brow. As a result of his efforts, it was evident that the professor's curious state had become more curious still. Fentiman made the position plain. "You understand, Professor Hurle, that my will is to be yours; you are to have no wish in opposition to mine. You are to do as I tell you, exactly, at once, and without comment. You are to say nothing unless I bid you. Take that pen." The professor took it. "Write the date on the top of that sheet of paper." The professor wrote it. "Now write what I am going to dictate to you; I will speak slowly. Begin. This is the last will of me, Hammond Hurle, of St. Clement's College, Camford, in the county of Camford. I devise and bequeath all my estate and effects, real and personal, which I may die possessed of, or entitled to, unto my nephew, Cyril Wentworth, absolutely. And I revoke all former wills and codicils. Dated this tenth day—repeat the date again."

Mr. Fentiman spoke slowly, as he said he would do. With docile accuracy the professor wrote down each word as it fell from his lips. The dictator, taking up the paper, read what had been written. It met with his approval.

"That'll do. It only requires to be signed and witnessed, and I flatter myself it will be as sound and valid a will as ever yet was drawn. I haven't studied *Every Man His Own Lawyer** for nothing." He replaced the sheet of paper in front of the professor. "There. Leave that where it is; don't touch it. Sit still; don't move; and don't speak. I'll step over to the porter's lodge and bring as good and responsible a pair of witnesses as any judge could desire; and if I can't bamboozle them into believing that the whole business is open and above board, I've less influence over you, Professor Hurle, than I imagine."

Leaving the paper on the table in front of the professor, he turned his back on him, and crossed the room. He already had his hand upon the handle of the door when a voice—a feminine voice—addressed him from behind, as he had addressed the professor.

"I fancy, Mr. Fentiman, that you may find that the matter is not quite so simple as you suppose."

CHAPTER V

THE SIX

HAD the painted ceiling of the room come tumbling down about his ears, Mr. Fentiman could hardly have been more surprised. As has been hinted, experience having accustomed him to disagreeable surprises, it needed something really remarkable to upset his equilibrium. That little remark nearly did it. He swung round and stared; the more he stared, the more his amazement seemed to grow. In front of the door which led into the lumber-room stood a lady—a young lady; charmingly dressed; good to look at. Between the fingers of her left hand dangled the handle of a parasol. She wore a veil. From behind this veil she glanced at him, out of two bright eyes, with a smile. Her self-possession was as obvious as his was not. When—if one might take it so—he had learnt as much of her as could be learnt by the sense of sight alone, he spoke.

"Who are you?"

"Ah, that's the question: Who am I?"

She swung her parasol, having balanced the handle on the end of one finger. It was a fantastic construction of light blue silk, harmonizing well with the pale blue muslin gown which she was wearing.

"Are you—Miss Mason?"

"No; I'm not Miss Mason."

"Where do you come from?"

"Just now, this very moment, I've come from in there."

She flicked her parasol towards the lumber-room.

"Did he know you were in there?"

The allusion was to Dr. Hurle.

"Poor dear! I should say not. What is there he does know?"

"Then what do you mean by going in there? or coming here? What is it you want?"

"Well, you see, I happened to learn from Mr. Cyril Wentworth that you were coming here to play some hankey-pankey tricks on poor dear Dr. Hurle, so I thought I'd come and see you play them. And here I am."

"Do you mean to say that Cyril Wentworth told you that I was coming here this afternoon?"

"I obtained the information from his own lips."

"Then—what is there between you? What have you to do with him?"

"I have a great deal more to do with him than, at present, he imagines."

Moving a little from the door, glancing at her all the time, Fentiman began to snap the finger-nails of his left hand against his teeth, an unpleasant habit in which he sometimes indulged when he was puzzled. At that particular moment he was very mystified indeed. He admitted it.

"You are beyond my comprehension altogether. Have you the cheek to hint that Cyril Wentworth sent you here to spy on me?"

"That is a question which I would rather you addressed to Mr. Wentworth himself. It is rather a rude one, isn't it?"

Advancing to the table, she took up the sheet of paper which was in front of the professor, who, while these remarks were being exchanged, remained as rigid as a poker, and apparently as unconscious of what was taking place.

"Is this the will he asked you to obtain for him?"

"Yes, that's it. What beats me is why Wentworth should want you to put your finger in the pie. I'm beginning to wonder if he's not more of an idiot than I thought he was. Come, be open with me. You know who I am. Tell me who you are. What is your little game?"

"Mr. Fentiman, for all information, on any subject, I must refer you to Mr. Cyril Wentworth."

She was folding up the sheet of paper.

"That will's not completed."

"It's as complete as it ever will be."

"What do you mean? It has to be signed and witnessed. I was just going to fetch the witnesses when you came out of that hiding-place of yours."

"Did I stop you? Perhaps you would like to go and fetch them now."

"And leave you alone with him? and with that will? I'm beginning to smell a rat—to suspect that this is a little plant of your own; that Cyril Wentworth has no more to do with this game you're playing, whatever it is, than I have. Give me that will."

"Thank you, Mr. Fentiman, I think not."

"You think not? So that is the game! It's some infernal bluff you're trying on! My girl, you're not going to bring it off quite so easily as you supposed. Give me that will."

"I've already told you, Mr. Fentiman, that I think not."

"Don't you make any mistake. Don't imagine, because you wear a skirt, that I'm going to let you monkey with me, because I'm not. If you won't give me that will I shall take it, with or without your leave—you can bet on it—and then those pretty clothes of yours will get themselves rumpled, which will be a pity. Now, for the last time, are you going to give me that paper, or am I to take it?"

"Oh, Mr. Fentiman, look at Dr. Hurle!"

The girl's voice had in it a note of sudden terror. Fentiman swung quickly round towards the professor to see what caused it. As he turned, the girl slipped past him, lightly and swiftly as some young deer. Before the more slow-moving Fentiman had perceived her purpose, and the trick which she was playing, she had reached the door. With creditable rapidity he was after her; but before he could stop her, she had turned the key and flung the door wide open.

"Gentlemen," she exclaimed, "would you mind stepping into this room for the space of just one minute?"

It seemed incredible that sounds could have penetrated through the two closed doors, or that her ears could have detected footsteps coming up the stairs; certainly Mr. Fentiman had heard nothing; yet if it was an unlooked-for accident that when the door was opened, Mr. Sharratt and no less than five of his friends were revealed without, it was a curious one. The surprise of Mr. Sharratt and his friends, at the vision which greeted them, was undeniable. In a moment each man had his cap in his hand, and, what was more astonishing, his hands out of his pocket. The young lady's bearing was imperious.

"Is not one of you named Mr. Sharratt?"

Dick admitted it.

"My name's Sharratt."

"I believe, Mr. Sharratt, that your rooms are over these?"

Dick bowed.

"That's so."

"Then may I ask you and your friends to come in and protect Professor Hurle from this man? The professor has been made the victim of a dastardly outrage."

Dick and his five friends went in to find themselves confronted by Mr. Fentiman, who did not seem to be altogether pleased to see them. Dick shook his head at him, more in sorrow than in anger.

"I knew I should be running up against you before very long. You're a beauty!"

Mr. Fentiman endeavoured to assume an air of dignity, with not quite so much success as he might have desired.

"Young gentlemen, I warn you, you are trespassing. As you are perfectly well aware, these rooms are private. This young woman, who is unknown both to Professor Hurle and to me, is herself a trespasser. She has no more right to ask you to enter than you have to presume upon her impertinent invitation. I must ask you to be so good as to withdraw at once, and to take her with you."

Dick shook his head at him again. His remarks were apparently addressed to no one in particular.

"He will do it! There's no stopping him! It's bound to be another case of sprinting down the High Street!" He turned to the vision in blue, with the big hat, and the veil, and the sparkling eyes. "What lark's he been up to now?"

"He has thrown Professor Hurle into a hypnotic trance, although he knows that, in the present state of the professor's health, it's an extremely dangerous thing to do; and then he has obtained from him, while in that condition, all sorts of information on his most private affairs, of which he has taken advantage to compel him to draw up a document, which, I am perfectly certain, he never would have drawn up had he been conscious of what it was that he was doing."

Dick advanced towards the chair on which the little professor, wholly oblivious of his surroundings, still sat rigid as a poker.

"Professor Hurle——"

Fentiman interposed.

"I warn you that Dr. Hurle is under influence, at his own request, as this young woman can testify, if she is as honest as she would wish you to suppose. You may subject him to serious, and even fatal, injury if you interfere with him while he is in that state."

"Then uninfluence him, or whatever you call the little dodge of bringing him back to his senses."

"I require no instructions from you on that point, Mr. Sharratt. I recognize no one in this matter except Dr. Hurle himself. In order to show you what view he will take of your conduct, and of this young woman's conduct, I propose to remove the influence of my own initiative, when you will quickly find yourselves ordered to quit these rooms."

The performance which Mr. Fentiman went through with those six pairs of eyes watching him was no more agreeable to witness than the one which he had gone through in private; but it was, fortunately, shorter, and before long the professor gave signs that he was returning to his everyday self. He grew limper and limper. Presently, his eyeballs turned right round in their sockets, as they had done before, only this time in the reverse direction. With a little gasp he looked about him.

"Have I been to sleep? Where am I? What has happened? Who are all these people? What do they want?"

Although his squeaky little voice suggested a certain amount of irascibility, he was so weak that he sank back in the big chair, a pathetic little figure of helplessness. The vision in blue, entirely ignoring his questions, assumed complete control of the situation.

"Will you be so kind, Mr. Sharratt, as to request Mr. Fentiman to leave the room? I will attend to Dr. Hurle."

Dick did what, in our childhood, we are told it is rude to do. He pointed.

"Fentiman, door!"

Mr. Fentiman showed extreme unwillingness to take advantage of the hint. He drew closer to the professor, or, rather, he tried to do so; as it chanced, Dick was in the way.

"Professor Hurle, I must ask you to exercise your authority; I even appeal to you for protection. Mr. Sharratt has already behaved to me in a manner which makes me fear that at his hands I may receive treatment——"

Dick interrupted the speaker's voluble expression with three words.

"Gentlemen—Fentiman—outside!"

In a surprisingly short space of time, those six young men were bearing Mr. Fentiman towards the door; if not with reverence, then at least with alacrity. Mr. Fentiman kicked and struggled, delivering himself of objurgations and strange words. He was a big man, capable of putting up a fairly good fight, if a fight was possible and there was nothing else to do. But these were six; all young, trained athletes, bent on doing a lady's bidding. In their hands he was helpless. So that presently the door closed on him, and he was seen no more. Only still, for a few moments, his voice came up the stairs.

Dr. Hurle, still huddled up on his chair, had been watching the proceedings, and the sudden disappearance of his professional colleague, with a sort of bewildered stupor, as if he was not quite sure if he was yet under that gentleman's influence or not. When the six with the one had vanished, he inquired, in stammering tremulous accents—

"What—what's it mean? What—what are they going to do with him?"

The lady bent over him, and smiled sweetly.

"It only means that they are going to take him into the fresh air, and give him—perhaps—a little exercise."

CHAPTER VI

AN EVENING'S ENTERTAINMENT

AT Mr. Tallis' ball Cyril Wentworth found himself rather awkwardly placed. Among the guests was one lady whose society he was desirous of enjoying, and another to whom he felt that it would be the part of wisdom to devote the whole of his attention. This second lady was Miss Bradley—Ellen Bradley—the only child of her father, and he was a widower, whose "Stomachic

Pills" are known, at any rate by name, to every English-speaking person on the surface of the globe; such frequently unintentional knowledge being one of the ills which modern flesh is heir to.* She was youngish, somewhere in the early thirties, and she was intellectual—really intellectual. Her novels were not only clever— some of the most respectable critics called them "brilliant"—but they had achieved considerable popularity. Her plays had been produced at various theatres, some of them with much success. Her gifts as an essayist and preacher to the world at large—on nothing in particular, and everything in general, in "literary circles" and sometimes outside of them—were a byword. And then, of course, there was her father's money. Under which circumstances personal appearance was of no consequence, though, at the same time, she was not absolutely ugly. If she had chosen, she might have married again and again; that is, if she had been fortunate enough to bury her husbands as fast as she had them. But she belonged to that genus of latter-day women which does not marry, not believing either in men as men, or in matrimony as a feminine vocation*— that is, she had belonged to it until she met Cyril Wentworth.

Mr. Wentworth was not so much attracted by her personality as she was by his, which is the way in which fortune likes to manage things. None the less, he was quite conscious that as a wife she would be, in many respects, a most excellent investment, and he was not a man to let a good investment slip through his fingers if he could help it.

Matters had, indeed, gone with him so far that he had come to Mr. Tallis' ball with the deliberate intention of asking her to marry him before the night was over. Under which circumstances, Mrs. Van der Gucht's presence "on the festive scene" might almost have been regarded as a stroke of bad luck, to such a degree did she divert his thoughts from the business he had in hand.

Mrs. Van der Gucht was a Boer. It may not be, as yet, so widely known as it one day will be, but—physically, to look at, to talk to, and so on—some Boer women are among the most delightful women in the world. Mrs. Van der Gucht was, admittedly, one of them. She was the wife of a prominent Boer* who had thrown in his lot with the English, and she was on a visit to England. Her husband remained in Pretoria. She always spoke of him most affectionately, and had brought with her some excellent introductions. Mr. Wentworth, who had been everywhere, had been to the Transvaal, and had there known her before she was Mrs. Van der Gucht—known her very well, so well, in fact, that she figured as the central figure in one of the romances of his life; there were more than one. Sometimes, after he was far away, he would think of her, and would close his eyes, and clench his fingers, and wish that he could see her as clearly with the actual eye as with the eye of memory—that she was within reach of him, close at hand. When she appeared in London the flame, which had once burnt pretty strongly, if anything blazed more furiously than ever. She cast a glamour over his senses, bewitched him, as she did in the old days on the veldt. Now that she had put her actual girlhood behind her, which even yet was all she had done, she had become beatified, more delightful than before. The lovely girl of the veldt transformed into a lady of fashion was, to him, a revelation of things which, in a woman, are to be desired. Her tall, slim, childish figure; her beautiful, big eyes; the glorious mass of her fair hair, which, as he knew, reached well below her waist, and in whose luxuriance she might, if she choose, clothe herself as with a garment; her pretty mouth, with the sweet red lips, and the small white teeth; the daintiness with which she moved—to see her dance was to realize what folks mean who talk of the poetry of motion; the grace which marked everything she said and did; the charming little gestures with which, when she was at all excited, and she was easily moved both to excitement and to laughter— how he loved to hear her laughter!—she would illustrate whatever she might be saying;—these trifles, being united together with other trifles, even sweeter, had cast on him a spell from which he had no desire to be free.

As he sat with her in the conservatory, through what was to have been one dance, but became two, his thoughts were with Miss Bradley—in no affectionate sense. He was aware that that lady was waiting for him in the ball-room, and that, when he did join her, she would ask him certain questions, and make certain remarks, in her well-known manner, which would jar upon his nerves. Still, he sat through the second dance, though her partner came to claim the lady—and had to be put off with a lie—saying things which he had no right to say, and to which she had no right to listen. And in the very middle of a sentence—which, beyond doubt, was better left unfinished—he stopped, and started, and sprang to his feet, and looked away from her, to her no small surprise.

"Why, what's the matter?" she inquired.

"I thought—but it can't be! And yet——!"

"And yet, what? And what can't be? And what did you think? What, all of a sudden, has happened?"

As he had been leaning towards Mrs. Van der Gucht, he had seen, as it were, out of the unoccupied corners of his eyes, a woman moving among the palms at the other end of the conservatory. He had paid little attention until, reaching the entrance to the ball-room, she had stopped, and turned, and looked in his direction. If he could believe his eyes, she was the woman whom he had found in his flat the night before; who had fallen to the floor when the revolver was discharged; whom he had carried, dead, to his bedroom; who had vanished when, after Fentiman's departure, he had returned to institute another, and more thorough, search for the missing examination papers. If his eyes had not deceived him, who was she, and what could she be doing there? He was so genuinely moved that, for a moment or two, Mrs. Van der Gucht was forgotten. When he did remember her existence he spoke to her in a strain which was very different from that which he had been using.

"Excuse me, but a—person has just gone into the ball-room whom I think I have seen before, and to whom, if I am right, I must speak at once."

Without another word, or even look, he left her there, alone, in the conservatory, staring. And as she stared, a flush dyed all her face, and tears came into her eyes.

Cyril Wentworth, rushing off as if in hot chase of some absconding creditor, gaining the threshold of the ball-room, stopped to look about him. The ball was at its height; the room was crowded, too crowded for comfortable dancing. In such a throng it was difficult to discover any particular person. And yet he told himself that, if that woman was anywhere within his range of vision, he would detect her on the instant. It was hardly more than a minute since he had seen her; she was moving slowly;

in that crowd she could hardly have gone far in so short a time. Being taller than the average man, he could see over other people's heads. His glance was rapid, unerring. His faculty for quickness of observation was not the least remarkable of his remarkable gifts. Somewhat to his surprise there was not a sign to be seen of the woman he was seeking. There was no one in the least like her. Not a person of whom he could say that, under certain conditions, she quite possibly might be mistaken for the woman of the night before. It was with a feeling almost of bewilderment that he realized that it was so. Had it been possible he would have satisfied himself by saying that he had been the victim of a delusion. But he knew he had not been. The woman had stopped, and turned, and looked, in his direction, of set purpose; he was sure of it. Then where was she, now, a minute afterwards? What did it all mean? He penetrated farther into the room, all agog for a glimpse of her. His search for the vanished lady went unrewarded, but he found Miss Bradley. And Miss Bradley, in a sense, found him. And neither party seemed in the best of tempers.

"I imagined, Mr. Wentworth, you had gone."

He looked at her with, in his eyes, a challenge.

"Would you rather I had gone?"

She slightly shrugged her shoulders, returning him glance for glance.

"My good sir, what does it matter to me? Does that mean that you're going now?"

He perceived that here was a lady with whom, if he was not careful, in her present mood, he might easily go too far, and this was an investment which he was anxious not to lose.

"You are cruel to me! Where have you been hiding yourself? I have been looking for you everywhere."

She knew he had been doing nothing of the kind. But her feeling for this man had reached such a stage that she was even willing to aid and abet him in a lie.

"I wonder if that is true? I certainly have not been looking for you; why should you have been searching for me?"

"Because—but you know why. Come"—he was going to say, "Come into the conservatory;" but he remembered that it was possible that Mrs. Van der Gucht was still there, awaiting his return, so he checked himself in time—"somewhere where we can be away from all these people. There is something which I—I must say to you."

"Is there? Indeed! Your tone is a trifle arrogant. Is it something to which I necessarily must listen? It is hardly likely that anything which interests you can interest me."

But she knew better. She was almost painfully conscious of a sensation which was strange to her. Possibly for the first time in her life she realized that she was in danger of losing her mastery over herself, her self-control. This man affected her as never a human being had done before, in a physical sense of which she had not supposed herself to be capable. He slipped her arm through his, possibly the better to steer her through the crowd; the near contact with him caused a sort of vertigo to pass all over her. She had to lean upon him to enable her to keep her equilibrium till the wave of feeling had passed; the closer she pressed to him, the stronger her emotion grew. From head to foot she was one curious thrill. She let him lead her where he would, incapable of remonstrance, only too willing to be led. He took her to a recess formed by a square bay window. Placing her on a seat, he seated himself beside her, leaving a space between them of several inches. She had a ludicrous desire—which, in its strength, almost amounted to anguish—that he would come closer, that she might feel him at her side. More than once, in her novels, she had made fun of women who had entertained such feelings, particularly women of her own age. The least disparaging thing she could say of them was that they—and their feelings—were vulgar. Now she was conscious that, for the first time in her life, she was beginning to live.

If Cyril Wentworth was scarcely any more self-possessed than she was, it was from altogether different causes. There were more reasons than he would have cared to admit why he should lose, at any rate momentarily, his mental balance, one being that for the woman near whom he was seated he felt an absolute physical repulsion, which was unfortunate, since it was his immediate intention to ask her to be his wife. He had not supposed that the task would have been so difficult. He was a man of much experience in such matters. He used to tell himself that he understood women better than they understood themselves.

He was conscious of having had a power over some of those with whom he had come in contact of which he had not hesitated to take advantage, remorseless, monstrous advantage. He had not imagined that he would find it any trouble to take advantage of an old maid's fatuity. He had done it before; he had taken it for granted that it would be easy to do it again. Only a few foolish words and a lie or two, and the thing was done. Yet, though he was aware that this woman—clever, shrewd woman of the world though she was—would swallow his hook, however it might be baited, greedily, eagerly, he found himself apparently physically incapable of even casting his line into the water. Words, which were to him the merest counters, declined to come.

He leant forward, resting his elbows on his knees, asking himself what had happened that he should be behaving like such an utter fool. The woman at his side, possibly supposing herself to be conscious of the cause which tied his tongue—the irony of the supposition—desirous of offering him that encouragement of which he stood in need, edged herself closer to him. The movement not only added to his feeling of aversion, it made him angry. For a moment he could have struck her. He would certainly have liked to push her from him. To have risen there and then, and left her, without a word, sitting on the seat alone, would have afforded him the keenest pleasure, if it had not been for other considerations. By long habit he had trained himself not to allow his feelings to get the better of his interest; never to show what was actually in his heart if it paid him not to, and it generally did. Because he would so much have liked to overwhelm the woman with some public mark of his contempt and scorn he did nothing of the kind. The mere strength of his desire brought him to his bearings. There would be opportunity, and to spare, for that kind of thing after she had become his wife; let him make her his wife to begin with. So, screwing himself to the sticking-point,* he was just about to commence his perjuries when—he was interrupted.

The woman of last night stood in front of him—radiant, charmingly gowned, as much at her ease as she had been when he had first encountered her. She assumed an air of being surprised to see him; whether it was feigned or not it was impossible to tell. Nothing could be more contemptuous than her manner of addressing him.

"You here! You! Incredible! It shows that you must have gone some distance to have been able to force yourself into a respectable house. If it were known, as it ought to be, who and what you are, even the servants would hesitate to soil their hands by throwing you out into the street."

Although these very frank observations were not made with unusual loudness, they, at least, were clearly spoken. There was that in her air which made them more conspicuous. People turned to see who the speaker was, and, having turned, were disposed to observe the scene with growing interest. That night something must have ailed Cyril Wentworth. In the days which followed, he told himself so. Ordinarily he would have been equal to the situation, and more than equal. Then he was beaten by it. Already nonplussed by his unexpected awkwardness in asking Miss Bradley to be his wife, this sudden apparition took him at a disadvantage; the manner in which he found himself being addressed was so unlooked for, and so surprising, that it completed his discomfiture.

His tormentor turned to Miss Bradley.

"I am afraid you don't know who this man is. He is a blackguard adventurer, who was convicted of theft, and who had to flee for his life to save himself from being charged with murder. In certain parts of West Australia he was known as Jack the Chemist. Ask him why. If he tells you truly, you will never permit yourself to be in the same house with him again.—Well, my man, what have you to say for yourself?"

The air of insolent assurance with which she put to him the question was, in its way, superb. In a fashion he found his tongue.

"I have only this to say: that, if there were a policeman within reach, I would give you into charge for burglary."

"There is one outside. Shall I send for him?"

"I will choose my own time and place; but before long you will find yourself in the dock, you may take my word for it." He turned to Miss Bradley. "I found this woman, who is a perfect stranger to me, in my rooms last night. She had made a burglarious entrance. Before I could have her arrested she escaped." The woman in question merely laughed. "I am making inquiries as to what her presence in my room meant, whether her intention was merely felonious, or whether she was sent there—as I think is possible—for a certain purpose by certain persons who have no cause to love me. When I am satisfied on the point, the police will be at once instructed to take action. As to the statement she has just now made—with what malicious intention I am at a loss to divine—not one syllable of it is true. My record is open to all the world. I need not tell you that I am not such a man as she has said I am."

The woman laughed again.

"Well brazened! Brass has always been your favourite metal next to gold." Then to Miss Bradley. "He has lied, as he always has lied, till it has been brought home even to his understanding that lying was no longer of any use. I have merely hinted at the sort of man he is in order that you may be warned and on your guard. You can scarcely wish to find yourself the wife of a notorious scoundrel. If you are wise, you will insist upon his telling you why he was known as Jack the Chemist, though, probably, before very long the reason why will be as household words in the mouths of all men."

CHAPTER VII

PROFESSOR FENTIMAN IS TRANSFORMED

WHEN, later that night, Cyril Wentworth let himself into his little flat in Sloane Street,* it was not strange that he was in a bad humour. Lately, many things had been going wrong with him; that night, in particular, had been a lamentable *fiasco*, and he had intended it to have been the occasion of his triumph. His assailant had borne herself off with flying colours. It appeared that she was unknown to the hostess, Mrs. Tallis. How she had gained admission was a secret of her own. It was a point on which no information had been obtained from her. To avoid further scandal it had been thought better to let her depart in peace; and she had departed, still completely at her ease.

Mr. Wentworth had not enjoyed himself after she had gone; Miss Bradley's manner towards him had been distinctly chilly.

The idea of asking her to be his wife that night was out of the question. She had quitted the assembly almost immediately after his unknown enemy, even declining to allow him to escort her to the door. But Mr. Wentworth had some acquaintance with what he called the feminine mind, as if all women had the same mental equipment! He did not despair of Miss Bradley merely because she had snubbed him. He would call to-morrow and explain, and would keep on explaining till he got within reach of her. Then he did not doubt that the matter would be settled. Where she was concerned, he had a strong conviction of the potent influence of his physical neighbourhood.

But after that "female devil"—that was how he thought of her—had gone, he was conscious of something much more ominous than Miss Bradley's coolness. He felt that in the whole atmosphere of the room there was, towards him, a feeling of aloofness. People avoided him so far as they could. When he spoke to them they answered with as few words as possible, and hastened away. It seemed that, if they had been able, they would have cut him. He had a feeling that the first opportunity which offered, they would. Even his hostess seemed to have been plunged into a refrigerator since he arrived. He descended the staircase with a grim consciousness that not improbably that was the last time he would go either down or up it. And after the pains he had taken to gain the freedom of that house, and to be on terms of something like intimacy with the people, who, he did not doubt, would experience a sensation of relief so soon as they were certain that he was really gone.

And all because of an unknown "female devil" who had descended on him, he knew not whence nor why.

Returned to his own rooms he asked himself—as he had done all the way from Mrs. Tallis', and, indeed, ever since the night before—who she might be, and what it was that she was after. There were so many things which she might be after. It was essential for his own comfort—not to say safety—that he should know which particular incident in his eventful history was being aimed at. If he could only identify his antagonist it would be something. To all intents and purposes he was without a single clue. He had spent hours, after she had vanished on the preceding night, in going laboriously through the papers with which she had taken such amazing liberties. So far as he was able to judge, not one of them was missing. Nor could he find anything to show what she had been looking for, nor what there was in them which could have been of interest to her. He racked his memory in his endeavours to recall her face, or one like hers; or a voice, a form, a gesture, anything which would enable him to link her with some particular association—in vain. Yet that hers was an entity which would have to be dealt with at once, and forcibly, events of that night had made sufficiently plain, or he might be destroyed before he knew what was striking him.

While he still kept trying back, there came a ring at the bell.

"Is that her? She's capable of it. I wish it were; this time she'd find me also capable of a thing or two. But I rather fancy it's my friend Fentiman. In either eventuality it's just as well that I should be prepared."

He took out of his waistcoat pocket a small leather case, which, having opened it and glanced within, as if to make sure that its contents were intact, he at once put back again. Then, since the bell still continued chiming, he admitted the ringer. It was not the lady—as he had anticipated; it was Professor Fentiman.

"You might give that bell a rest, Fentiman. You're not bound to keep your finger glued to the button."

"I like to feel that I am giving you no excuse to pretend that you were not aware that I was ringing it, which is an amusing little game I have known you to play before to-day."

"Don't be an ass! If I didn't want to hear it I could disconnect it in an instant. You were perfectly well aware that I was not likely to deny myself to you tonight. It's rather the other way round. I was just beginning to wonder if you meant to come."

"You may thank your stars that I have come. It's certainly no fault of yours that I'm alive to do it."

"Don't hint that it's my misfortune; that would be unkind. Talk sense, Fentiman; you occasionally can. What luck? Have you brought my dear uncle's very last will and testament?"

"On my honour, Wentworth, for sheer impudence you take the cake. To look at and to listen to you, one would think that you were the most straightforward creature breathing, while I

know you—and you know I know you—to be the most infernal
hypocrite and humbug that ever walked the earth."

"Fentiman, have you been lowering it even more than usual?"

"Lowering it? I've been lowering nothing, except, God knows,
how many gallons of water!"

"If it really is water which you have been absorbing, that
possibly may explain the singularity of your language, because
beyond doubt so unusual a liquor would affect you strangely. Be so
good as to tell me plainly, have you brought with you my uncle's
will, drawn up in the terms which we agreed upon?"

"You pretend to ask me such a question, you treacherous
hound, after setting that infernal woman to spy on me? When I
think of it, I feel like taking you by the throat and choking the
life right out of you; I'm more capable of doing it than you may
imagine."

At the mention of the word "woman," Mr. Wentworth did not
exactly change countenance, but a flicker passed across his face, as
if some muscle had been involuntarily twitched.

"Setting what infernal woman to spy on you?"

Mr. Fentiman explained, with considerable force of language,
how, at a delicate point in his interview with Professor Hurle, a
woman had, as he put it, "popped on to the scene like a damned
Jack-in-the-box," which was rather a crude way of setting forth the
actual manner of the lady's appearance.

"But what's the use," he went on, "of telling you what you
know already, since she was your own infernal spy."

"On what grounds do you say she was my spy?"

"She told me that she was, in so many words."

"Did she? The beauty! Then she lied. Reflect, Fentiman. Ask
yourself what conceivable reason I could have had for setting her,
or any one else, to spy on you, when the whole transaction was of
so eminently delicate a character that the first essential was that
the knowledge of it should be confined to our two selves?"

"That is what I have been asking myself: what reason could you
have had, unless you did it out of pure cussedness, which is quite
possible, because, anyhow, it was you who informed her that I was
going down to Camford, and on what errand I was going."

"I who informed her!"

"She said that she obtained the information from your own lips; and she obviously must have done, since she certainly never had it from me; and she could have got it from nobody but one of us."

Mr. Wentworth reflected. It occurred to him as possible, nay, probable, that the information had been obtained from his lips, though it had been very far from his intention to convey it. The statement which he made was distinctly accurate.

"I assure you, Fentiman, that I have not breathed one syllable on the matter to any one but you. If this woman of yours is the one I suspect, then she has been the cause of considerable annoyance to me already. If I can once get within grips of her, I promise you that I'll quickly bring her to a final account. Where is the will you induced my uncle to draw up?"

"She has it; that fair friend of yours."

Mr. Wentworth's face darkened. "Then, in that case, it may be the cause to me of serious injury. You had better have torn it up rather than let it get into her hands."

"You don't understand; I was helpless. She set a gang of ruffianly undergraduates on to me, who, at her instigation, threw me into the college fountain. If it had not been for the intervention of an individual, who was apparently of the don species, I might have been drowned—actually drowned. What I have endured at the hands of those cowardly blackguards, you have no conception."

He shuddered at the thought. Mr. Wentworth smiled, a fact which the sufferer possibly noted. He went on.

"But if I have been subjected to treatment on the details of which I do not care to dwell, and if I have left the draft of the will which was to make you your uncle's heir in the hands of your lady friend, I have brought something away from St. Clement's College which I think may prove to be of some value—at least, to me."

"What is it—the recollection of a pleasant dip? Seriously, Fentiman, you have my hearty sympathy. I understand what your feelings must have been at finding yourself introduced to cold clean water."

"I am glad my experiences amuse you, Mr. Wentworth. You enable me to perceive the more clearly that that young woman was not such a liar as you would wish me to believe. However, I fancy I have acquired a piece of information which may not amuse you quite so much. I told you last night that it was beyond my comprehension why you should be so anxious to be your uncle's heir, since he had nothing to leave. Now I begin to have the glimmering of an idea."

"Indeed. What is it?"

"Have you ever heard of the Great Harry Gold Mine? But you needn't trouble yourself to answer, because, as a matter of fact, I know you have."

"What of it?"

"What has become of the five thousand shares in it which you hold in trust for your uncle?"

"How do you know that my uncle has, or ever had, any shares in it?"

"He told me so himself, this afternoon, while under influence. But he's such an addle-headed old idiot that he takes it for granted that because they were worthless once they must be worthless always, and therefore is entirely unconscious of the fact that, owing to certain accidents, they are worth, we will say, a good deal more than the sum he paid for them."

"Well, Fentiman; what next?"

"You and I, Mr. Wentworth, are the only persons in existence who know that your uncle holds those shares, and what their value is. How much do you think it would be worth to you to keep the real facts of the case, say, from him?"

Mr. Wentworth smiled. "You want me to pay you to keep still?"

"That's about the size of it."

"I will be candid and admit that it is a matter of almost vital importance to me that those facts should not become generally known; had I guessed that you would have got upon their track, I doubt if I should have introduced you to my uncle."

"You underrated my powers. I always told you that you did."

"I suppose that was the case—I suppose it was. As you have shown that I was wrong, and since matters are as they are, all that remains for me to do is to face the situation, and to treat it from a business point of view."

"Quite so. You are right enough there."

"I am glad you feel that also. All that remains for us is to understand each other thoroughly. My experience is that as a means of oiling the wheels a whisky and soda is not to be despised."

"I'm still with you." From a cabinet which he unlocked, Mr. Wentworth took out a decanter and a tumbler. "How do you like it?"

"Stiffish."

Wentworth poured out a generous modicum of whisky, which he diluted with but a modest proportion of the contents of a syphon of soda. He mixed another drink for himself on less heroic lines.

"Here's to our understanding each other better, Fentiman."

He raised the tumbler to his mouth, but whether any of the liquor passed his lips was doubtful. On that point, as regards Mr. Fentiman, there could be no doubt whatever, he nearly emptied his glass at one great gulp. As he did so a startled look came on his face.

"What—what's the matter?"

That was all he said. The glass slipped from between his fingers. He reeled, and fell to the floor, and where he fell he lay still. After a moment's pause, Wentworth, putting down his own tumbler on the mantelshelf, advanced and stood over him.

"You said you wanted it stiffish, and you've got it." He again took out of his pocket that small leather case, and from it he produced a tiny syringe. "If you'd brought me the will, all signed and settled, I'd have given you your discharge in full, as I promised, since I did not propose to allow you to hold the knowledge of how it came into existence over me. As, although you have permitted yourself to be bluffed by a woman, you have got hold of information which I would rather you hadn't, you shall still have your discharge in full. Here it is."

Kneeling on the floor beside the prostrate man, with his left hand he brushed the hair away from his forehead. He drove the nozzle of his syringe, which was unusually long, and of needle-like fineness, right into the head, among the roots of the hair in the centre, between the temples. Then he injected the contents.

That was all. But the following afternoon there was brought before the magistrate at the Hammersmith Police Court an individual who had been found wandering, in an irresponsible manner, about the streets. He was unable to give an account of himself, for the sufficient reason that he was speechless, being apparently a deaf mute, and also, unmistakably, an imbecile. He was remanded to the imbecile ward of the Hammersmith Workhouse, to be medically examined, and pending certain inquiries. The doctor certified that, while he was beyond doubt a lunatic, his case presented features of a most unusual kind.

The certified lunatic was Professor Fentiman.

CHAPTER VIII

A CHANCE ENCOUNTER

FOR those who are fond of exercise, there are few more agreeable playthings than a free-wheel bicycle; only, even in the most skilful hands, unfortunately, they are liable at times to behave in unexpected fashions. When John Banner, turning the corner on his motor-car,* pulled up just in time to avoid running over what was left of a young lady who was apparently mixed up with her machine, he realized that this was probably a case in point. The young lady was half-sitting, half-sprawling on the road, in an attitude which she certainly would not have chosen of her own accord; and under her, and over her, and round about, were some of the component parts of what once had been a bicycle. Mr. Banner sprang down to her assistance.

"Are you hurt?" he inquired.

That the lady was still in possession of her faculty of speech, her reply made tolerably clear.

"Am I hurt? Of course not. No one who is thrown over the handle-bars of a bicycle and nearly killed ever is. I don't know if every bone in my body is broken, but I'm sure that most of them are."

Mr. Banner's eyes twinkled. There was that in the speaker's tone which was hardly suggestive of great suffering.

"I'm sorry it's so bad as that. Can I help you up? Or don't you think you'll be able to stand? I've attended classes for first aid to the wounded; perhaps I may be of some assistance."

The young lady's answer was to rise quite unassisted. She gave herself a little shake, as if for the purpose of ascertaining what portions of her remained intact.

"Perhaps," suggested Mr. Banner, "it is not so very bad, after all."

"Thank you. You are very kind. I don't know what you call bad. My bicycle is done for!"

Mr. Banner examined the machine.

"It does seem rather the worse for wear. I am afraid that for the present you will have to put it on the retired list. How did it happen? Something went wrong with the brakes?"

"Something went wrong with everything, I should say. I was free-wheeling down that abominable hill."

"Which has a 'Dangerous' board at the top."

"It ought to have a 'Murderous' board; I am sure it is absolutely deadly. I don't know how many miles it is, or how many gradients there are; and it keeps turning and twisting among the trees and the high hedges, so that you can't see where you are going. I was just thanking my stars that I had reached the bottom alive when, as you put it, something went wrong, and then you found me. What I should like to know now is, how I am going to manage. I can't very well leave my machine here; I can't carry it; and there doesn't seem to be a soul within miles."

"I am afraid that this district is scantily populated. May I ask for what part of it you were making?"

"I was going to call on Miss Lettice Mason, of The Croft, which I understand is somewhere hereabouts; though, according to the lucid nature of the directions I have received, I have not the faintest notion where."

"This, though a fortuitous, may prove to be rather a fortunate encounter, since Lettice Mason is my niece, and The Croft is my home."

The girl gazed at him in undisguised astonishment.

"Is your name Hurle?"

"No, my name is Banner; John Banner."

"Then Professor Hurle is not your brother?"

"The relationship is rather remote. My half-brother, Charles Mason—my mother's son by her first marriage—married one of his sisters. Lettice is their daughter and only child. Her father and mother are both dead; so it happens that Lettice is to me as if she were my daughter."

"I see. Now I begin to understand. When I heard that Miss Mason lived with her uncle, I supposed that he must be the professor's brother; but—I should never have taken you for that. You are not in the least bit like him."

"That sounds like a doubtful compliment. Professor Hurle is a very clever man."

"Is he? I know that he is a great scholar; but—are the two things synonymous?"

Mr. Banner laughed.

"I am afraid that that is a point which you can scarcely expect me to decide off-hand. May I ask to whom I have the pleasure of speaking?"

The girl hesitated, as if in doubt to what extent to give him her confidence, searching his countenance with her bright eyes as if to learn from it what manner of man he was. Apparently the result was, at least in a measure, satisfactory.

"My name is Capparoni, Agnes Capparoni."

"That sounds Italian."

"My father was Italian, but my mother was English, and I am English."

"There is a note in your voice which seems to say that you are glad of it."

"Of course I am. Everybody would be English if they could be."

"You believe that! I wonder—— However, Miss Capparoni, since we are not acquainted, I think, under the circumstances, that I am at liberty to offer you a seat in my run-about, since your bicycle is—resting. My car is two-seated; as you perceive, I am my own chauffeur; there is room in it both for you and your machine. You will find that that is the quicker way to The Croft."

Presently the two were bowling together over the road. For some distance both of them were silent. Then Mr. Banner asked—

"Are you a friend of Letty's?"

"I am, in one sense—and I hope that you will think me so—though I have never seen her."

"Then she does not know that you are coming?"

"So far as I am aware, she is not even conscious of my existence."

There was another interval of silence. Then the girl spoke again.

"Mr. Banner?"

"Miss Capparoni?"

"I think, now that I have seen you, and have had an opportunity of judging what kind of person you are——"

"Don't jump at conclusions, Miss Capparoni."

"I don't, as a rule. I was merely about to observe that, on the whole, I incline to the opinion that before I see Miss Mason I had perhaps better speak to you on the subject on which I proposed to speak to her, if you don't mind."

"Not in the very least. I think you will find me a tolerable listener, especially if, as your tones would almost suggest, you have a horrible tale to unfold."

"It is, at any rate, a curious one. Only, as I may have to occupy your attention for some minutes, I think I could say my say much better if the car were not going quite so fast. Would you mind giving your car a little rest?"

"There!" The car stopped dead. Its driver leaned back in his seat and turned to her. "The car is resting. Since I doubt if a dozen persons pass along this portion of the road in the course of an average day, I don't think that we need fear interruption. So now for your tragic story."

"It may prove to be more tragic than you imagine, Mr. Banner. In the first place, will you please look at that?"

She handed him a paper which she took from the little bag which was hanging at her waist. He realized its nature with evident surprise.

"Professor Hurle's handwriting; his will, leaving everything to that scamp, Wentworth; but with no signature attached. Miss Capparoni, I don't understand. How do you come to be in possession of this, and why do you show it to me?"

She narrated how the will had been extracted by Fentiman from Dr. Hurle. Mr. Banner's amazement plainly increased as he listened.

"You must pardon my bluntness, but—I am still at a loss. How came you to be where you say you were; and what business had you to be there, anyhow?"

"On the preceding night I was in Mr. Wentworth's rooms. I heard him form his plans with Fentiman, so—I thought I'd intervene."

"But—without inquiring what you were doing in Wentworth's rooms at night—what have Cyril Wentworth's movements and plans, however nefarious, to do with you? In other words, Miss Capparoni, who are you, that you should go out of your way to play so curious a part in what—if I understand you rightly—you admit is no concern of yours?"

The girl seemed to consider.

"If you don't mind I'll tell you my story. Then you will understand how closely I am concerned in everything which concerns the man whom you call Cyril Wentworth; and how through him I became associated with Professor Hurle, and through the professor with Miss Mason. Also, by the time I've finished my story, I think you will admit that, in telling it, I had no egotistical intention."

"By all means tell me anything which you think will throw light upon the puzzle. I confess that, so far, you have only filled me with bewilderment. But since tobacco seems to clear what I call my brain, if you'll permit me, while you talk, I'll smoke, and I'll get out of the car to do it."

Descending to the ground, he lit his pipe. Planting himself immediately in front of the car, he kept his eyes fixed on her face while she told her tale, she remaining apparently wholly unmoved by the fixed intentness of his gaze. No one coming along the road, seeing how each was absorbed in the other, would have guessed that they were strangers, who had met each other, for the first time in their lives, by the merest chance, only a few minutes before.

CHAPTER IX

PIETRO CAPPARONI

"My father was, as you have surmised, an Italian. When he married my mother, he came with her to live in England. My mother always had delicate health. While I was still a child, the doctors told her that if she wished to continue to live, she would have to leave England. My parents thereupon commenced a series of wanderings to and fro upon the face of the earth in search of health for my mother. They never found it. In the end she died—in Australia.

"At that time the world was full of stories of the gold which had been found in West Australia. Hundreds, thousands of people, coming from all quarters of the globe, were rushing into the waterless desert in search of it. In Australia itself the gold fever was in the air. It attacked my father. It was not because he was in need. Although he was not rich, neither was he poor. My father and my mother had both had means. It was certainly not pecuniary stress which drove him out into the salt swamps and arid wastes of the Victoria Desert.

"Not only had theirs been a love match, my mother and father continued to be lovers to the end. The more I look back the more clearly do I see that each only lived for the other. The nearer my mother came to death, the more beautiful she grew; I suspect with a beauty which was in itself unnatural, and, if the thing was possible, the more my father loved her. When she died, everything in the world which was, to him, worth living for went with her. If he could, I believe he would have had himself fastened in the same coffin. While he was still half beside himself with grief, there came the tale of the West Australian gold,* that will-o'-the-wisp which lured so many to a quest which ended in destruction. Before I realized what it was that he proposed to do, he was off in search of it, leaving me at a Melbourne boarding-school.

"I never saw him again. For months I had from him a weekly letter; strange and wild letters some of them were; I have them every one; and then—came silence. His letters ceased. I continued to write to him, but there came no answers; instead, after a time, my own letters came back to me. They had never reached him. According to the legends on the envelopes, he was 'unknown,' 'not to be found.'

"The last letter I had received from him was addressed from Darlot City Camp. It was the seventh that I had had from the same place. He had been the usual round which men went in those days: through the Coolgardie district, and then up north and east. I have letters from most of the places which, then, were famous. His idea was not to mine himself, but to develop other people's mines, and to speculate in claims on his own account. He was no simpleton, although, in his letters, he used to tell me how my mother had come to him in the night, and ridden with him across the desert. Whether he himself believed in her visitations I cannot say; I think myself it is possible that great love works miracles. Certainly on all other subjects his brain was clear enough. He had a good general knowledge of the business on which he was setting forth. Geology had always been his hobby. He knew as well as any man the kind of ground in which gold is found, and the best means of getting at it when it is there. He seemed, so far as I was able to judge from his letters, to have met, on the whole, with at least his share of success. He had entered into several speculations which had turned out well; and, indeed, his last two or three letters had contained hints that he was even then engaged in a venture which might not improbably have great results.

"In each of the last nine communications which I had had from him, one particular individual was referred to by name—Charlie Walker. This Walker seemed to have made on him a considerable impression. It was through him that he went to Darlot City Camp. It was in partnership with him that he was engaged in the venture which promised so well. The earlier allusions said nothing but good of him. Later, a tone crept into them which made me wonder. It was not that my father began to think less of him, in a certain sense; indeed, on the score of his abilities, the impression grew, instead of waned. My father once wrote, 'I believe Walker's the cleverest all-round man I ever met,' adding, as if by an afterthought, 'and the wickedest.' I wondered in what direction his wickedness lay, since it must have been very obvious to have struck my father, who made it his habitual rule to think ill of no man. His language grew stronger as the weeks went by. In the very last letter I have he says, 'Walker belongs to a type of man I have never before encountered. He is like a being out of a fairy tale. I am sometimes in doubt as to whether he is a man or a devil. I believe that, in certain directions, he has the powers of a devil. The men in camp credit him with using his powers with devilish cruelty. Some very queer tales are told of him. I hope, for his own sake, and mine, that none of them are true.'

"The words are stamped on my brain in indelible letters. When it began to dawn on me that my father had ceased to write to me; that, apparently, there was an end of him, those were the words which recurred to me again and again. His silence meant that he was ill; that he was dead; or—what else? That was the question which I had to put to myself and answer. If he was ill, it was hardly likely that he was too ill to dictate at least a note to an acquaintance; for instance, to his partner, Walker. He knew that I should be greatly worried if I heard nothing from him at all; and I knew him well enough to be certain that, however ill he might be, his first thought would be for me. I was sure that he would get some one to tell me that he was still alive, lest, from his silence, I should infer the worst. Therefore I concluded that he was not suffering, and had not been suffering, from any ordinary illness.

"On the other hand, I did not believe that he was dead. I told myself that if he were dead, his papers would have been left behind; my relationship to him, and my address, would have been learnt from them, and, at any rate, the broad facts of his fate would have been communicated to me. Supposing them to have fallen into bad hands, then still I might have heard. Among his papers was a cheque-book on a bank in which he had a large balance. An ordinary thief would have drawn a cheque and cashed it, which, under the circumstances, would have been an intimation of an unmistakable kind. But nothing reached the bank; the account remained untouched. It happened that one of his letters had contained a list of the securities which he had with him in the camp. It struck me that it was rather odd that he should have thought it necessary to send me such a list, though he explained the proceeding by saying that in certain company one never knew what might happen, and that therefore it was desirable that I should have a duplicate list of the more valuable of his belongings. Inquiries were made, which showed that the securities had been entered in his name, and still continued to stand in it. As time went on, nothing transpired to show that any attempt had been made to deal in them. If the papers had been stolen, even supposing the thief to have been unwilling to forge a cheque, he would surely have endeavoured to turn the securities into cash, especially as they might, one and all, have been easily negotiated.

"The more I thought, the more I felt persuaded that my father was neither ill nor dead. Then what alternative was there? People about me answered that there was none. They said that he must be one or the other. As time went on they decided that, beyond the slightest shadow of a doubt, he was dead. My mother had left me all that she possessed. My father had seen that all her affairs were put into proper order before he started. I remained at that Melbourne boarding-school until my twenty-first birthday, the silence having remained unbroken for more than two years. Having come into possession of my small property, and having become, to that extent, my own mistress, I went to look for my father. People laughed. Some tried to stop me. They said that he was certainly dead; that to go and look for him in Western Australia was absurd, since the place was played out, and all traces of him must have been long since lost. But I paid no heed to any of them. I went. And I may tell you that I have been looking for him ever since. Some would say that I am no nearer him than I ever was. I, however, am of a different opinion."

For the first time Mr. Banner interrupted her.

"How long is it since you started?"

"More than three years. I was twenty-one when I began. I shall be twenty-five next birthday."

"Twenty-five?" Mr. Banner looked at her, as if to learn how she bore her years. "I am glad you're twenty-five."

"Why should you be glad?"

"Because you look younger, and I was afraid you were."

"Why should you be afraid of that?"

"Well, you see, I'm not so young as I once was; and when a man has arrived at my age, he finds that very young women are apt to regard him as advanced altogether into the sere and yellow.* But sometimes, when a young woman has attained to the dignity of twenty-five, she takes a more reasonable view of his position."

"You don't seem to be at all old to me, and, of course, you're not old. It's only for the sake of saying so."

"I'm glad you think so." Mr. Banner sighed. "And do I understand that although you have been looking for your father for more than three years without finding him, that you still hope to do so?"

"Emphatically."

"Alive?"

"Certainly. I should not expect to find him in this world if he were dead. But I am convinced that he is not."

"What grounds have you for your conviction?"

"You shall hear. You may think them slight, but they suffice for me. I reached what, in my father's time, had been known as Darlot City Camp, which I found, having shed two of its names, had become simply Darlot. More than once on the way there I had lighted on traces of my father, and more particularly of Charlie Walker. At Darlot itself my father's name had already become little more than a tradition. Walker's was as alive and fresh as it had ever been, though I discovered that he was more widely known under a sort of pseudonym, 'Jack the Chemist.'

"Jack the Chemist was still a notorious character in all that region. The nickname had come to be used almost as a bogey with which to frighten children. It was not long before I came to the conclusion that his reputation must have grown with the efflux of time. Such a monster as they portrayed would never have been allowed to live. They would have killed him, with or without sanction of law, just as they would have destroyed any other dangerous animal. Some of the tales they told of him were hideous; on the face of them, almost incredible. And yet, that some of the most apparently incredible parts of them were true, I have now begun to believe."

She paused, as if to think. Mr. Banner intervened with a comment.

"Not seldom the seemingly impossible proves to be true. It has been so over and over again in the history of human progress. When you come to deal with the actions of individual men you approach a subject in which the word incredible should be sparingly used. One is compelled to believe that some men are capable of anything, and that to them all things are possible. It is rather a question of evidence. I should prefer rather to hear what evidence was offered you than what tales were told against him."

The girl still continued silent. Then, leaning forward on the seat of the car, clasping her hands together in front of her, she spoke of Jack the Chemist.

"I will tell you one tale which I heard, not from one person only, but from certainly a dozen persons, and then you will begin to understand how it is that that apparently silly nickname, 'Jack the Chemist,' has to me become associated with nightmare horrors; and, also, you will be able to guess why I believe that my father is still—alive."

CHAPTER X

JACK THE CHEMIST

"IN Darlot City Camp, in those early days, labour was the scarcest thing there was. The workings were mostly alluvial; the miners had to find the gold with their own picks and shovels. When a shaft had to be sunk, to deal with anything like a deep lode, to all intents and purposes the mine was at an end. Few would work for pay. It was practically impossible to take in a sufficiency of partners to deal with such a mine on business-like principles. When a certain distance was reached working ceased; that is, in the majority of cases. My father's mine was an exception, a singular one.

"I call it my father's mine, because everything goes to show that it was his. Walker was his partner, and shared in the profits. But it was my father's money which developed it, and it was he who bought and paid for the machinery which was used in working it. He must have known all about the claim before he arrived upon the scene, because, when he came, he brought the machinery with him. It was rudimentary enough, but there it was regarded as wonderful, not the least wonderful thing being that he had been able to get it there at all. I do not know how many horses had been used up in the process, nor how many men. The greatest marvel of all was that men should have been found who would undertake such work; but they had, Walker had found them. The arrival of the outfit was regarded in Darlot City Camp as a latter-day miracle. It comprised my father and Walker, and nine men—working men. A stranger lot, if what I was told was true, surely never were seen. There were five blacks, two half-breeds, and two whites, and they were all of them not only speechless but imbecile."

The girl paused, as if to enable Mr. Banner to grasp the full meaning of her words. He repeated them after her, contemplatively.

"All of them not only speechless but imbecile?"

"All of them."

"Then, if that was the case, as workmen they were worthless, because, as doctors will tell you, the one impossible thing is to get lunatics to do work that counts."

"The only thing they could or would do was work for Walker. No one had any influence over them but him; they paid not the least attention to my father. I was told that my father's attitude was not the least singular part of the whole proceedings. He wore a continual air of bewilderment, of being mystified, as if all that was going on was clean beyond his comprehension. I believe that up to a certain point it was.

"A well was sunk, water found, the machinery set up, a shaft made, by those nine men. They worked as few men could ever have worked before—all day and every day, and sometimes far into the night, under Walker's supervision. He would have worked them on Sundays, if my father had not interfered. The partners quarrelled because my father insisted on their having one day's rest in seven. The nine men offered no remonstrance, showed no sign of unwillingness. When Walker was there, they worked unceasingly, like so many automata. When he was not there, they became like so many stocks and stones. They did nothing, and nothing could be done with them. The strain on him must have been almost as great as it was on them."

The listener interposed a question.

"Are you suggesting that this was another case of the man Fentiman you were telling me about, and that those nine men were under some sort of hypnotic influence."

"That was the idea which first gained credence in the camp. When questioned, and you may be sure that Walker was freely questioned, he used to say with a laugh that he had hypnotized them. But it was soon realized that any theory of that kind offered a very insufficient explanation.

"In less than a month the mine was in full working order; in a rudimentary sense, no doubt, but in a sense which was altogether beyond anything which had been hitherto seen in Darlot City Camp. Then the nine men began to die—what of, was never known. There was no doctor to certify. One thing was certain, they died very much against Walker's will. He regarded their deaths as so many personal injuries, which, no doubt, they were. He offered fabulous wages to men who would take their places. My father went from claim to claim; guaranteeing payment out of his own pocket. I think that some might have worked for him; but for Walker, no. Already they regarded him with something more than feelings of distrust—as a being to be both feared and shunned.

"It had been noticed, among other things, that he was fond of making what would be to use the language of hyperbole to call experiments—on animals. Animals of all sorts seemed to regard him with a mixture of fear and hatred. His horse had to be kept constantly tethered, because directly he approached it, it went half mad in its efforts to avoid him. Directly he was on its back it began to sweat and shiver. The three or four dogs which were in the camp would retreat as he approached, and snarl and snap if he tried to touch them. A miner had a bull-dog of which he was very fond. Although an inoffensive creature, as a rule, given to make friends with all and sundry, it flew one day at Walker, without apparent cause, and bit him in the leg. That night the dog was missing. Two days afterwards it was found at some distance from the camp; but something had happened to it. It seemed to have lost its wits. It did not recognize its own master, and moved sideways, with a sort of crab-like progression, as if incapable of walking straight. Its owner went straight to Walker, and charged him with having played tricks with the dog. Although Walker denied it, no one believed him.

"Seven weeks after their arrival, six of the nine men were dead. Walker, who claimed to be possessed of medical knowledge, asserted that they had died of some sort of fever. If that was the case, it was odd that it should have only attacked the six. Work at the mine was perforce suspended. Since no labour was to be obtained in the camp, Walker set out in search of some, though where he expected to find labourers within hundreds of miles of where they were, no one was able to guess. My father told him, publicly, as he was starting, that he was setting out on a wild-goose chase, since it was certain that his errand would be fruitless. He turned savagely upon my father, telling him that he did not know what he was talking about, declaring, with an oath, that he would return with a dozen men inside a week.

"The very day after his departure, a man—a stranger—appeared in the camp, who told a singular story. He said that he had been making for Darlot City Camp with a companion. They had pitched, on the preceding night, what they hoped would be their last camp before arriving at their destination, and were eating their supper when they were joined by another traveller. Bush hospitality is proverbial; the new-comer was warmly welcomed. So soon, however, as he came right into the light of the fire, the narrator declared that he recognized in him a man who had been known in quite another part of the country as Jack the Chemist. He had borne so diabolical a reputation that his sudden appearance startled him almost into speechlessness. He endeavoured not to allow any signs of recognition to escape him, awaiting an opportunity to put his companion privately upon his guard. That opportunity never came. After supper the traveller, taking a flask out of his satchel, suggested that they should drink his whisky as a night-cap. 'You'll sleep more soundly after this than you ever slept in all your lives before,' he said, pouring some of the contents into each of the three drinking cups. 'Now, all together; gentlemen, here's to you.' Something in the speaker's words and manner put the narrator on his guard. He endeavoured to convey a warning to his friend. 'If you take my advice. Bill, you won't drink any more of this stuff than you can help; it comes out of a chemist's shop, I guess, this does.' The friend, supposing him to be jesting, only laughed, and swallowed the contents of his cup. To his horror, the other man—who had abstained from tasting what was in his cup—saw him, immediately after he had drunk, fall to the ground as if he were dead. Before his companion could move to go to his assistance, the traveller was on him, and had him by the throat. Struggling for more than life, he picked up the iron pan in which the meal had been cooked, and, more by chance than anything else, struck a blow with it which knocked his assailant senseless. He could not have been a very courageous person, because, without stopping to see what had really happened to his friend, he jumped on to his horse and rode off through the night. But I was informed that the tales he told of Jack the Chemist were quite sufficient to explain why any one should flee from him as if he were the devil himself.

"There could be no doubt, from the description he gave, that Jack the Chemist and Walker were one and the same person. This story cast a lurid light upon his methods of recruiting labour. The whole camp sat upon him in a sort of committee. A *posse* was formed to chase and bring him back before more evil was worked. But he never was brought back—at least, by that *posse*. The next morning, when the camp awoke, the stranger who had brought the story was found lying dead. In his tightly-clenched hand was found a tiny strip of steel, which was afterwards known to be the nozzle of some unusual form of hypodermic syringe. The three remaining workmen were dead. My father's tent was empty; he had vanished with all his papers. In the first wild burst of rage it was taken for granted that my father was a criminal. But facts which came out later more than hinted that he was only another of Jack the Chemist's victims. Two men had been seen making across the desert eastward—in those days so desperate an adventure that men would need to be very hard driven to attempt it. The natives who had seen them said that one man was sitting jauntily on a horse, while he led another, on which was his companion, by the bridle. The second man was incapable of leading his own horse, he could hardly keep his seat upon the saddle; he was apparently blind, speechless, and imbecile."

The girl ceased to speak. She sat, with tightly compressed lips and gleaming eyes, looking into space, as if she saw, with the eyes of the mind, those two lone travellers. Mr. Banner watched her for a moment, and then said—

"You conclude that the one man was Walker, and the other your father?"

"I am sure of it. I have no doubt that Jack the Chemist—I prefer to call him by that name, it marks him as with a brand—returned to the camp that night for some purpose of his own. My father charged him there and then with being the manner of man he was, whereupon he used my father as he had used those nine men, and Heaven only knows how many more beside. Gathering together my father's papers with his own, towing him after him as if he were a chattel, he fled for his life across the desert. You can have no idea, and I can give you none, what in those days such a journey, under such circumstances, must have meant. More than two years afterwards, under much more favourable conditions, I did that journey myself. I never want to do it again. After all that lapse of time I found traces of them by the way. Whoever saw them once never forgot them. They were so strange a pair—in particular was my father so striking a figure.

"When they reached South Australia they seem to have parted; thenceforward I only found traces of my father. Blind, dumb, imbecile, he roused compassion wherever he went. It seems that, though always tired and way-worn, he was unresting, always going on, as if some one was calling him, bidding him to haste. I believe that some one was calling him, even from afar off—the monster who had transformed him into his worse than slave—and that he had no option but to obey."

Again the girl stopped. Once more her listener seemed to choose his words before he spoke.

"I quite understand what your feelings are, and the tragic meaning all that you have told me has for you. But you must pardon me, Miss Capparoni, if I am so dull as still not to perceive what connection this has with Professor Hurle and the unfinished will which you have handed me."

"It has at least this connection—Cyril Wentworth is Jack the Chemist!"

CHAPTER XI

MR. BANNER TAKES MISS CAPPARONI HOME TO TEA

"MISS CAPPARONI!" Mr. Banner stared at the girl as if wondering if she knew what she was saying. "Are you conscious of the monstrous charge which you are bringing against a person who, I have reason to believe, has both means and reputation, and who is of some standing in society?"

"It is not merely a charge which I am making, I am stating a fact."

"I fancy you are forgetting, also, that Cyril Wentworth is, in some degree, my relative."

"I don't see how. Even if he is Professor Hurle's nephew, he is not yours; that is, if I followed correctly the explanation of your genealogical tree which you just now gave me."

"He is Lettice's cousin, and I have always regarded Lettice as my daughter."

"All the same, she is not your daughter; and one can't help having a cousin who's a scamp, which you yourself admitted that he was. I am only showing you that your doubts of him were justified. Please understand me, Mr. Banner; I am making no wild feminine charge against this man, based on prejudice or rumour. I come to you with proofs of every word I say. If you wish, I will say no more. I will go away as I have come; Miss Mason need never see me. I have evidence that her cousin is almost as much her enemy as he is mine. I hoped that, when you had learned what that evidence is, in return for the help I can give Miss Mason, you would help me—as I believe you can help me—to find my father, who is still—somewhere—at that man's mercy. But if you will not do this, then I must work without you, and I will, though I may probably have to move on different lines than I should do if I had the advantage of your aid. So, Mr. Banner, which is it to be? Do you wish to have the truth, or don't you? Am I to go on, or stop? Will you help me to unmask a scoundrel, and rescue from his clutches at least one of the victims of his iniquity; or am I to fight him single-handed? I'm not afraid, I assure you, and in the end I'll win; but, if you'll help me, I may win quicker. You do not need me to point out to you that this spoiler of men is not only Miss Mason's enemy and mine; he is in an even greater degree the enemy of humanity. Now, Mr. Banner, please, which is it to be!"

John Banner knocked out the ashes of his pipe against his heel, looking at her half quizzically as he did so. He commenced to pace to and fro across the road. The girl, sitting motionless on the seat of the car, watched him. At last, still moving from side to side, he spoke.

"You forget. Miss Capparoni, that although to you what you have said is ancient history, to me it is as if you had suddenly pointed a pistol at my head and fired it."

"The analogy doesn't seem to me to be a very good one. Do you mean that you want time to consider?"

"I do."

"To consider what?"

John Banner stopped in front of the car. This time there was no doubt that the glance with which he regarded her was wholly quizzical.

"You are a very shrewd young lady, Miss Capparoni, and a very persistent one. I can well believe that you'd be a match, and more than a match, for any man—however bad that man might be. But might I ask you to remember that every question has several sides, and that some folks see some sides clearer than others?" He looked at his watch. "And one of the sides which just now appeals very strongly to me is that at the present moment Lettice is waiting for her tea. Do you know that you and I have spent the best part of the afternoon here, in the middle of the road? I'm sure a cup of tea will do you no harm. Let me take you where you'll get one, and we'll leave your story to be continued in our next."

"You are very good. But although there is but little more of it, that little is not the least essential part. I'd rather continue it now to an end. When you have heard me out, we shall each of us know better where we stand."

John Banner gave a grotesquely exaggerated sigh. He assumed an air of resignation and refilled his pipe.

"Very well. Anything to know better—as you phrase it, where we stand. Only if we find Lettice in a state of nervous palpitation, under the impression that the car has been blown skywards and borne me with it, the blame will be yours, not mine."

"Certainly; if I do see Miss Mason I will make that clear to her. I'm going to hurry, leaving out everything but the absolutely essential."

"Thank you very much."

Mr. Banner expressed his thankfulness in such tones of meekness that, in spite of herself, the girl had to smile. She went on rapidly, as she had promised, leaving him to put in for himself, if he chose, what she left out.

"At Darlot City Camp there was, even then, the inevitable man with a camera. He snapped everything—my father, the nine workmen, Jack the Chemist; Jack the Chemist he snapped over and over again. When I reached Darlot that photographer had become one of the leading citizens. He still had those snapshots. He allowed me to have copies made of them; I have those copies now.* With their aid I looked for the original all over the world. I almost lighted on him again and again, never quite. I thought I saw him in a motorcar at Monte Carlo; a second time at a Parisian theatre. At last, only a few days ago, I was sure I saw him in London, in Hyde Park. I followed him home. I found that he had a flat in Sloane Street, where he called himself Cyril Wentworth."

"His name—this is by the way—is Wentworth; to that fact I myself can vouch."

"To me, as I have said, he will always be Jack the Chemist. I gained admission to his flat, during his absence, by means of which I will say nothing; in dealing with him I don't propose to stick at trifles. I ransacked every paper I could discover in search of something which would tell me what had become of my father, wholly without success. He came in and found me there."

"And sent for the police?"

"He talked of doing so, but he only talked. I charged him with being Jack the Chemist; he attempted no denial. I think he was too taken aback to think of a plausible lie."

"Did you question him about your father?"

"Not I; I knew better. My object was to mystify him, not to afford him information. I dropped no hint as to who I was or what I wanted; to have done so would have been tantamount to signing my father's death warrant. I heard him instruct Fentiman to cozen a will out of Professor Hurle; how that came about I may tell you some other time, it will amuse you. As I have told you, I was at St. Clement's before Mr. Fentiman, and heard him extract from the professor a piece of information which, quite possibly, places Cyril Wentworth between my finger and thumb."

She held out her hand with a significant gesture. Mr. Banner shook his head.

"You play the eavesdropper to perfection, Miss Capparoni."

"Situated as I am, all means are justified. I assure you I mean to stick at nothing—nothing. Are you acquainted with Professor Hurle's financial position?"

"I know that, although he has always said that Lettice will be his heiress, he has also confessed that he has nothing to leave her."

"Some time ago he purchased some shares in an Australian gold mine."

"A pretty gold mine! He bought them off Wentworth, who cheated him finely. The mine was bogus; the shares were worthless. Poor old Hurle lost every farthing."

"The mine was the one which belonged to my father, and in which Walker was a partner. After my father's disappearance it had an eventful history. At one time it was known, not inappropriately, as the Old Nick. When the Westralian boom began in England, it was re-christened, turned into a company, and launched on the London market as the Great Harry Mine. I don't know how it was managed, but I am quite sure that Wentworth was careful to let no one on the other side guess that he was in any way connected with it; the risk would have been too great. Soon after the company was floated the mine went wrong; the shares went to zero. Wentworth chose that moment to plant five thousand of them on his uncle."

"The model nephew!"

"By degrees, however, matters improved. My father was justified. The mine showed itself to be one of the richest in the country. The shares went up and up. At this moment they are worth more than fifty pounds apiece."

"You don't mean it!"

"You have only to look at the first list of mining shares you come across to have all the proof you want. You see now why Wentworth wanted that will. He still holds the professor's five thousand shares, their owner not having the faintest notion that they are anything more than waste paper. Soon after the will was signed the professor would have died, you may be sure of it, and Mr. Wentworth would have come into undisturbed possession of a great fortune, whose very existence nobody but himself suspected."

Mr. Banner, who had taken off his cap, was rubbing his head, as if to rub the news which he had just heard into it.

"Miss Capparoni, you amaze me. If what you say is correct—and do not suppose I am doubting it—what a blackguard the man must be!"

"The language you apply to him is laudatory, Mr. Banner; he is very much more than that. To sum up, my position is this: If I place Miss Mason, whom you regard as a daughter, within reach of more than a quarter of million of money, then I think that, as a sort of a *quid pro quo*, you ought to help me to find my father; help me by all and every means in your power."

Mr. Banner still continued to rub his head.

"I am beginning to think that you are right; I am, I admit it freely. It is being borne in on me more and more strongly every moment, not only that you are an excellent pleader, but that you have a sound case to deal with. But, at the same time, what you have said has so taken me by surprise, and is of so startling a character, that I can't take it all in at once—I really can't. You must give me time to digest it. My mental processes may be slow, but they are all I've got; and if you want to make the best of me, you must allow me to make the best of them. I propose that, without further discussion, you now let me take you to where we both of us can get some tea, on the understanding that I am on your side."

"I shall be very glad to come—if you are on my side."

"I hope to be there literally very shortly. There is, however, one condition which I must make. You are to say nothing of all this to Lettice without my express permission. Nor, indeed, are you to say anything more about it to me; the subject and all its branches is to be tabooed until I have had my tea, and my digestion has been advanced at least another stage."

On that understanding the car was restarted. As it sped through the leafy lanes they talked together as if they were old acquaintances. She soon perceived that he was far from being so slow-witted a person as it pleased him to pretend; that what he called his "mental processes" moved as rapidly as any one could possibly desire. She suspected that under the guise of easy, effortless conversation, on all sorts of themes, he was finding her out, learning what sort of person she really was. She had a comfortable feeling that, on the whole, he was content with what he learnt.

When at last they stopped at the door of The Croft, a young girl came running down the steps.

"Uncle, you bad man! Where have you been? I thought that you were never coming." Perceiving that he had a companion, she drew a little back. "I beg your pardon; I did not notice that there was some one with you."

"Lettice, this is Miss Capparoni. I hope she will allow me to speak of her as a friend of mine, and I trust you shortly will be able to look on her as a friend of yours. Hollo! who's that in the hall there?"

Lettice answered. "It's Dick Sharratt. He's come over to see you."

The young gentleman appeared on the steps.

"Has he? Dick Sharratt, what do you mean by absenting yourself from your university in term time?"

"As Lettice says, I ran over to find out how you were getting on. It's so long since I saw you."

"Is it? Was it yesterday, or the day before?"

"Rubbish! It's a jolly good week. Why——" Dick recognized the lady who was descending from the car. "I believe that we've met before, quite recently."

Miss Capparoni smiled.

"Mr. Banner, it was Mr. Sharratt who threw Fentiman into the fountain."

Dick protested.

"I say. Really, it isn't fair to give a chap away like that."

Lettice spoke.

"I am glad, Miss Capparoni, to hear that you have met Mr. Sharratt before; but I am sorry to learn that it was under discreditable circumstances. I hope that he was not behaving very badly."

"On the contrary, he was behaving very well indeed."

"Then I'm afraid it was by mistake. It's not his custom to behave well. Do you know that it's frightfully late? Are you people coming in to tea?"

They went in to tea, all four of them.

CHAPTER XII

MORNING CALLERS

CYRIL WENTWORTH was just starting to call upon Miss Bradley when, at the very door of his flat, he met Mrs. Van der Gucht, who, evidently, was just coming to call on him. Than such an encounter, to his mind, scarcely anything could have been more inopportune. That the lady thought quite otherwise she speedily made clear.

"How lucky that I've just caught you! Why, in another minute I might have missed you."

He wished she had.

"I've an appointment. I was hurrying off to keep it. You might walk with me part of the way if you don't mind."

Even while he was speaking he was wondering in what direction he could take her, so as to keep her from suspecting that the supposititious appointment was with Miss Bradley. She made a little grimace.

"Cyril!" He glanced round. He wished she would not call him Cyril out there upon the landing. "I don't want to walk—at least, not just yet. I want to come in and talk to you."

He hesitated. The prospect of such an interview offered delightful possibilities. And yet he had the feeling strong upon him that Miss Bradley was a lady who must not be kept waiting.

"Unfortunately, I'm pressed for time."

"Pressed for time! What's it matter? Let the people wait, whoever they are. I'm pressed for time. Do you know that it's very rude to keep me waiting outside your door? Do let me come in, please!"

Such a cadence came into her voice, and such a look into her eyes; and, moving towards him, she laid her small hand upon his arm with such a bewitching grace that he yielded. As soon as they both of them were in his sitting-room, he began to administer to her a lecture, or what was meant for one.

"Do you know that you've no right to be here?"

"I suppose not. I suspect that that's one of the reasons why I've come. I never was in a bachelor's rooms before."

"You oughtn't to be in one now."

"I dare say; not in some bachelors' rooms. But—in yours? Oughtn't I to be in yours?"

She looked at him with meaning in her eyes.

"Bertha!"

"Cyril! I've always understood that bachelors' rooms were comfy; and certainly this room is that, though I don't believe it

contains a single cushion. Then, again, I've always understood that
even a man's room suggests the character of its occupant. Do you
know that any one, even of an observing turn of mind, who saw
it for the first time would say that it was difficult to decide what
manner of man it was who lived in it. And that's exactly how I feel
about you. Although I've known you all this time, and pretty well,
I'm always conscious that there are ever so many sides of you of
which I know nothing at all, and probably never shall."

"Possibly it would be better for you if you never do."

"You think so? Perhaps you're right. I suppose if a woman ever
did know the whole of a man she would rather she didn't. How do
you think I'm looking?"

"Wicked: being of opinion that it is wicked for a woman to
look as charming as you are doing now."

"Thank you very much." She swept him an enchantingly
malicious curtsy. "A compliment from Mr. Cyril Wentworth is
such a very difficult thing to capture. Don't frown like that! You
look as cross as two sticks; as if I were some dreadful thing. What
do you think I am?"

"You know very well what I think you are; you know that I
think you are everything which in a woman is most to be desired."

"Cyril! that's really very nice of you, especially as your behaviour
has been quite beyond my comprehension lately. The other night at
Mrs. Tallis's dance you jumped up in the very middle of a sentence,
and left me in the conservatory all alone, and never came near me
again the whole of the evening; and you've never been near me since
to beg my pardon. Now perhaps you'll tell me what explanation you
have to offer. But never mind; I'll forgive you. I always do forgive
you everything. Do you know what I've come for?"

"I flattered myself that you'd come to pay me a morning call."

"It was nice of me to come—wasn't it? Please say that it was
nice."

"You witch!"

"Am I a witch? Do you really think that I am a witch? Aren't
witches rather horrid things? I'm sure that I'm not horrid. Since
you won't ask me why I've come I'll volunteer the information.
I've come because I want a holiday."

"You want a holiday—whose whole life is one long holiday!"

"Yes, I dare say. But there are holidays and holidays, and I want one of a very special kind. To be perfectly candid, Mr. Cyril Wentworth, I want you to take me on the river."

"My dear child, I've a dozen things which I must do!"

"Then don't do them. This is exactly the sort of day not to. It's perfectly lovely weather; the idea of wasting it in doing things! Please, Cyril, take me on the river—Cookham way; up one of the back-waters, you know, where everything is lovely and serene."

"It sounds inviting."

"Sounds inviting! It will be delicious, man! We'll get a punt, and I'll pole. You told me yourself you never saw any one pole better than I do. You shall enjoy the ravishing spectacle of seeing me pole—until I'm tired. Please, Cyril, take me in a punt, and let me pole."

When he spoke it was not in answer to her petition. He gave the conversation a sudden turn. He had been looking at her pretty hands, as she held them up in front of her, pressed together in mock entreaty.

"I see that you are still wearing the ring I gave you."

"Of course; I have never taken it once off since."

"Really?"

"Not once. You made me promise never to take it off, and I never have, not even to wash. I've kept my promise to the very letter. Do you know, I've a feeling about that ring as if it were different from all other rings; not merely because you gave it me, but—because it is. You may laugh at me, but sometimes it almost feels as if it were alive; as if it were caressing my finger. And when it's like that, a most singular sensation goes not only right up my arm, but all over my body. Isn't it funny?"

"Let me look at it!"

"Do you mean take it off?"

"Yes; take it off and let me look at it."

"Really, Cyril, if you don't mind I'd rather not. Can't you look at it while it is in its proper place upon my finger?"

"How can I, goose? Do as I tell you."

"I've a superstition that if I take it off something will be taken from me with it—something which I don't want to lose. Oh, Cyril, don't make me take it off!"

"You silly girl, I want to examine it closely, and how can I do that while you have it on? Do as I tell you. Take it off; or should I take it off for you?"

"Cyril, don't! Oh, you have taken my ring! Give—give it me back! What has happened? I—I hope I'm not going to be ill. Cyril, please give me back my ring! What's that?"

While the man peered closely at the ring, which he had removed from her finger even against her will, holding it with his right hand, while he kept her off from him with his left, the bell sounded. Both started, as if it had been a sound of dread.

"It's some fool," said Wentworth.

"Is it your door bell?" He nodded. "Will one of your servants answer it?"

"I keep no servants. I'm seldom here in the daytime; often not at night for days together. The woman who does for me when I am here went an hour ago."

"Are we alone in the flat together?" He nodded again. "Is it some one you are expecting; or perhaps it's a tradesman?"

"I'm expecting no one. All parcels are left for me in the porter's room. As I said, it's some fool." The sound was repeated. "I'd let him ring, only if I do he may hang about for a deuce of a time; and then if I were to go out and find him, it would be awkward." The sound came a third time. "I'll go and see who it is; but before I go I'd better pop you out of sight, it may be some inquisitive idiot. Whoever it is, he'll get short shift from me. I'll be rid of him inside five minutes, I promise you that. In with you!"

He had led her from one room to another.

"But—Cyril, this is your bedroom!"

"That's all right, it's only for a minute. You'll find plenty of books; get something to read."

Half thrusting her in, he drew the door to after her.

"Cyril, you've my ring, and you're locking the door!"

It was his frequent custom, before going out, to lock each room separately. Finding the key on the outside of this door, he turned it.

"You'll be perfectly all right. You don't want to have some stupid ass come blundering in. I'll let you out in a dozen seconds."

She spoke to him again from the other side of the door, but, possibly because the bell was making itself once more audible, he strode off unheeding.

CHAPTER XIII

THE PURSE

It might have been any one at the door, and Mr. Wentworth would probably have betrayed no symptoms of surprise, except the person who actually was there. The visitor was a man of about thirty. Cyril Wentworth stared at him with astonishment which, both in degree and quality, was almost comical.

"Quannell! What on earth brings you here?"

"I have something, Mr. Wentworth, which I wish to say to you in private."

"In private? What the deuce can you have to say to me which needs to be said in private? Is it something in the City—business?"

"No; it is a personal matter. If you will allow me to come in I will explain."

"But, my dear sir, I've an appointment for which I'm already overdue. Can't you write me, or meet me somewhere later in the day?"

"I'm afraid not. What I have to say must be said at once. If you will let me pass, Mr. Wentworth, I will not detain you one moment longer than I can help."

"Really, my good fellow, your tone's peculiar, and your manner's almost more so. However, if it is so pressing, in you come. I will give you five minutes by my watch; after that, however reluctantly, I am afraid I shall have to clear you out."

Mr. Quannell made no reply. He followed Wentworth into the sitting-room, where he stood for a moment looking at his host. He was tall, broadly built, not ill-looking, although stern-featured. In the eyes of some people his habitual gravity was his chief defect. Life to him was a serious thing. If he had a sense of humour he held it in subjection. Few of those who knew him claimed to have seen him laugh. He was the son of an Englishman who had settled in the Transvaal, and had himself been born and bred there. Although acquaintances of some years' standing, both in Africa and England, the two men, having nothing in common, had rather gone out of their way to avoid each other. To Wentworth's keen perception, Max Quannell's presence there, just then, was pregnant with significance.

When Quannell did speak, it was in the cold, measured tones which were in keeping with his character and deportment; but Cyril Wentworth fancied that on this occasion he detected something in his manner which was neither cold nor measured.

"Let me first point out to you, Mr. Wentworth, certain facts which justify my presence here, and which entitle me to say what I am about to say."

Wentworth thrust out his elbows with a gesture of remonstrance.

"My dear Quannell, you're not going to inflict on me a long preamble. Remember, you only have five minutes; hasten quickly."

But Mr. Quannell preferred his own gait.

"I have known Mrs. Van der Gucht all her life. She is ten years younger than I am; but when she was a child she and I were playmates. As you know, we were neighbours; her people were my people's friends. Her husband is, I think, the dearest friend I have."

"Mrs. Van der Gucht? Is it possible, Quannell, that you have forced yourself upon me in order that you might talk to me of Mrs. Van der Gucht?"

"When you were in South Africa your relations with her were the subject of injurious comment. As you are aware, her relatives and friends resented your conduct very strongly. Indeed, it so affected her father that he has never been the same man since."

"Hasn't he? Then, if I were you, I should be warned by his example."

"After you had gone, she married."

"Do you know, Quannell, that I always fancied that you rather wanted to marry her yourself. Odd how one does get such fancies, isn't it?"

The words conveyed a sneer. Mr. Quannell was silent. It would be incorrect to say that he changed colour; but something did happen to his face, and when he spoke again it was with a new light in his sombre eyes.

"I did want to marry her, but—she preferred my friend. Van der Gucht is the most indulgent of husbands. When she wished to visit England, although he could not accompany her, he let her come alone. Thus it happens that, in a very real and most unfortunate sense, in England she is alone; though it is true that decent men and women would consider her loneliness as her chief protection. I am afraid that it is not in that light that you have regarded it." He paused. If it was to afford the other man an opportunity of speaking, Wentworth did not avail himself of it. He stood, straight as a ramrod, his hands hanging at his sides, regarding his visitor with a peculiar smile. "From all quarters stories have reached me in which her name was coupled with yours—unpleasantly. Some of these stories have reached her husband."

"You acting as a medium?"

"No. I should not be easily induced to repeat stories to Mrs. Van der Gucht's disadvantage, even to her husband. None the less, stories have reached him. It is, to some extent, in consequence of a communication which I have received from him that I am now here."

"All this, to you, possibly is interesting; but as the five minutes which I conceded you is more than up, I must ask you to take yourself away at once."

"I trust that it may not be necessary for me to detain you more than another minute. Give me your word of honour that all acquaintanceship between Mrs. Van der Gucht and you shall cease, now and henceforward, and I will instantly withdraw."

"You are a modest man, Mr. Quannell. Permit me to show you to the door."

"If Mr. Van der Gucht does not receive telegraphic advice that you have given me such an undertaking he will immediately leave Pretoria for London, a proceeding which may result in ruin to him and to her. You perceive the position?"*

"Your friend Van der Gucht will possibly be able to speak for himself when he reaches London. In the mean time you may inform him that in matters of this sort I prefer to deal with principals only. Now, sir, please go."

"You understand clearly what your refusal to give me such a promise involves?"

"Do you understand that I am asking you—not for the first or second time—to leave my rooms?"

"Mr. Wentworth——"

"Mr. Quannell, if you wish to bring a shower of scandal down upon this lady, you are going the shortest way to effect your purpose. If you won't go, I shall put you out; if you resist, there'll be a row. Although that may amuse you—and, possibly, me—do you suppose that it will do any good to the lady?"

The cogency of this line of reasoning seemed to influence Quannell, almost against his will; although one might suspect that every pulse in his being urged him to take this gentleman by the throat, and consent to spare his life only in exchange for the required promise. If he did entertain such a desire, he kept it well in hand. Turning slowly, with his eyes fixed upon the other's face, he began to move towards the door. As he went, his foot kicked against something which was lying on the carpet. Stooping, he picked it up. Glancing at it for a second, he then looked quickly up at Wentworth.

"You blackguard!"

Mr. Wentworth said nothing. He also glanced at what the other was holding, then up at the finder's eyes. For perhaps six seconds the two men regarded each other in silence, like two animals who have reached a point at which it has become a case of either to fight or to retreat. Evidently Quannell had to put pressure on himself to enable himself to speak. His voice had assumed a sudden quality of hoarseness.

"This—this is Mrs. Van der Gucht's purse."

He was holding out the article in question at full length of his arm, almost as if he was afraid of letting it come into too close contact with his body. It was one of those small bags made of gold mail, which some foolish women wear dangling from their waists, in which to carry their money and odds and ends. Wentworth looked at the speaker with that peculiar fixed smile, like a continual sneer, which had been on his face since the commencement of the interview. His tone was not only cool and clear, it was flippant.

"Well, what of it?"

It seemed as if Quannell supposed that the other had not grasped the full drift of what he had said. He repeated his own words, with additions.

"This is Mrs. Van der Gucht's purse. I am sure of it. I know it to be hers."

"I hope you are not suggesting a criminally intimate knowledge of the lady's belongings, Mr. Quannell?"

"Wherever she goes she nearly always carries it with her; I know that also. I called on her before I came here——"

"Quannell! Fie! And Van der Gucht your dearest friend!"

"She was not in. They told me that she had probably gone out for the whole day. You blackguard! She has either been here quite recently, or—she is here now. Wentworth, is—is Mrs. Van der Gucht here now?"

He asked the question almost as if he roared it. Beyond doubt, the man was growing dangerous. Cyril Wentworth merely gave to his smile a more aggressive twist.

"Admitting, for the sake of argument, that Mrs. Van der Gucht is here now, doesn't it make your offence still ranker that you should have forced yourself, not only upon me, but upon a lady too?"

What Mr. Quannell saw, or imagined that he saw, in the other's words and manner, he alone could tell. But his conduct was suggestive. With his clenched fist he struck the other a swinging blow on his right cheek. That the attack, at that moment, was unexpected, is probable. Wentworth reeled backwards, as if taken unawares, and was only saved from falling by being brought up against the wall. But he still smiled. Putting his hand up to his cheek-bone, he brought it away with the fingers dabbled with blood. The skin had been cut, possibly by a ring which the other was wearing. He put his blood-stained fingers into his waistcoat pocket, keeping them there for some moments, as if feeling for something which it contained. Withdrawing them, he moved swiftly across the room. Precipitating himself on Quannell, when he was within a foot or two of him, like some wild creature, heedless of the blows which the other hailed on him, he caught at his hair with his left hand, and began to fumble his scalp with the fingers of his right, as if feeling for some particular point. There was a gleam of something bright. Then, loosing his hold, Quannell ceased to strike at him. Instead, he went blundering backwards, retaining his perpendicular position only with an effort. He was attacked by a curious and continuous shuddering—the sort of shuddering, almost amounting to a convulsion, which often precedes an epileptic fit. Wentworth watched him with a vague, impersonal something in his bearing which was almost horrible, as if he had seen that sort of thing so often before that, for him, it had lost all interest.

The man seemed to have been all at once attacked by some hideous form of paralysis. As the trembling ceased, it was followed by twitching of the limbs and head, which suggested that the spinal cord was not performing its proper functions. The form, just now so upright, had become limp and fibreless, the shoulders were hunched, the head had dropped forward on to the chest. The whole man had not only decreased in height, but, obviously, in manhood also. His jaw, which hung open, was slightly contorted; he showed his tongue; his partly closed eyes were lustreless, void of meaning; in the expression of his face there was not a trace of anything which had the slightest claim to intellect. He had, all at once, become a grotesque, dreadful caricature of what he was—a brute beast, rather than a sentient being.

Cyril Wentworth took a little flat leather case out of his waistcoat pocket; out of it a small silver tube. From the top of the tube he removed a cap. In the tube he inserted the nozzle of a tiny hypodermic syringe, which he apparently re-filled from the contents of the tube. He returned the tube and syringe to the leather case, and the case to his waistcoat pocket. He smiled at the uncouth creature in front of him, perverting, as he did so, a well-known saying—

"'It is good to have a giant's strength, but it is better, sometimes, to use it like a giant'—eh, Quannell? what do you think?" Stretching out his arm, placing the palm of his hand against Quannell's broad chest, he gave him a fairly hearty push, the big man giving way as if he were so much unresisting matter. "The question now arises, what am I to do with you? I can't send you out as you are into the open streets in the broad daylight; complications might arise. I think—yes, on the whole, I rather think that, to begin with, I'll dismiss the lady."

CHAPTER XIV

THE CURIOSITY OF A LADY

HE crossed towards his bedroom door as nonchalantly as if nothing had occurred to disturb his equanimity. He turned the key; in the doorway stood the lady. She was perturbed enough—all doubt, tremor, and concern.

"I thought you were never coming. Who was it? What has happened?"

In reply he held out the purse, the discovery of which had been the immediate cause of disaster to Mr. Quannell.

"You've dropped this, you careless child!"

"Did I?" She glanced at her waist. "So I did; I never noticed." She returned to the subject of her complaint. "What have you been doing all this time? You said you'd only be five minutes; I'm sure you've been an hour."

"Have I? I don't think so; not quite so long as that. You see, after all, I'm a business man; one, moreover, on whom business— of sorts—makes many and unexpected calls. I'm afraid that little jaunt of ours upon the river will have to be postponed. Or, stay; do you think that you could find something to do with yourself during, say, the next two hours, and then meet me at Paddington, or let me pick you up somewhere? We still might pay a visit to the glades of Cookham."

She seemed to give a little shiver.

"Somehow I don't think I care for the river now. I'm—I'm all of a twitter; don't you see I am?" Across her pretty face flitted what was but the ghost of a smile. "Cyril, you mustn't laugh, but I believe I miss my ring. Since you took it off my finger I've felt all—all mops and brooms, as if—as if something had happened. Give it back to me at once."

It was as if she tried to make her tones imperious, although they quavered. He regarded her with the same keen, half-amused, wholly impersonal scrutiny which had marked his bearing a few minutes before.

"Your ring? I haven't got it."

In her voice there was a note almost of terror.

"You haven't got it! Cyril, what do you mean?"

"My dear child, don't shriek out like that. I only mean that I've left it in the other room. If you'll get back inside there I'll fetch it, and bring it to you inside thirty seconds—this time an honest thirty seconds, not one tick over."

He put out his arm as if he would thrust her back into the bedroom. She remonstrated.

"Cyril, can't I come with you?"

"No; I don't think you had better come with me."

"Why? Is—is there still some one in there?"

"Yes; there is still some one in there."

"Who—who is it?"

He left her question unanswered.

"If you'll wait just where you are I'll bring it to you here."

"Yes," she said, "I'll wait."

He looked at her, smiling; then, turning, moved away.

The door in which she stood opened into the small apartment which he called his study. On the opposite side of the study, almost facing her, was the door which opened into the sitting-room. Reaching it, Wentworth, gripping the handle, found himself confronted by what was evidently unexpected resistance, which prevented him from opening the door. It sounded as if he said something to himself under his breath. Then, placing his shoulder against the panel, he shoved; and, framed in the doorway, stood Max Quannell.

"Damn you!" he exclaimed, with sudden rage.

Taking him by the throat, he would have hurled him back into the room, had not a cry from Mrs. Van der Gucht warned him that if his object was to evade discovery, he already was too late. Releasing Quannell, he turned to confront the lady, who, having advanced into the centre of the room, was staring at the man in front of her as at some dreadful vision. Having, as it seemed, waited for him to speak to her in vain, she spoke to him, in a half whisper.

"Max! Max!" When he yet was silent, she exclaimed, as if impelled by the sudden terror of some frightful memory, "Cyril, he looks just as father looked—that night!"

"I rather fancy that he has been taken suddenly unwell."

"That's what you said when I asked you what had happened to father."

"My dear child, it's a coincidence. Perhaps their constitutions are in sympathy."

"Cyril, what have you done to him? You know I told you that I thought I saw you do something to my father—in the darkness? You denied it, and I believed you, but—you did. And now—Max. What have you done to Max?"

"If you desire information as to what ails the gentleman, I can only refer you to a medical man, or to the gentleman himself."

"That, also, is what you said to me when I asked you what you had done to father. But I will ask Max. Max, don't you know me? I am Bertha. Don't you remember Bertha? Max, look at me, and speak to me, and tell me. What has he done to you? Max!"

Although she stood within a few inches of him, it was doubtful if he either saw or heard her. He kept moving his head fatuously from side to side; his whole frame continually twitched, as if he were affected by some variety of St. Vitus' dance. She turned to Wentworth with a new glitter in her bright eyes.

"What have you done to him?"

"My dearest girl, do let's leave Mr. Quannell and his little peculiarities alone. I assure you I've had enough of him. I'll get your ring, and we'll start for the river."

"The river—with you—alone? I daren't!"

"Isn't it rather late in the day for you to talk of not daring to be alone with me, anywhere?"

"Cyril, what have you done to Max?"

"Bertha, after what I have already had to go through on your account, your persistence gets upon my nerves. If you will have it, you shall. This is what comes of calling on a bachelor in his chambers. If anything has happened to Mr. Quannell, it is you who are responsible."

"What do you mean?"

"You know perfectly well what I mean; don't try to play the

baby. Quannell came asking questions about you, especially when he found that you were here. I'm a person who dislikes interference. When he tried to interfere, I stopped him."

"What do you mean—you stopped him?"

"If you'll look at him you'll see."

She looked, and shuddered. When she spoke again, her voice was pitched in such low tones it was scarcely audible.

"Did you—stop—father?"

"My dearest girl, I'll be candid, since we've got so far, and you will insist. I suppose you've sense enough to hold your tongue, for your own sake. I had to, or he'd have stopped me."

"Cyril! And I—I—— Oh-h-h!"

Covering her face with her hands, her sentence ended in a stifled scream.

"Now, Bertha, don't behave like a fool, and let me have any nonsense! I'm very fond of you."

"Fond of me!"

The words were screamed rather than spoken.

"Yes; you know I am. It's my fondness for you which has been the cause of all the trouble, and your—your silliness. But I've my own methods when I find myself in a nasty place. Self-preservation is nature's first law. If you think you can behave to me like an ungrateful little wretch, I'll take care you don't, because, rather than you should do that, I'll stop you too; so be warned in time."

He paused and looked at her. She looked at him, and saw in his eyes something which robbed her of her few remaining senses. Shrieking in a sudden agony of terror, she ran towards the door which opened into the passage, meaning, no doubt, to rush along the passage to the front door, and so out on to the landing, where she would be within reach of help, and might find safety. But she never got so far. Before she was out of the room, throwing his right arm round her, he lifted her from the ground as if she were a doll, gripping her slender throat with the fingers of his left hand to stay her shrieking.

"Stop that noise, you little fool!"

He bore her towards the sitting-room. Quannell still stood in the doorway. Charging him with his shoulder, as if he were so much dead matter, he sent him blundering backwards. Following him, with Mrs. Van der Gucht still in his arms, with his other shoulder he pressed against the door and shut it.

CHAPTER XV

IN THE CARRIAGE

AFTER an interval of probably not more than half an hour, Mr. Wentworth came out of his flat, alone. He was immaculately dressed. His frock-coat fitted him without a crease. His beautiful silk hat was set just at the proper angle, a shade of a shadow upon one side. His grey suede gloves fitted him as well as did his coat. He twirled his cane with the air of a man who is without a care in the world. And as he went he smiled. In the entrance hall, as he was descending into the street, he was saluted by the porter.

"A lady came and asked for your flat, sir; and then, about half an hour afterwards, a gentleman. As they didn't seem to know whereabouts it was, having received no instructions, I directed them. I don't know whether they found you; I haven't seen either of them come out again."

Mr. Wentworth nodded affably.

"That's all right. I fancy they came down the other staircase."

Again the porter touched his cap. Mr. Wentworth departed. The porter stared after him.

"That's queer. Came down the other staircase, did they? Then I don't know where they went to after they did come down. He so seldom does have visitors that I particularly noticed those two—a nice-looking girl she was—and I've kept my eyes open for them ever since, thinking that it might be a case of calling a couple of cabs, and a bob for me."

As he strolled, Cyril Wentworth indulged in reflections of his own.

"One of the chief points which one always has to keep in mind is, that this is a world of eyes; there is always some one who notices. That porter man will have it in his mind all day that he has not seen my visitors depart. It will worry him." He was passing a florist's, and paused to glance in at the window. "Shall I get her some flowers as a peace-offering? Or shall I trust to myself to make peace in my own way? The flowers might be construed as a confession of weakness. I'll trust to myself." He turned into Hyde Park, and had been there only a minute or two when he recognized a victoria which was coming up the drive.* He stood and observed it as it approached, hesitating. "Shall I? or shan't I? I will!"

Moving through an opening in the railings on to the drive, he placed himself in such a position that the victoria in question was bound to pass close to him. He signalled to the driver as it neared him, who reined in his horses. Hat in hand, he advanced to greet Miss Bradley, who was driving alone.

"Won't you give me a lift?" he asked.

It was not difficult to guess that her intention had been to greet him with all possible coldness, to the extent, even, of practically ignoring him. Undoubtedly his manner of address, his assurance, took her by surprise. She was not prepared for the easy air of confidence with which he asked her to show him so marked a sign of her favour, one, indeed, which would signal him out for notice in a fashion which those who had an inkling into the situation could hardly fail to appreciate. Had she been asked only ten seconds before what answer she would make to such a request, she would have replied that she would merely accord it the treatment which such impertinence demanded; it was unfortunate that the question had not been put to her, for having given it such an answer she could scarcely have stultified herself directly afterwards. It is certain that she intended to snub this man; and there were few women who could snub a man more effectively than she could. Yet when she found herself, unexpectedly, thus face to face, her intention wavered, tottered, fell. The influence his personality had on her exerted its force, most agreeably, the moment she knew that he was close at hand. Just now she had been brooding; dull, depressed, conscious that her mood was hardly genial—that the world was drab. When she saw this good-looking fellow—as many women did, she held him to be good-looking, though no man had ever been able to perceive it—with the singular face and eyes, and small mouth with its pouting lips, she realized all at once that whatever the world might be, it offered possibilities which certainly were not drab. The grey eyes, which were, before all else, shrewd, looked coolly into hers with—although she did not know it—an easy dominance which suggested the over-lord; the eyes of a man whom no woman would ever turn from his purpose. She was a strong woman, or thought herself one; and, indeed, had proved herself to be more than a match for the average man. But here the mystery of sex came in. He knew, though she did not, that in him she had met that physical something for which—although unconsciously—for years she had been craving; and, as usual, he was prepared to take the fullest advantage of his knowledge, and her ignorance.

Yet she was not disposed to give him, at once, all that he demanded. She regarded him, from under the shadow of her parasol, with an air which was intended to be supercilious, and a lip which was meant to be curled, being oblivious of the fact that her eyes had suddenly grown brighter, and that a faint flush had appeared upon her cheek. It was her wish that even the tone of her voice should convey a suspicion of disdain.

"I was just going home."

"Then take me with you."

"Father will be at home; he has business which keeps him at home this morning. He will be waiting lunch."

"Isn't there a third chair for me? I'm sure Mr. Bradley wouldn't mind my occupying it; and I don't believe you would either; and I'm quite sure I should be delighted."

This was a difficult man to snub, especially since—although not for the world would she have admitted it—the easy fashion in which he took her for granted afforded her a subtle pleasure. Still she demurred.

"Are you not forgetting, Mr. Wentworth, that you owe me some sort of explanation?"

"For what? I'm sure I owe you many explanations, and I'm always ready to give them you, every one, at the utmost length. But, in particular? Oh!"—as if with a sudden burst of recollection—"you mean that insane young woman the other night. I'll tell you all about it as we go along."

With perfect calmness he mounted into the victoria, speaking to the coachman as he did so. "Home!" The horses started as he was settling himself against the cushions at her side. She offered no remonstrance; under the circumstances it would have, perhaps, been hard to do so; and then, with the consciousness of his near neighbourhood, she began trembling—delightfully—from head to foot. So far from proceeding with the narrative to which he had referred, almost as an excuse for his intrusion, he addressed to her an extremely personal observation.

"How well you're looking!"

"Do you think so? I'm not feeling well."

"I can hardly credit it. Shall I tell you why?"

"Why?"

The monosyllable was iced. She studiously kept her face turned from him, though she longed to look into his eyes; but she wished him clearly to understand that he was still suffering from her displeasure—at least, until the required explanation had been given. He, on his part, showed no sign of smarting under a sense of her coldness as, possibly, he was meant to smart. On the contrary, he could scarcely have seemed more completely at his ease or more self-confident.

"I am so foolish as to believe, at any rate, in physical sympathy."

"I'm afraid I don't follow your meaning."

"As I sit here by your side I feel as well, nay, better, than I ever felt in my life—more content; I don't believe that I should feel like that if you did not feel well also."

"You have no right to speak to me like that, Mr. Wentworth. You take a great deal for granted. Besides, do you expect me to believe what you say?"

"It is not a question of belief, but of knowledge. You know that I feel well—happy, when I am beside you; since it is because of the virtue which proceeds from you, you must know it. Ellen, why are you so cold to me?"

On the instant there came rushing over her, with overwhelming force, a perception of the fact that he intended to propose to her, in the carriage, there and then. She, who, as a rule, flattered herself on the way in which, as she would herself have phrased it, she "kept her head," found herself, on a sudden, the struggling, and nearly helpless, victim of a dozen conflicting emotions. The sheer impudence of the man she saw quite clearly. That, things being as they were, he should intrude himself into her carriage, and, practically without preamble, ask her, there and then, to be his wife;—it would surely be hard to find a more striking example of pure insolence than that. No punishment could be too great, no reprisal could be too merciless. If she were to have him thrown out upon the road it would serve him right. But she was conscious that if he was thrown out she would not improbably be moved to throw herself after him. That she ought to resent his conduct she was aware, yet momentarily the desire—even the power—to do so was growing less and less. An insurgent something was stealing through her veins, rising higher and higher, becoming stronger and stronger, till she had to grip the handle of her parasol with both hands, and bite her lips, in order to retain sufficient command over herself to keep herself upright. As to answering him, all at once she had become as incapable of speech as of flying.

Of which facts he had not impossibly as clear a notion as she had. The Bradleys lived in Hyde Park Gardens.* The carriage was speeding up towards Victoria Gate. The crowd had been left behind. Where they were it was more private. Wentworth, drawing closer to her, leaned forward, so that, although her head was still turned from him, his eyes were on her face. He saw the strained look it wore, and read its meaning.

"Why won't you speak to me? Why are you so cruel?" He spoke so softly that the words could only have been audible to her, the very softness of his tone suggesting an intimacy which constrained her more and more. When she still was silent he commanded. "Look at me, Ellen."

The petition—if it was meant for one—uttered so gently, yet with such intensity, completed her subjugation. As if unable to help herself, she turned her head round slowly, until she confronted him face to face; and he saw the lines upon her countenance, which were almost lines of pain; the wide-open, dry eyes, which ached with the yearning she was powerless to conceal. He remembered, as he thought that he had never seen her look less inviting, that it is not in our moments of sincerest, deepest feeling that we look our best. He had seen that truth illustrated before in others. But he was not going to allow a trifle to keep him from the sticking-point then.

"Ellen, will you be my wife?"

Actually tears came into her dry eyes; one stood in the corner of each. She spoke—under pressure from him—with faltering lips.

"Do you—do you want me to be?"

"You know that I want you. Ellen, tell me that you will be my wife!"

"If you—if you want me to, I will."

It was impossible, seated in an open carriage, in broad daylight, in the middle of Hyde Park, to kiss her—impossible even for him; or to indulge in appropriate raptures of that kind, for which he thanked his Maker. But he took her left hand and pressed it between both of his, murmuring—

"Thank God! thank God!" Ejaculations of that sort meant nothing to him, and he was aware, from experience, that they pleased the woman. He went on, on well-known lines. "You have made me the happiest of men!"

"Is that—is that true, Cyril?"

That spontaneous, although timid use of his Christian name, affected him almost like a douche of cold water. It was not a name he cared for himself; he thought he had never heard it sound more banal. He increased the warmth of his language lest she should perceive the coldness of his feelings.

"Darling! don't you know it's true? If you—if you dare to hint a doubt, I'll take you in my arms—out here in the park—and squeeze the life right out of you."

He was capable of doing it, not in a sense which she suspected. Her face flushed like any young girl's.

"Cyril! you mustn't—in the park!"

"Don't I know I mustn't! Worse luck! But it's all I can do to keep myself from doing it; so you look out!"

"Cyril, you mustn't talk like that! They'll hear you on the box."

She gave an upward glance.

"Let them! I don't care! They'll soon know."

She flushed again.

"Cyril, do you—do you—care for me?"

"Do I care for you—do I! The doubt is all the other way. Do you care for me?"

The accent was on the first word of her reply.

"Care for you?" She shut her eyes, opened her mouth, drew

a long breath, a performance which did not make her more prepossessing. "Care for you! Cyril, I care for you so much that I—I'm afraid."

She had cause to be, though, when he laughed at her, she felt as if—though they were driving through the park—she could, like any housemaid, have laid her head upon his shoulder to hide from him her face of happy shame.

CHAPTER XVI

A FATHER'S BLESSING

MR. BRADLEY was at home—a solid-looking gentleman, whose appearance hardly suggested stomachic pills. He was in the library, as his daughter discovered by opening the door to see. Before she had an idea of his intention, Wentworth had taken her by the hand and was leading her to her father.

"Mr. Bradley, I have asked your daughter to be my wife, and she has said Yes, so I have brought her to you to secure your blessing."

Taken wholly by surprise, Miss Bradley went red as fire.

"Cyril, how could you—without a word to me of warning!"

Snatching away her hand, she ran out of the room, the happiest woman in Hyde Park Gardens. Left alone with her impetuous wooer, her father stared.

"Are you serious, Mr. Wentworth?"

"Perfectly, Mr. Bradley. I never felt more serious in my life, or more light-hearted."

In proof of which statement Mr. Wentworth smiled, while Mr. Bradley stared still more.

"I can only say, Mr. Wentworth, that the communication which you have just now made to me has taken me completely by surprise, as, to me, it is entirely unexpected."

"I thought it would take you by surprise, though I have been hoping to find myself in a position to make you such an announcement for some time. Let me make my position in this matter to some extent clear to you. I don't pretend to any intimate knowledge of Miss Bradley's financial position."

"She possesses a considerable fortune of her own, which she inherits from her mother. I thought, Mr. Wentworth, that that fact was public property."

"I have heard, generally—since, as you suggest, I could hardly help but hear it—that Miss Bradley was not a pauper; and I was glad to hear it, for her sake. So far as I am concerned, her fortune will continue to be her own. I want no woman's money. What I want is a wife, who shall do me credit as the head of my establishment."

"I was not aware that you had such a thing."

"I have not at present. What is the use of a great house to a bachelor? But I propose to have one shortly. I may inform you that I am in a position to place Miss Bradley at the head of an establishment which shall be, at any rate, the equivalent of the one to which she has been accustomed, entirely out of my own resources. I wish, as the French say, to range myself, to solidify my position, which has been, so far, a little at loose ends. I am an ambitious man, Mr. Bradley. I intend to take up politics. By the way, I have heard your name mentioned in connection with politics."

"By whom?"

"I hear that Dering proposes to retire from the representation of South Essex, and that your name has been mentioned in connection with the prospective vacancy."

"Who was your informant, Mr. Wentworth?"

"While matters of this sort are still in a fluid state—and, as yet, it is only known to one or two that Dering has any intentions of the kind—it is as well to name no names. But I may tell you that I might have stood for South Essex;* but when I heard that you had inclinations in that direction I at once withdrew any claims I might have had, since, regarding you as my prospective father-in-law, it was very far from my wish to stand in your way. I may add that I believe my action has made you safe."

"You surprise me more and more. It is perfectly correct that I was informed that there was another Richmond in the field, and that he had retired in my favour; but I had no notion it was you."

"I made a particular request that you should receive the information from no one but me."

"Then, in that case, I can only say, Mr. Wentworth, that you have placed me under a considerable obligation."

"I trust, Mr. Bradley, that that word obligation may never arise between us. I am about to marry your daughter, therefore what will be to your advantage will be to mine. There is another point on which, since we are between ourselves, I may as well touch. A little bird has whispered in my ear that you are about to transform your business into a company."

"Pray, Mr. Wentworth, what is the name of that little bird?"

"Again, if you don't mind, no names. I won't even ask if it is true. I will only remark that if such is your intention, I shall be glad if you will accept my name as an applicant for a substantial number of shares. You can scarcely object to having your son-in-law as one of your largest shareholders."

"I shall certainly object to nothing of that kind, Mr. Wentworth, but you must allow me to remark that I find you a trifle overwhelming. You appear to me as a sort of god out of the machine. A comparative stranger,—and, to me, you are a comparative stranger—you tell me, without the slightest ceremony, that you intend to make my daughter your wife; and, in the same breath, that you have practically ensured my becoming a member of the House of Commons; and that you propose to take up a large number of shares in a company, the very possibility of whose coming into being I have the best of reasons for being certain is only known to two or three. I say again that I find all this—coming all at once—a trifle overwhelming."

Cyril Wentworth laughed. He seemed to find Mr. Bradley's surprise, which obviously almost amounted to bewilderment, amusing.

"I merely wish to make clear to you that my position is, in all respects, equal to your daughter's, and that in becoming my wife she will lose nothing."

"All this is entirely satisfactory, so far as it goes; I am the last person to deny it. But, Mr. Wentworth, there still is something. Although she has had opportunities enough, and to spare, I have always understood from my daughter that it was not her intention to marry."

"Fortunately, for me, up to the present she has preserved that intention intact."

"Quite so; but you, it seems, have gone some distance towards inducing her to break it. Even if I take for granted that your position is, in all respects, everything that could be desired, there is still something which I should like to know. When I married my wife I loved her. I am still old-fashioned enough to wish to be assured that your feelings towards my daughter are such as a man ought to have towards the woman whom he intends to make his wife."

"On that point, don't you think, Mr. Bradley, that the person who has first of all to be satisfied is the lady herself? No man living could have a higher opinion of your daughter than I have. And, because I do esteem her so highly, I am quite sure that she would not have anything to do with any person whatever, in a matrimonial sense, for whom she did not entertain those feelings of which you speak; and who, she had the best of reasons for knowing, did not entertain those feelings for her. I am pretty certain that she loves me, and perfectly certain that she knows that I love her. If you wish it, I have pleasure in announcing the fact of my affection for her to you, and am even willing to announce it from the housetops. Indeed—what is practically the same thing—I did almost make public announcement of it in Hyde Park just now."

"Cyril!"

The voice, which came from the neighbourhood of the door, belonged to the lady who was the subject of their discussion. Mr. Wentworth, turning towards her, gaily held out his arms in her direction.

"Here, Mr. Bradley, is Ellen herself. If you ask her, I think you will find her willing to admit that, even in the middle of Hyde Park, I nearly relieved my feelings to what might have been an inconvenient extent."

"Cyril! you're not to talk like that! I won't have you tease me! Papa!"

She fluttered across the room quite lightly, considering her age, and the dignity which generally marked her movements, blushing as she had never supposed she could have done. Mr. Bradley and his daughter were not, in general, moved to either public or private exhibitions of feeling. It was, therefore, with no little surprise that that gentleman—and father—found himself with his daughter in his arms, and her face quite close to his. Under the circumstances he rose to the situation with much presence of mind, and, indeed, came out of it with flying colours.

"I am glad to hear, Ellen, that you have at last made up your mind to enter into that condition in which, as you are aware, I have always held that a woman is most at home. I hope, my daughter, that yours will be a happy marriage."

He kissed her on the lips, a thing which he had not done for years. Altogether, it was most affecting, and it had all come about with such surprising suddenness.

CHAPTER XVII

THE MAN IN THE ROOM

WHEN Mr. Cyril Wentworth parted from his betrothed—for the first time since she had been his betrothed—in her father's mansion in Hyde Park Gardens, he paid a visit to an establishment of quite a different kind. A cab took him back across the park to Westminster Bridge. Alighting near the district railway station, he strolled over the bridge on foot. At the corner of the Lambeth Road he climbed on to the roof of a tram, in his beautiful apparel. His neighbour on one side was a lady who nursed a large and mysterious parcel, and who smelt of gin; on the other was a plasterer, whose propinquity might have been more desirable had he borne the marks of his calling less conspicuously about with him, and if he had not pertinaciously smoked a foul clay pipe which was loaded—notoriously loaded—with an ineffable brand of shag. Attired as he was, in such company, Mr. Wentworth seemed a little out of place. To do him justice, he showed no consciousness of anything of the kind. On the contrary, he seemed completely at his ease, which, as a matter of fact, in all places, under all circumstances, he invariably did do. On the present occasion he carried his affability so far as to inquire of the plasterer what tobacco he was smoking, which inquiry the smoker seemed to regard as a compliment. He explained, to begin with, that it was the very cheapest tobacco in London, which one could easily believe. He bought it at a quarter of a pound at a time, for which quantity he paid elevenpence, receiving as a bonus a box of matches with each four ounces.

"And if there's any cheaper tobacco to be bought in London, I don't know where it is." He stated this fact in a tone of voice which made it evident that it was intended for the public advantage. "Not, mind you," he added parenthetically, "that I wouldn't sooner smoke it, no matter what it cost. If you was to bring me tobacco what you'd paid a pound a ounce for, I'd sooner smoke this what I am smoking. You can taste it."

Mr. Wentworth observed that he was convinced of that. He added that you could also smell it. This, also, the plasterer seemed to regard as a compliment.

"It is a bit whiffy, ain't it? My missis, she sometimes says that by the time she's smelt me through a pipe of it, she almost feels as if she had been smoking it herself." Mr. Wentworth admitted that to him that seemed extremely probable. Whereupon that plasterer waxed more confidential still. "You wouldn't hardly believe it, but my missis she buys me this here tobacco herself. I gives her the money, and she goes and buys it; at a shop in the Falcon Road, where she buys her groceries, she gets it. She says you can smell it as soon as you gets inside; but I expects that's her joke."

His listener thought that, if that was the case, the lady's humour was grim.

Along Wandsworth Road, down Lavender Hill, past Clapham Junction, the dingy horse-drawn tram-car wended its slow and dreary way. At the top of St. John's Hill Cyril Wentworth descended. He turned into a road on his right until he entered one of those mean streets which cluster about the York Road. Here, if anything, he seemed more out of place than on the roof of the tram. The houses were small and ill-kept. Children were in the streets here and there, but for the most part the whole neighbourhood wore an air of desolation. Although it was packed with human dwellings, and, no doubt, most of them sheltered more than their proper number of inmates, it affected one as if it were a desert; possibly because one was conscious that, in such an atmosphere, life, necessarily stunted, could with difficulty attain to natural proportions.*

At the door of one of the meanest of all the mean houses, and, outwardly, one of the most ill-kept and most untidy, Cyril

Wentworth stopped. He glanced to the right and left, as if to learn who was watching; then, opening the front door with a key which he took from his waistcoat pocket, he disappeared inside, shutting the door behind him the moment he was in. Although he had entered directly into a room the light was dim. A faded yellow blind veiled the interior of the room from the street, though the window hardly needed its assistance, every pane of glass in it was so obscured by grime. The room was scantily furnished, as one would have expected an apartment in such a house would be furnished; but it bore no signs of recent use or occupation. Dust was everywhere, and there was that musty odour which is the result of no ventilation. As one perceived it, one began to understand how it was that Cyril Wentworth had not objected more strenuously to the odour of the plasterer's pipe.

He stood, still within reach of the street door, and listened. At first it seemed that silence reigned, that there was nothing to which to listen; but, by degrees, a sound was audible overhead—a faint sound, such, for instance, as might have been made by a rat. Wentworth recognized it on the instant. As he heard, he smiled.

"Resting. How fond he is of—resting. Each time I come inside this door I wonder if, at last, he is at rest—for ever; but he isn't. I never can make up my mind whether I am glad or sorry. Wonderful how a man can live on long after he is dead; and, positively, thrive. I take it that the vital organs are, as it were, held in suspense; and so, since they are subjected to no strain, although dormant, continue—like some tubers, which, under certain conditions, can be stored for an indefinite number of years, and though, to all seeming, dead, still retain vitality. Wasn't it a seed which was found in one of the pyramids, which grew into a flower and bore fruit, after lying dormant in a mummy's sarcophagus through countless centuries? But I suppose that, in the case of the dormant human animal, there does come a time when the vital organs do decay, and expire, if only of dry rot."

As he communed with himself he ascended the stairs to the floor above, throwing open the first door to which he came. An altogether indescribable odour came rushing out at him. Here, also, a yellow blind screened the window, so that again the room was all in gloom. Picking his way gingerly across the floor, putting his hand behind the blind, he opened the window to its fullest extent, without moving the blind. Then he turned and looked about him.

There was something in the room; but a stranger would have found himself at a loss if requested to decide upon the instant what. The something was on the floor in a corner, and kept swaying slightly to and fro; it was the abrasion produced by its languid movements against the wall which caused the faint sound which had been audible below. It had paid no attention to Wentworth's entrance; but, heedless of his presence, continued its gentle swaying until he spoke.

"Well, old partner, how fares it with you? Still going strong? Stand up, old friend!"

As Wentworth spoke he gave an upward movement with his outstretched right arm, and the something in the corner rose and stood up, and one saw that it was a man; or, perhaps, it would be better to write, something that once had been a man.* His feet were bare. He wore, indeed, but a single garment, made, apparently, of some sort of canvas. His hair, beard, and moustache were a snowy white, or would have been had they been clean. Evidently it was many and many a day since they had received the ministrations of a pair of scissors. Not only were they unkempt and dishevelled, but the hair on his head and the beard on his chin were each of them more than a foot long. It seemed as if he could not stand upright. His head dropped forward on to his chest, his arms dangled aimlessly at his sides, as if he was not only gone at the knees, but weak in the back. Whether he had heard Wentworth's voice, or meekly followed the direction of his arm, was not plain. That, in the ordinary sense, he neither saw nor heard was certain; that, in some way, when he chose, Wentworth made his presence felt by him, even to the point of constraining obedience, was equally clear.

As he stood there, his head swaying from side to side, his limbs twitching, his whole body in slight, continuous movement, Cyril Wentworth surveyed him—and he smiled.

"To look at you, Peter, who, who doesn't know, would think you were a millionaire? And nobody does know, except you and me. Gold has not brought much to you. The longer I live, the clearer I perceive that it does not bring much to any of us; but to you it has brought less than nothing, since it has brought you this. One thing is clear, my dear old partner, that before long I shall have to set to and valet you, even to the extent of washing and bathing you, and cutting your hair. And you must have a new suit of clothes. And I really must superintend you while you make your dwelling-place something like fit for human habitation, or we shall have the neighbours noticing something peculiar in the air, and that would never do. I would set about the job at once, only it will take some time, and at the moment I don't happen to have the time to spare. But we will make him nice and sweet and clean very soon, I promise you; because, whatever happens, we must avoid all risk of scandal. Now, Peter, you shall have a little exercise. You shall come and see me in that pretty room of mine next to yours, and I will talk to you."

Cyril Wentworth, quitting what was, in very truth, a den of filth, unlocked the door of the room adjoining with still another key, which he took from his waistcoat pocket, calling, as he threw it open—

"Capparoni!"

The something that had been a man came shuffling after him.

CHAPTER XVIII

THE MAGICIAN

THIS other room which Wentworth had entered, and across the threshold of which the something which had been a man was stumbling, although distinctly an apartment of a conglomerate, if not nondescript, character, did contain possibilities of comfort. It contained, for instance, a large, old-fashioned couch, which was capable of being used as a bed, as the folded rugs and cushions showed; a roomy armchair, which, like the couch, was no worse for being old; two ordinary chairs, with stuffed leather-covered seats. A well-worn writing-table stood in one corner. Near it was a small square table with a plain deal top. A metal sink was in another corner, with a waste pipe and a tap. On a row of shelves over the table were a number of queer-looking bottles, and a variety of chemical apparatus which was undoubtedly worth much more money than all the other contents of the room put together. On other shelves, by the fireplace, were books—learned-looking books, for the most part, and not a few of them German. On the other side of the fireplace was a tall, oak cupboard, which was locked.

Once in the room, Cyril Wentworth began to remove his silk hat, his gloves, his frock-coat, his beautiful fancy waistcoat—he even turned up his shirt-sleeves. And all the time he kept up a continual flow of talk, as if the creature in the doorway understood every word he said.

"What's the first thing I always do every time I come to see you, Pietro? I think Pietro sounds better than Peter, don't you? And, after all, it is your name. I don't wish to deprive you of everything, Signor Capparoni; oh dear no! Don't I always begin by giving you food—food, old partner? Not only enough to serve you for a single meal, but sufficient to sustain you for an entire week; or longer, if it came to a pinch? You may not credit it, but I don't know why I give you food; you certainly have no idea how often that little question of sustenance or no sustenance hangs in the balance. You see, the mischief is, I never can decide whether it would be better—for me; though perhaps it would be more polite to say for both of us—to keep you alive, or to have you dead. Sounds silly, doesn't it? And yet the matter is not so simple as you suppose. Of course, the advantages of having you dead are so obvious that I need not dilate on them; they are, indeed, so plain as to be plain even to you, and to be that a thing has to be very plain indeed. And, no doubt, before very long you will have to be dead. Every time I see you I long to perform the happy despatch, you miserable beast! But the fact is that it's quite on the cards that contingencies might arise which would render it extremely advisable that you should not be dead. It is possible that circumstances might arise in the chequered history of the Great Harry mine which would make it a matter of the first importance that both partners should figure on the scene instead of one. Frankly, the possibility of such a contingency ever arising is becoming more and more remote; so that, between ourselves, I think that before long you will be dead.

Still, as—being caution personified—it has not yet become quite remote enough for me, permit me, Signor Capparoni, to present you—free, gratis, and for nothing—with another week's rations."

All the time he had been speaking, Mr. Wentworth had also been busy with his hands. Having unlocked the oak cupboard, he had shown that at least part of it served as a larder. From it he had taken a tin of corned beef, which he had opened and divided—with a very professional looking knife and fork—into slices. From another tin he had taken twenty-one large whole-meal biscuits, counting them carefully as if to make sure that the tale of the number was right. He had supplemented these with fourteen fine apples, and three water-melons, which, with considerable ingenuity, he had cut into seven portions. He had taken fourteen spoonfuls of meat essence out of a bottle, each of which he had put into a small earthenware cup. He now turned to this display of provisions with a little flourish.

"Now, Pietro, say grace, and be thankful that there's food for another week for you; a carefully considered dietary which is best suited to the conditions under which you live and have your being. Come; here's meals for to-morrow—breakfast, dinner, supper! Take them and put them in their proper places."

The creature in the doorway came shuffling forward, as if drawn by some influence of which he was unconscious, yet against which he was incapable of offering resistance. He closed his nerveless, tremulous fingers about a small tray, on which Wentworth had arranged, in three separate saucers, an apple, a biscuit, and a spoonful of essence; three slices of beef, a biscuit, and a piece of melon; and again, on the third saucer, another apple, biscuit, and spoonful of essence. With this tray, which lurched and swayed as he shambled forward, he made his devious way out of the room and into the next, presently returning with another tray, on which were three saucers and a cup, all empty. Seven times was this performance repeated, Mr. Wentworth uttering audible comments all the while.

"Curious, Peter, isn't it, how a poor old looney like you, who, so far as intelligence goes, isn't worth a row of pins, can be persuaded—by the proper person—to feed himself, in solitude, almost as decently as if he were sane, and with much more regard to system? Breakfast at eight; dinner at one; supper at seven. Those are your hours; and, although you have no clock, I'll be bound that you keep to them nearly as closely as does the average cook. Such regular habits, in one placed as you are, almost suggest a special providence; don't they, Peter? You shall have your proper provision of water later on, before I go, in those nice air-tight cans I brought for you. We neglect nothing, do we, Peter? Never was a child more carefully looked after. In the meantime, partner, here's that little pick-me-up, of which you are so fond."

The creature drank the contents of a glass which Wentworth passed to him, emptying it down his throat as if he were pouring it down a sink.

Then, out of the same cupboard, Wentworth took a glass mask, such as chemists wear, to guard their mouths and nostrils when engaged in delicate and dangerous operations. His hands he covered with a pair of thin wash-leather gloves. Setting out his apparatus on the square deal table, he half filled a retort with some colourless liquid out of one of the bottles on the shelves, and placed beneath it a curiously fashioned lamp. Presently he was engaged in compounding some mixture, whose preparation involved the greatest care and watchfulness. Yet, though it was evident that his attention never relaxed, he managed to find opportunity to keep up a running series of remarks in the form of a monologue, as if the something that had been a man had been the most intelligent of listeners.

"Magic and spells! that's what we are mixing now, Peter; and never had a magician an elixir more wonderful than the one which I am brewing. With it—why, a man's master of the universe, practically, as things are; he's certainly a master of men. To it I myself owe everything, as you yourself know, dear friend. And what, in my case, everything means, it would require a volume to tell; the truer every word in it was, the more they'd say it was full of fairy tales. To it—in one of its forms, for its forms, old chum, are many—I owe some very charming women, and, also, what is of quite as much importance, to it I owe their silence. To keep a woman silent, under certain circumstances, requires a magician, and here is the magician that does it every time. Silence! that, sometimes, is what I think my magician really ought to be called.

Until one has been its master, one can have no notion of what miracles silence works, if brought to bear at the mathematical moment. Silence has made me rich. Between ourselves, Peter, folks don't guess how rich I am, and—still between ourselves—I'm not sure that I'm not more than half afraid to let them. Caution goes hand in hand with silence. There's a copy-book axiom for you, Peter. If it were generally known in how many channels my riches lie, there might be quite a stir, and I do hate fuss. So I let one person know that I own this, and a second that I own that, and a third that I own the other; but I'm not particularly anxious that any one should know that I own all three, besides lots more. Questions might be asked how I came to own them, and silence is one of those things which loses its virtue if it's broken."

The liquid, in the distillation of which he was engaged, was passing—in one of its phases—in the form of vapour from one retort to another, a process which he observed with such intense interest that even his tongue was still. When, however, the operation had reached a satisfactory point, he began again.

"You've no idea, Peter, what a difference it makes if everything doesn't go just as it ought to at this most exquisitely delicate stage; what a difference to the powers of the magician, I mean. And do you know, Peter, that if the fragile glass of this retort were to be shattered, say, by the heat, as it very easily might be, as I am bending over it like this, in spite of the mask which I am wearing, it is very possible that in less than thirty seconds I should cease to be a man, and become a mere brute beast, as you are. Wouldn't you like to do a little smashing, Peter? Am I not rash to trust myself, in the face of such awful, imminent peril, alone with a lunatic? And yet I'm not a bit afraid; no, Peter, not one little bit."

Again there came a point at which the chemist was too much absorbed in his task to indulge in speech; and again it was past.

"This is the first time I ever breathed a word to you upon the subject, Peter, but it so happens that this would be rather an inopportune moment in my history for this retort to break; I am not sure that, as a sort of by product, it wouldn't result in the breaking of a lady's heart. Because there's a lady who loves me, Peter—yes, one more; and who, this time, is to be my dear, dear wife. My wife, Peter! Think what I shall seem like with that appendage. To every man there comes a time when he must marry. Of course she's money, Peter; and not in any ordinary sense, but in heaps and heaps. Then there's her father; he's a multi-millionaire, actually. And I'm willing to lay you a little sporting wager that before I've finished I not only have her money, but her father's too. And quite soon. Because, candidly, I shan't be able to stand either of them very long, the father or the child. Child!—my wife that is to be, Peter, is not in any sense a chicken,—which, since where women are concerned my taste is decidedly for veal, is perhaps unfortunate! And yet I don't know. If my wife that is to be was very young and very sweet and very pretty, it would be with positive reluctance that I should call in the services of the magician, so far as she was concerned. But as things are, I shall hail his approach with rapture. So you see, everything's for the best in this best of all possible worlds." He was holding up before his eyes a phial which was filled with a dark-coloured substance, which was only partly fluid. "There's the magician, Peter. Like the jinn in the fisherman's story, he's at present in a bottle, but when he's released and applied to the proper spot in the proper manner, he's a wonder-worker, partner, as you, of all men in the world, did ought to know."

CHAPTER XIX

AT THE CROFT

AT The Croft, Agnes Capparoni was as if she were at home with John Banner and his niece, Lettice Mason. She laughed at herself because of it. It was absurd of them to allow her to stop, to persuade her to stop, to make her stop. Not, she admitted, that she required much making. But there it was. A spill off a bicycle; a chance encounter in a lane; a long drawn-out story told within ten minutes of their meeting, in the middle, actually in the middle of the road! She told Mr. Banner that she wondered how it was that he had ever listened; at least, he must have taken it for granted that she was absolutely devoid of a sense of humour, to have played the Ancient Mariner* at sight on an inoffensive stranger. What had he thought of her? Mr. Banner did not seem to be able to say, or he was unwilling to put his opinion into words. He simply told her that she was at The Croft, and that at The Croft she would have to stay, until Lettice let her go. That was how he put it, until Lettice let her go. And that Lettice declined to do. So trunks came down from town until, as Agnes put it, it looked as if she was about to become a member of the family. Whereat Lettice laughed.

Lettice was just a girl, in the enjoyment of the best of health, and, therefore, the finest spirits. She assured Agnes that she was just the person she had been looking for, for years; when Agnes found that she insisted on making her her mother-confessor and confidant in general, she began to think that this must be so. Not that Lettice had anything to confess, or any confidences to make, but when there is a Dick Sharratt in the air, it is surprising how much a girl like Lettice does find to reveal to another girl under a pledge of inviolate secrecy. And Lettice revealed it all, or thought she did, though it was exactly what she did not reveal that Agnes saw most clearly.

Did not Agnes think that every man ought to marry? For instance, ought not Uncle John to marry? Agnes was of opinion that that was a point on which he was entitled to please himself. Perhaps Agnes thought that he was too old? No, Agnes did not think he was too old; indeed, he seemed to her to be quite young. Of course, he was years and years older than Dick. Undoubtedly, since Mr. Banner was a man, and Mr. Sharratt was only a boy.

It is to be feared that Agnes said this with some improper intention of provoking Lettice, who, although she was continually informing Dick to his face that he was the merest child, liked other persons to regard him as if he was almost patriarchal.

"I don't think it's quite fair to call Dick a boy."

"He's a very nice boy."

Lettice condoned the one word for the sake of the other.

"He is nice, isn't he? And he's so clever. He thinks a tremendous lot of you."

"I'm not prepared to admit that that's a proof of his cleverness. For all he, or any of you, can tell I may be a frightful fraud. You none of you know anything about me except what I've told you myself, and you've only my word for that."

"My dear Agnes, we're not all of us perfect idiots; certainly

Uncle John isn't, nor Dick, though you can call me what you please."

"Lettice! when did I call you a perfect idiot!"

"You as good as call me one when you say that I've made a friend of a frightful fraud. But of course, you poor thing, I know it's only the silly way you have of talking. I forgive you. Don't you think that Dick has rather a well-shaped head?"

"Not bad, for a man."

"Agnes, what do you mean? Aren't men's heads as well-shaped as women's?"

"I dare say. But I don't fancy one notices that sort of thing in a man."

"I suppose not. Of course there are things which are much more important in a man. I wonder—I wonder what a man notices in a girl?"

"Her intellect."

"Really?" Lettice glanced up from the work which she was doing to find that Miss Capparoni was smiling. "You're laughing at me. I suppose you said that because you know I've none."

"No intellect?"

"Only the weeest, tiniest morsel; not enough to count. But I don't believe that it is her intellect which a man notices most in a girl."

"What do you think it is?"

"I could tell you, only it would take a tremendous time; at least, I think I could tell you; but—here's Uncle John."

Since that first day, the subjects of Jack the Chemist and Miss Capparoni's father had not been referred to, by special command. John Banner had assured Miss Capperoni that he would make the fullest inquiries into what she had told him, and, at the earliest possible moment, would acquaint her with the results, until when, under no circumstances, was any reference to be made to King Charles's head.* For the moment Agnes was content to leave the matter in his hands, being well aware that she had reached a point in the case at which the sort of assistance which he might be able to offer was just what she required. A week ago he had gone to town. The two girls had been left alone, with the exception of flying visits from Mr. Sharratt and calls from neighbours. Letters had been received from him, in which no particular mention was made of Agnes, except by way of expressing a wish that she was not growing tired of The Croft and Lettice. He had said that he might return without notice, at any moment; and here he was. Lettice sprang at him.

"Uncle, do you know that the tip of my little finger has been itching all day long, and I wondered if it meant that you were coming."

"It didn't. It meant that Dick Sharratt was going to bring me over from Camford on his run-about. I've been spending the morning with your uncle, the professor. You'll find Mr. Sharratt at the door, wondering if that run-about of his is ever going to run about again; as a car, it's not to be compared to mine."

Later in the day Miss Capparoni heard from John Banner all that he had to tell. They were alone together in the drawing-room after dinner; Lettice, assisted by Mr. Sharratt, was looking for a thimble which she was nearly certain she had lost somewhere in the garden. No doubt the darkness explained the difficulty they had in finding it.

Mr. Banner began.

"I am gratified to find that you bear no outward and visible signs upon your person of being unduly tired of The Croft."

"That's because I'm not tired, though I've no doubt that The Croft is heartily sick of me."

"On a remark of that kind comment is needless, especially as Lettice informs me that she doesn't know what she would do without you, and I'm sure I don't. But I don't propose to tell you again what you know very well without my telling you, how glad I am to find you still an inmate of my home. I want to make clear to you what I have been doing since I saw you, and I am sorry to have to inform you that it amounts to very little. But I suppose you hardly expected me to perform in a few days what has occupied you years, and in one or two directions I have made progress. I have ascertained, for instance, that beyond all doubt Mr. Cyril Wentworth is a thoroughly bad lot."

"That is something to have learned."

"As you say; but I am not sure that, considering all things, it is a very pleasant something. Those five thousand shares still stand in Hurle's name; Wentworth has not gone quite to the extent of having them transferred to his own name, but he has been drawing dividends on them, thumping dividends, not one penny of which has reached the professor."

"How has he managed that?"

"So far as I can learn, he practically runs the Great Harry mine, and does as he likes."

"He can be made to disgorge."

"Certainly, if Hurle chooses. I have been to see him to-day; the old gentleman's breaking up. His medical attendant, whom I interviewed, says that that villain Fentiman nearly killed him, and probably would have quite if you hadn't pulled him up."

"It was time that some one pulled him up."

"By the way, the scoundrel is either in hiding or else he's disappeared. I've found out where he lived, in lodgings at Notting Hill. He has never returned to them since that historic day at Camford, nor has anything been heard of him of any sort or kind."

"For information about Fentiman apply to Cyril Wentworth."

"You don't suspect him of keeping a fellow like that up his sleeve; why should he?"

"I suspect him of anything and everything. But go on; what about Professor Hurle?"

"His business capacity never was his strongest feature; to-day it struck me as having ceased to exist. I had the greatest difficulty in making him understand what had happened to his shares. So far as he is himself concerned, I doubt if he cares a wag of his finger what has happened to them; but I managed to get from him a power of attorney authorizing me to deal with them exactly as I please."

"That's good. With that in your pocket you may be able to make yourself agreeable to Mr. Wentworth. What else have you done?"

"I have arrived at a decision, to go to Germany either to-morrow or the day after, and to take you with me, and Lettice."

"Have you? And pray why, without being consulted, are we to be bundled off to Germany?* I am not your chattel, Mr. Banner."

"No, I—" He was about to say, "I wish you were," but altered his intention in time; "I never suggested that you were. It's in this way. Cyril Wentworth was a student at Heidelberg."

"Well, is that any reason why I should be bundled off to Germany to-morrow?"

"Not exactly, but you'll understand if you let me finish. I was talking to a man who was at Heidelberg with him. I mentioned casually that I had heard that he has something of a reputation as a chemist. The man said at once, as if it were a matter of course, that if he hadn't a reputation then he ought to have. I asked him how that was. He told me, what I never knew before, that his special study at Heidelberg was chemistry; and that, moreover, he was the favourite pupil of Professor Ehrenberg. I am, doubtless, an ignorant man, but until that moment I had never heard of Professor Ehrenberg, and I confessed as much. Whereupon my German friend grew eloquent. He declared that Ehrenberg was the greatest chemist the world had ever seen; so far as I could gather in a very peculiar sense, his knowledge of chemistry being reputed to be so great as to be almost unholy. Tales were told of him which put the necromancers of old to shame. He was commonly reputed to have the power, if he chose to exercise it, of turning the world—and all the men and women in it—upside down. If ten per cent. of what that German told me has any foundation in fact, then Professor Ehrenberg must be a truly remarkable man. But to me, the most interesting statement which he made was this, that it is believed that Cyril Wentworth is the only student who was ever admitted to his private laboratory."

Miss Capparoni, who had risen from her seat, broke in the moment he had finished.

"Then that is where Jack the Chemist acquired the knowledge which in his hands has proved so dangerous a possession. And you propose?"

"To start for Germany, as I say, to-morrow; or, if not, the day after."

"To interview the Herr Professor?"

"Precisely; to learn from him exactly how much Cyril Wentworth knows. To put it mildly, the powers with which you credit him sound as if—well, as if they were peculiar. Ehrenberg may be able to tell us if such things are possible, and in other matters he may be to us of the most material assistance."

"We'll start to-morrow! I shall be ready! I've no doubt Lettice will be also."

CHAPTER XX

A PARTY OF FOUR

ON the morrow they started, a party of four. Mr. Sharratt was the fourth. He explained that as term was over, or as good as over, and there really was nothing to keep him at Camford, absolutely the best use which he could make of his time was to take the fullest advantage of so excellent an opportunity of polishing up his German. It appeared that his father was particularly anxious that he should master the language colloquially; so was his mother, and his sisters—it would be so very useful when he took them abroad; while he had an uncle who was always preaching that the one indispensable thing for a young man nowadays was a practical knowledge of modern languages. To throw away so excellent a chance of becoming almost as German as the Germans, it was not to be thought of. Moreover, a change would do him good. He was rather run down; he did not say what had run him down, because John Banner had his eye on him, but a change always did do him good, besides enlarging his mind. And, anyhow, they would be away so short a time that he might as well go with them as not.

When he had made it quite clear, after some stumbling, why he was going without being invited, Mr. Banner fixed him with his glance.

"Then do I understand, Sharratt, that the sole reason why you are favouring us with your company is that you may improve your knowledge of the German language?"

Mr. Sharratt seemed uneasy.

"I don't know about its being the sole reason, but it's one reason. German's a lot of help to a fellow."

"No doubt. Then I presume that you don't propose to speak a word of any other tongue but German from the moment you quit the English shores."

"Oh, I say! that's a tall order. As a matter of fact, I only do know three or four words of German, and I'm not sure which they are, and, anyhow, you can't get along very fast with only three."

"That's true. Then I take it that you intend to gain at least a nodding acquaintance with the other two or three hundred thousand words during the two or three days that we propose to be away. Dick, your intentions do you credit." Mr. Banner turned to Miss Mason. "You know, Lettice, you are not compelled to go with us, if you prefer to remain behind; for instance, if you have any engagements in the neighbourhood which you think you ought to keep."

"Uncle, you know I've no arrangements! Of course I'm going!"

"As you please. It only struck me as being possible that, as Sharratt was going, you mightn't care to join the party."

Dick and the young lady exchanged glances of a rather complicated kind.

"Uncle! how can you be so absurd! And I'm sure I think Dick is most sensible in taking advantage of every opportunity of self-improvement; and no one can go to Germany, if it's only for two or three days, without learning something."

So it came about that they were four. As John Banner put it to Miss Capparoni—

"It's just as well that that young man should come. So far from being in our way, he'll take Lettice off our hands, and that'll give us a better chance of interviewing Ehrenberg without exciting observation."

It was a somewhat singular fact that Miss Mason asked no questions as to what might be the cause of their so suddenly rushing abroad. Her life was, in general, such an uneventful one, that under ordinary circumstances she would have bombarded Mr. Banner with inquiries as to why he was rushing off to Germany in red-hot haste. As it was, when he informed her that he was going to pay a flying visit to Heidelberg, she displayed a quite unusual lack of curiosity as to his motives. Possibly the announcement which Dick Sharratt promptly made, of his fixed intention to avail himself of so excellent an opportunity to improve his knowledge of the German language, had something to do with it. It is even conceivable that when John Banner allowed Dick to bring him over from Camford on his run-about, at the back of that gentleman's mind there was a dim idea that his young friend might formulate

such a proposition. It is not only in extreme youth that there are
wheels within wheels.

The university city of Heidelberg is one of the most romantically
situated cities of Europe. Its university is in some senses, and for
the most part, one of the quaintest and queerest of its educational
resorts. And, as neither of those four persons had ever been there
on a previous occasion, to them everything was new. Lettice was
in ecstasies. She thought the river lovely, the heights on either side
lovely, the town itself lovely; it all was lovely. There happened to
be no students there just then, or she might have thought them
lovely; in which case it is within the bounds of possibility that, on
at least that one point, she and Mr. Sharratt might have disagreed.
On all other points they were at one, or almost as good as at one.
Of course, Heidelberg was not Camford, and, unfortunately for
itself, it was in Germany, and therefore as a university it was not
to be taken seriously; but in all other respects, he allowed that it
was decent as a place in which to chaperon Miss Mason. So, for
the most part, he took her one way, while John Banner took Miss
Capparoni quite another, which was precisely what all parties
most desired.

The fame of the Herr Professor Ehrenberg filled all the place.
Miss Mason and Mr. Sharratt, not being interested in matters
of that kind, remained in ignorance of his existence. But Miss
Capparoni and Mr. Banner had only to put a few ordinary inquiries
to learn that all the world in Heidelberg knew everything about
him, or thought it did.

He was a very old man. His exact age was not generally known,
but he must be eighty. Still hale and hearty, and in possession of
all his faculties. It was true that he did not go much abroad now,
and did but little walking. But then he never had cared much for
physical exercise, and always had maintained that the ordinary
man could get all he needed within the precincts of his own
apartments. That was one of his ideas. Yet he could smoke his pipe
and drink his wine, or beer, with any one, and even occasionally
attended the meetings of his old corps*—of course, *incognito*—
where he was both a welcome and an honoured guest. He had
been a famous fighter in his time, and had not always fought for
fun. He had always been of opinion that the finest physical training

a man could have at Heidelberg resulted from a knowledge of how to use the two-handed sword as a master should. As for singing, he gloried in the ancient songs which dead and gone members of his corps had sung for centuries; sometimes now his great voice, which began to be a little tremulous, could be heard shouting them out through the open windows of his house. Was he accessible to strangers? Well, that might be. He had been known to see strangers, especially if they were provided with proper credentials. Enough of them came to see him from all parts of the world. But he was a man of moods. If he choose he would; if he did not choose he would not, and there it was.

John Banner put the matter, so far as he was concerned, promptly to the test. Did the Herr Professor speak English? Why, certainly; he spoke all languages, but English as if he were an Englishman, which was comforting information for Mr. Banner, who was doubtful about his German, especially when it came to the composition of a letter. So he wrote to the Herr Professor in the language with which he was most familiar, mentioning that circumstances had arisen in connection with Cyril Wentworth, who, he understood, had been one of his pupils, which made it desirable that he should have some conversation with him on the subject of that gentleman; and that, therefore, he should esteem it a very great favour if he would grant him, at his earliest convenience, a personal interview. The messenger who took the note brought back a reply, couched in irreproachable English, to the effect that Professor Ehrenberg would be pleased to see Mr. Banner that same afternoon. Mr. Banner handed it to Miss Capparoni, who commented on it.

"He says he will see you, in the singular; he says nothing about seeing me. Didn't you tell him that I wanted to see him also?"

Mr. Banner shook his head.

"I thought that if we went together we might be able to explain better by word of mouth how it is that your interest in the matter is even greater than mine."

The lady looked doubtful.

"But the professor's a bachelor, and may object to women, and he may regard my unexpected appearance as an attempt to steal a march on him."

"There isn't a man in the world, bachelor or anything else, who wouldn't be willing to have a march stolen on him on those terms any day of the year."

But Miss Capparoni was not so sure.

CHAPTER XXI

THE HERR PROFESSOR

MOST of the houses in Heidelberg are old; the Herr Professor lived in one of the very oldest. A great, ramshackle old place, which stood on the very edge of the Neckar: the back windows being convenient for any one who wished, with the least possible exertion, to take a header into the river. An old gentleman answered Mr. Banner's ring.

"Is Professor Ehrenberg in? I have an appointment with him. My name is Banner."

The old gentleman looked askance at the lady. He began his reply in German, then drifted into English.

"Aber das Fräulein? But the Fräulein—the young lady?"

"It is more important that the young lady should see him than that I should, as I will explain to the Herr Professor. Will you be so good as to tell him I am here?"

The old gentleman shook his head.

"The Herr Professor sees no women—never! He will not allow that I let one in."

As Miss Capparoni was glancing at Mr. Banner with an I-told-you-so air, there came a stentorian voice from behind the old gentleman, which spoke English with a slight accent and an occasional recollection of a German idiom.

"Johann, what is it you are chattering about? Every chance you have your tongue clack, clack, clacks—you old fool! Who is it there? Is it some one who wishes to see me? Is it Mr. Banner? Then why don't you show him in? Out of the way!"

A big hand was laid on the old gentleman's shoulder. He was moved to one side, and the door was swung wide open. In it there stood a huge man, whose appearance—though he was of almost

Falstaffian proportions*—suggested, in an unusual degree, both physical and mental health and vigour. His hair was white, his face clean-shaved, blue eyes looked out undimmed from under shaggy eyebrows. He was in his shirt-sleeves; in one hand he held a cherry-wood stem, to which was attached a porcelain pipe.

"Are you Mr. John Banner? I am Ehrenberg."

"Permit me, Herr Professor, to introduce to you this young lady."

"Young lady? What? She comes also with you? This will not do! I have nothing to do with women; I do not care for them." He paused, staring at Mr. Banner's companion as if suddenly struck by something in her appearance. "Ah! With you it is perhaps different. What is your name?"

"Agnes Capparoni."

"Capparoni? Then you have in you Italian blood, although you are English. Is it a lot of drivel which you wish to talk to me?"

"I wish to speak to you on a subject which is of the utmost importance to me, and of considerable interest to you."

"So, if you do not wish to say to me a deal of nonsense, enter." When she was in he put his big hand on her shoulder. "You are pretty, very pretty; therefore it does not so much matter, this time. It does a man good to see sometimes what is pretty, even if it is only a woman—it pleases his eye; to give pleasure to the eye generally benefits the brain. It is your ugly women I will have nothing to do with, and your learned women. An ugly and a learned woman— is that not the superlative of the ridiculous? It is sufficient for a woman to be a woman; and to be a woman, it is necessary that she should give pleasure to the eye. I am a chemist. I sometimes think that to every ugly woman I would like to give a little powder. What a good thing for the world that would be, because you must understand that it is the ugly woman who is the cause of the ugly man."

While he talked—as if he were addressing a class a thousand strong—the Herr Professor led his guests along a broad, winding staircase to a room at the back of the house, a large room, with four great French windows, which all stood wide open, and led on to a wooden balcony. To this balcony he immediately conducted Miss Capparoni, still retaining his hand upon her shoulder.

"You see, here I am at home. In front the hills, the trees, the beautiful country; below, the Neckar—it is to me as an old sweetheart, this river; behind, about me, the ancient city, which my whole life long I have known and loved. It is not a paradise, Heidelberg—no, I do not say it—but to me it means much. Below you there is much water, as, if this were to give way, you would find. But have no fear, it is strong enough both for you and for me. This great house—you think it is too big for one old man? Well, perhaps; but you must remember that it is as a museum that I use it. In it are some very extraordinary things. I would show them to you, only some of them are not nice for a woman to see; not even if she is my wife—and that you will never be. Alas! I am too old. But I am yet young enough to recognize a pretty girl. Now that I have begun, it is for you to go on. But let us go back into the room; we shall, perhaps, there talk more at our ease. It is this room I like best when I am not working; it has air, it has light, it has space—for me three important things. It is here also that I dream—oh, how I dream!—of the heights and the depths, the mysteries and the wonders; but it is when I am widest awake that I dream. So far it is only I who have talked. Which of you two is to talk now? Only do not both of you talk together; one at a time is enough."

The lady and the gentleman exchanged interrogative glances, then Mr. Banner made a slight movement with his head, which, apparently, the lady understood.

"I am," she said.

"So! I have heard that it is generally the woman who does the talking, though sometimes I suspect that I myself can talk as much as any one. Now, Miss Capparoni, if you please! Mind, no nonsense; it is forbidden! I am the only person in this house who is allowed to talk nonsense."

"I understand that an Englishman, a Mr. Cyril Wentworth, was once a pupil of yours."

"Well—what of it?"

"This."

She told, as succinctly as possible, the story of her father's disappearance, and the reasons why she believed that he was still alive, at the mercy of the man whom she called Jack the Chemist. With his blue eyes fixed intently on her face, he heard her, without interruption, to an end. Then he put her through a sort of catechism.

"Is that all?"

"It is as far as the story has gone, at present."

"Why do you come to me? What for? What have I to do with a man I never saw, of whom I never heard, because he is your father; since you, also, are to me a stranger?"

"I come to you for several reasons!"

"Name one."

"In the first place, I believe that you know, and that possibly you are the only man in the world who does know, what that man did to my father."

"Well, if I do?"

"If you do, then it follows that Cyril Wentworth acquired from you his knowledge of how to work such monstrous wickedness!"

"Therefore?"

"Therefore, in a sense—a very real one—you are responsible for what he did."

"That is good reasoning, for a woman, upon my word! So if I tell a student, in the ordinary course of the instruction which it is my duty to impart to him, what are the qualities of prussic acid, if he uses it to poison his grandmother, it is I who killed her? We advance. This it is to be a professor—excellent! Let us return to the pre-historic age, when there was no one to know anything; we shall be safer."

"If a shopkeeper sells a loaded revolver to a person whom he knows to be a lunatic, he is held responsible by the law."

"Did I know Cyril Wentworth was a lunatic? Is he a lunatic?"

"You knew him to be a dangerous person."

"I knew him!"

"Did you not know him to be a dangerous person? I cannot believe that he was your pupil without your finding him out; you are too shrewd a judge of character."

The professor carefully emptied the huge bowl of his pipe, then with, if possible, even greater care refilled and lighted it. He had three or four whiffs, as if to make sure it was in good working order; then delivered himself of some observations, which could scarcely be called a direct reply to Miss Capparoni's questions.

"I thank my stars I never married. With women you cannot deal; the more pretty they are, the worse. An ugly woman you can take by the neck and throw into the river; but a pretty girl, a man cannot find it in his heart to use her like that, not even though he knows that is the only treatment which will meet the case." He shook his pipe at Miss Capparoni. "You are a pretty girl; therefore I am a fool. And it is because in the presence of a pretty girl I always am a fool that I will have nothing to do with women, nothing at all. The prettier the girl, the bigger fool I am. And it is because you are—as you English say—a devilish pretty girl, that I make of myself a fool the most complete. I treat you as if you were a reasonable creature. I speak to you as if you were a man—a man, also, with some brains in his head. I tell you some secrets, and about Cyril Wentworth, and about what he did to your father, and—other things. I speak to you quite clearly; so do not make me more ashamed of myself than I am already by pretending that the meaning of what I say does not enter your unintelligent head. Therefore, listen with as much attention as if I were talking to you about a bonnet-string."

CHAPTER XXII

A STUDENT OF PROMISE

THE professor took a few more pulls at his pipe. Then he made a suggestion to Miss Capparoni; thus far he had allowed John Banner to go altogether unheeded.

"It will take me some time to say all that I have to say, which is your fault, not mine, therefore you had better sit down."

He motioned towards a large, leather-covered, straight-backed chair.

"Thank you, I prefer to stand."

"As you will. If I had not offered you a chair you would have said I was a bear; since, however, I have, of course you prefer to stand."

"You appear to have a very poor opinion of women."

"Not at all. The female fills a high position in the scale of nature; it is only when we come to deal with the human animal that she steps out of it; that is why a woman is so inferior to a cow. However, we will not talk of it; it is a question of A B C. Now I will begin what I have to say. You see how you interrupt me continually, already how much time has been lost."

"It seems to me that you keep interrupting yourself to say rude things."

The Herr Professor glared at her through a cloud of tobacco smoke.

"If that is the way in which you used to speak to your father, he is perhaps better off where he is."

"My father loves me, and I love him, which two trifles make a difference. I am beginning to wonder whether, in spite of all your knowledge, you know anything of the greatest thing in the world—love. If you will be so kind as to commence, I will promise to listen with quite as much attention as if you were talking about bonnet-strings, in the plural; and I will keep still, however rude you may be."

For the first time the Herr Professor addressed himself to Mr. Banner.

"Yet I do not wish to drop her into the Neckar; that it is to be a pretty girl. An ugly woman, she would have gone long ago." Again he waved his pipe at Miss Capparoni. "Having exchanged these diplomatic pour-parlers, now I come to the point. I am a chemist." He announced this fact as if he were issuing orders to a regiment of soldiers. "A German is the most logical being in the world, his intellect is the best arranged, he begins always at the beginning, where I begin. Why am I a chemist? While I was still a lad, though already a student, I asked of myself. What is the most important study in the world? I decide, Chemistry. Therefore I became a chemist, which supplies an answer to my own question. Not the chemist of a chemist's shop; that is a pharmaceutist. What you call chemistry we in Germany call *chemie*, in France it is *chimie*, the difference of a letter. These words are from the same root, the Egyptian god, Khem, the god of generation, productiveness, vegetation. You see what a scope is there. The chemist has not only the whole world, but all the worlds for his province. But since no man can know everything, I say to myself, which particular branch shall I specially study, so that I may know something—one or two things worth knowing? I answer, Man. You inquire, what has man to do with chemistry? I reply, everything—with the kind of chemistry which I make my own special study. To explain fully what I mean by that would take too long, and perhaps would not to you be very intelligible; but I will give you an illustration, which is to the point, since it leads us to your friend, Cyril Wentworth."

"He is no friend of mine."

"You said you would not interrupt!"

This came like the roar of a bull of Bashan. Miss Capparoni smiled, inscrutably, possibly exasperatingly also. The Herr Professor glared, holding up his pipe in the air, as if he would like to use it as a weapon.

"Have you any more remarks which it is in your mind that you would like to make?"

"None, thank you; I am sorry I spoke."

"I also am sorry you spoke. Do not speak again till I tell you. Where was I when you interrupted? I was saying that I would give you an illustration which would lead us to your friend, Cyril Wentworth." He paused, as if to dare her to make further comment. Apparently she deemed discretion to be the better part of valour. He went on as if appeased. "I am told that there is in America a man whose name, I think, is Burbank. His study is plants and trees and flowers.* Out of an old flower he makes a new blossom, from an old tree he gets a new forest; he creates, in the vegetable world, new forms out of old ones, by the process of what he calls grafting. I asked myself, long before I heard of Mr. Burbank, if, in the animal world, it was not possible to do something like that, not by grafting, or cross-breeding, that has been tried; but by chemical processes, which have not been tried. Now I come to the secrets. You understand that, as a chemist, my work here at Heidelberg has had nothing to do with what I am about to tell you. I have tried to teach to a number of other men, of all ages, and more or less thick-headed, what is known already, for the most part, to all chemists. There has been only one person beside myself who has ever had any natural insight into the work which has been the real occupation of a pretty long life. Why I give

you my confidence I do not exactly know; yet before I come to an
end my reasons may be plainer both to you and to myself."

He crammed the tobacco tighter into the bowl of his pipe with
his little finger, and struck another match.

"If you cut off a man's hand he cannot hold a knife in it;
with the stump of his arm he can do little or nothing. I began by
ascertaining if, by chemical processes, you could not produce the
effect of the severed hand. That was very simple; I found that you
easily could. In a second, with a little prick, which was so slight a
prick that he was not always conscious that he had been pricked, I
reduced him to the condition of a handless man. More, also with a
prick I could give to his hand—at least for a time—qualities which
it did not have before. I could make his fingers keep on opening
and shutting, opening and shutting; and—I could do many other
things to that hand of his without, you understand, his having a
suspicion that it was I who had done it. I learned by experiment
that what I could do with his hand I could do with other parts
of his body—with all his limbs. I learned also, what was perhaps
the greatest thing, that I could both do and undo. With one prick
I took from a man his hand, with another I gave it to him back
again. When I had reached that point I had already gone far, and
yet I was only at the beginning."

The Herr Professor was silent. He went to the window and
stood looking out across the river, while he puffed at his pipe.
Miss Capparoni and John Banner exchanged glances. But they said
nothing, they waited for him to continue, which he presently did,
speaking with his back turned towards them.

"But, after all, the limbs of the human animal are trifles; it
is the animal itself which is of consequence. I ventured in many
directions. I found that, always with my pin-prick, I could change
the nature of a man or woman. They talk of love's philtres. Did I
choose I could sell to a man a ring which, when he placed it on a
woman's finger, would begin to affect her in a very singular way.
Or I could ensure to a wife that her husband should continue to
love her. She would only have to make him the present of a very
innocent-looking ring; before very long she would be able to do
with him precisely as she pleased. I also learned something which,
I will admit, at first a little frightened me."

He again, in silence, indulged himself with some extra vigorous puffs at his pipe; then went on, with his back still turned to them.

"I learned that, by touching a certain nerve in the eye, in a moment you could make a man blind, and he should not know, and an oculist should not know, what had happened. There was nothing in the appearance of the eye to show, the change having been brought about by the tiniest drop of matter which had been injected. I tried this experiment first on my own eye, the left. When I found how successful it was, and how, all at once, with my left eye I was blind, I was a little startled. Before I performed the experiment I had reasoned that if the one thing had one property, another thing would have exactly the opposite property. When I found myself blind, I was in a great hurry to snatch up the syringe in which already was the antidote which I had prepared. You may imagine with what care I applied it to just the same spot—the smallest fraction of difference in the locality might make all the difference in the world; with what delicacy I touched the piston, on the instant my sight was restored. I could see again with my left eye as well as with my right, exactly as before.

"It was then that I was conscious of a certain fear, like one who stands on the threshold of the unknown, that unknown which is always mysterious. How far was I going? Already I could change, in certain respects, that nature with which a man had come into the world; take from him his sight and restore it to him again; there were other things, equally striking, which I could do. What next? If I was master of his fate so far, why not farther; why should I not be master of it altogether?

"What I have told you sounds strange, wonderful. That is because you are ignorant. As I said just now, the unknown is always mysterious. As a matter of fact, it is all perfectly simple. Certain substances have certain properties, I had only learned that, if applied in a certain manner, under certain conditions, to certain parts of the human frame, they had certain results; in my note-book I had the formulæ under which these substances were prepared. Of course each operation requires a different formula. Do not suppose that I am a quack doctor, claiming that one pill will do all sorts of different things. One pill will only do one thing, that is what I have found. If you want to do another thing you must have a second pill, containing different constituents.

"What I had now to reach was the man himself. What is the man? His brain. Speaking generally, a man is what his brain is. If it is sound, he is sound; if it is unsound, mentally, morally, physically, he is the same. The brain is a delicate thing with which to try experiments; like a complicated watch, it is more easily put out of order than readjusted. I had reached a point at which I had a feeling that it would be as well that I should no longer work alone. A fellow-labourer in the same field might not only be an assistant, a coadjutor, he might—he might be other things besides. I looked round for such a one, and found him at once. Indeed, I had had my eye on him before I had even begun to think of looking.

"There was here at Heidelberg, at that time, a young Englishman whose mental equipment was, in many respects, of the first class. I do not use the language of hyperbole when I say that mentally and physically and, I may add, morally, he was a remarkable young man. In several ways he had distinguished himself. As a student in my own lecture class he was head and shoulders above his fellow students; he was of a different calibre. He had not only the desire, he had the instinct to learn, to know. To teach him was easy. His quickness was bewildering. In dealing with a cuneiform inscription you had but to hint at a key to one of the characters, he had the whole affair at his finger-ends in a flash.

"As regards my own class of work, it was not only that he surprised me by the agility of his mental processes; by the swiftness with which he would leap at the very heart of a fact, gripping the essential point; I could not but recognize that his mind was, in some ways, the correlative of mine. He saw, and was eager to reach, heights of whose existence his associates were unconscious, and for which they would have cared nothing had they seen them. In that respect he and I were absolutely at one, in his yearning to penetrate into the regions of the unknown. As regards capacity, I had reason to believe that in, at any rate, one sense he was my equal. I said to myself, here is the coadjutor I want.

"They will tell you, the people of this place, that Cyril Wentworth, the young Englishman, was my favourite pupil. It is a lie, they are mistaken. I disliked him so strongly that I told myself

I did him an injustice; that I was jealous of him; that because his genius promised to make him, in a very short space of time, my equal, and probably my superior, therefore I allowed my feeling towards him to become warped and prejudiced. It ill became me to allow myself to become the slave of a mere prejudice; so—I brought him here; I installed him in my private laboratory, the only creature, except my servant, Johann, and—and one other, who ever passed its door, either before then, or since, as my coadjutor, my associate, my friend."

The Herr Professor's pipe had again gone out; while he talked he forgot to smoke. Shaking out the burnt ash, he examined the condition of the tobacco which remained in the bowl, pressed it down a little tighter, and struck another match. For some seconds he enjoyed his pipe. Then, turning slowly round, he wagged his finger, solemnly, at Miss Capparoni.

"I am a German. They say you English, like us, are Teutons. If that is so, since it is true that quarrels among relations are often the bitterest, therefore I have never been able to take an Englishman to my heart since I took Cyril Wentworth into my private laboratory. When he left he left in haste; after I had fought with him with my hands and my fists, with every muscle in my body, for more than my life. He had tried to serve me as he served your father."

"Herr Professor!"

"Yes, you may well exclaim, I pardon your interruption. I had taken a devil into my laboratory, not a man. All my expectations of him had been realized, unfortunately all of them. His thirst for knowledge was insatiable; but it was not because he loved knowledge—for its own sake, not at all. He was like the student of whom I spoke, who takes advantage of his knowledge of the qualities of prussic acid to poison his grandmother. In a powder mill, having learned how to make gunpowder, he would have blown up the mill, with all his fellow workmen, in order that he might keep the knowledge of how to make gunpowder to himself, so that he might use it for his own benefit, for the destruction of whoever might stand in his way. I say again, he was a devil, not a man." The professor waved his pipe wrathfully in the air. "I could tell you tales of him, but one is enough. I learned, as I anticipated, that you could become the master of a man, the man himself, as well as of his separate limbs and organs. By injecting into the brain, at a given point, a given quantity of a given matter, you could, in a fraction of a second, deprive a man of sight, of speech, of reason; you could, in fact, transform him into more than a brute beast, with this disadvantage as against the beast, that he had only a rudimentary control over his own limbs and muscles. One of the curious features of his condition being that no one could tell— who did not know—what had happened to him. No doctor living could diagnose his case. As for doing him any good, for curing him, not all the doctors in all the world could benefit him one iota. I had one day occasion to remonstrate with Cyril Wentworth on the recklessness with which he conducted his experiments. When he was insolent I requested him to leave my laboratory, never to enter it again. Without a word of warning he sprang at me with the hypodermic syringe in his hand which I had just seen him charge with this particular matter. I had my pipe; I dashed the bowl into his face as he came at me. I fancy some of the hot ash got into his eye. He started back with a cry of pain; then came at me more furiously than before. His momentary hesitation had given me time to collect my wits. I closed with him as he came on that second time, and—we fought. It was a good fight, a hard fight, a long fight. The end of it was that I dropped him out of the window into the Neckar."

CHAPTER XXIII

THE ANTIDOTE

AGAIN the Herr Professor paused. He went to the window and looked out upon the stream, as if he still saw Cyril Wentworth plunging into the water. That he beheld the scene with the eye of memory his next words showed.

"It was a great splash he made—a great splash."

"And what did you do then?"

It was Miss Capparoni who put the question. The professor replied without any sign of being annoyed at its having been put.

"What did I do? I thanked God."

"Did you try to rescue him, or did you try to make sure that he was drowned?"

"I did neither. I wanted no scandal, or I might have drowned him; and as for rescuing him, I knew he could swim like a fish."

"Then what followed? Did he charge you with assault, or with attempted murder?"

"Mein Gott! Nothing followed. He vanished; that is what followed. He left Heidelberg that same afternoon. I have seen and heard nothing of him since—until to-day. I thought that I should have heard of him before this, knowing the man; and there have been——"

"There have been what?" inquired Miss Capparoni. The professor had stopped in the middle of a sentence.

"There have been cases, of which I have heard and read, which have caused me to wonder where was Mr. Cyril Wentworth, and what it was that he was doing. But there has been no proof. Nothing sure. Only surmise."

"Then I take it that what he failed in doing to you he succeeded in doing to my father."

"So it would appear from what you have told me. I know nothing of my own knowledge, but—it looks like that."

"If he did it, then you do know exactly what it was he did do?"

"Yes—but always in a sense. That experiment is capable of an infinite number of minute variations, one of which would make a material difference in the results. It is not easy, from a mere verbal explanation, to say which, if any, of these variations he adopted. If, as you suggest, your father was obedient to Cyril Wentworth, then he adopted one of them; the result of the simple and original experiment is that a man is made like a log of wood. No one can compel him to do anything, because he can do nothing either for or with himself—he cannot even convey food to his own mouth. Those men who you tell me were working in the mine—there was another variation; one, also, which he himself discovered. It was over that we had our final battle. He told me that he had discovered that, by an infinitesimal variation in the formula, you could make a man or a woman like a clockwork figure. That is, the operator could set him or her to do a certain thing, and that, unless the operator intervened, he or she would continue doing it, always less and less quickly, until death came and stopped the work. I doubted it—mind you, he would not tell me in what the variation consisted; he was impudent—so I said I doubted it. Then he was more impudent than before. He laughed in my face, and said that if I would go round to his lodgings I should have ocular proof. I asked him what he meant. He told me that he had set his servant-girl to sweep his room in the middle of the afternoon, and that she would keep on sweeping it until he returned to stop her. I said, if it was true, he had been guilty of a vile action. The end of it was that I dropped him into the Neckar. Afterwards, feeling curious as to the truth of his story, I went round to his lodgings to institute inquiries. He had not yet returned—indeed, to those lodgings he never did return. I found, later, that he had also other lodgings about here; he was a young man of many secrets. The door of the room was locked; I forced it open with my shoulders. There, sure enough, was the poor servant-maid, with a broom in her hand, walking round and round the room, sweeping each inch of the floor again and again and again, never stopping for an instant's rest. It was an extraordinary spectacle; it was quite amazing to watch her. I thought, after a while, that it was a trick, one in which she played a part. But, no; try how I might, I could not stop her. When I picked her up and held her tight, she offered no resistance, showed no consciousness of what was happening to her; but her arms and legs kept in regular, though convulsive movement, as though she still walked and swept. When I tied her to a chair, it was the same. It would have been most laughable had it not meant that her entire existence was destroyed."

"Cyril Wentworth had performed your experiment on her?"

"With a variation which he had himself discovered, and of which he would not tell me the secret."

"It occurs to be, Professor Ehrenberg, that it would not have been a serious misfortune if he had succeeded in the experiment which he endeavoured to perform on you."

"On the contrary, it would have been a very great misfortune."

"For you, or for the world?"

"For the world and for me, but principally for the world. In such a matter myself I should not count."

"I fear I cannot agree with you. It seems to me that it would have been simply poetic justice if this man had prefaced the long list of victims whom you had placed at his mercy—with you. Surely, to a volume of which you were yourself the author, you would have made a fitting frontispiece."

"You do not know what it is you talk about. I will not discuss with you; to argue with a woman is useless. I will point out one reason why it was fortunate for the world that your compatriot's experiment did not succeed—that one reason, I think, you will find enough. I had learnt, once more, how to do; I had yet to learn, again, how to undo. I had discovered the poison; now I had to find the antidote. The dreadful spectacle presented by the poor girl whom your fellow-countryman, caring nothing, had left in such a horrible condition——"

"I wish you would not keep on calling him my fellow-countryman."

The Herr Professor thundered back at Miss Capparoni—

"He is your fellow-countryman—is he not? Am I not entitled to call a spade a spade? Well, then, I say that the spectacle presented by the poor girl was to me the cause of great affliction. I had not hurt her, Heaven forbid! I do not conduct my studies for the purpose of working evil. Yet I could not bear to think of her condition. I said to myself, there is an antidote—there must be; there shall be. I will discover that also. I reasoned logically that since in nature everything has its contrary—so that we can always oppose heat to cold—here also must be one. And there was, and is. I found it."

Suddenly Miss Capparoni showed signs of being interested almost to the point of agitation.

"Do you mean that you cured her?"

"I do. With a touch—a pin-prick; in an instant she was as she had been before. That she has suffered no after ill effects she is alive to testify. She is married; has four children—strapping youngsters. She herself is immense, strong as a horse, always well; and to this hour she does not know what your compatriot did to her, and what I undid."

"Then—then, if you cured her, you—you could cure my father?"

"If Mr. Cyril Wentworth had succeeded in his experiment on me—what then? He knew nothing of an antidote; I will wager that he knows nothing of one now. He destroys—he thinks for ever. But let me come within reach of any that he has destroyed, I will restore; I will make them again as they were before—as by a miracle. Yes, as by a miracle! Was it not, then, fortunate for the world that his experiment failed on me, so that I might acquire this knowledge, and that it might be preserved? Was it not fortunate, if for that reason only?"

"Herr Professor, I beg your pardon. As you have more than once pointed out, I am only a woman; and sometimes women speak first, and only afterwards begin to think. What I said was said in haste, without any real intention. It was very foolish—unjustified, wicked. I ought to be, and I am, ashamed of allowing my tongue to carry me away. Will you, please, forgive me?"

The Herr Professor beamed. Miss Capparoni as a penitent was an entire success, if only from a spectacular point of view.

"My dear little girl, a man always forgives a woman everything—especially a pretty woman. What is a pretty woman for if she is not to be forgiven? My dear young lady, we are the best of friends; in token thereof I salute you."

He touched her forehead with his lips, which was a little unexpected. But the young lady showed no visible signs of being distressed. Indeed, she smiled, as if the surprise was rather a pleasant one. For a moment or two she became almost affectionate.

"And, dear Herr Professor, if I succeed in finding my father, as I know I shall do, will you perform a miracle for me—a miracle of healing—and restore to me the father I once knew and loved?"

"I will. I promise it. And that you may bear on your brow a mark of my promise, once more I salute you."

He did, a second time. She turned to John Banner, who all this while had been listening and looking on with what, no doubt, would be inadequately described as varied feelings.

"Mr. Banner, when we return to London we will put pressure on Mr. Cyril Wentworth together. We will dangle before his eyes certain shares on which he has been drawing dividends, and we will do other things as well. We will try a fall with him; if needs be, we'll take the buttons off the foils. Between us we may succeed in inducing him to give us a hint where my father is. And then—then when we have the hint, it will go hard with me, and with Jack the

Chemist, if I do not find my father before we are much older. And having found him, I will bring him to this worker of miracles here, and he will give back to me the father I have lost so long."

The Herr Professor took the cherry-wood stem from between his lips, expelled a cloud of smoke, and waved his pipe in the air, which, with him, seemed to be a favourite method of expressing emotion.

"Yes, that is true; I will work another miracle."

CHAPTER XXIV

A DOUBLE DISAPPEARANCE

EVERYTHING went well with Mr. Cyril Wentworth and Miss Bradley—particularly with Miss Bradley. It was strange that a woman could have lived so long in the world and yet not known what living really was; and she had not known, she owned it both to herself and to Cyril. He was the most delightful of lovers. The day after she had consented to be his wife he presented her with a ring; it was not an engagement ring, that came afterwards—a gorgeous affair, which Miss Bradley, whose taste in such matters was modest, was inclined to think almost too gorgeous. This was quite a simple ring, which had for setting a single ruby; not a bad stone, but nothing in any way uncommon. The gold hoop in which the stone was set was curiously thick; so thick as to be almost clumsy. Miss Bradley made something like a grimace when first she saw it.

"Do you know, Cyril, that that ring will make my finger, and indeed my whole hand, look as if it were immense. I shall scarcely ever be able to wear it, if only because I shall never be able to draw a glove over it."

"On the contrary, sweetheart"—he uttered the word in a tone which thrilled her—"you will always wear it."

"Cyril!"

"Always. I will give you some of the reasons why. First of all, that ring is a mascot; it will bring you luck—and happiness."

"Haven't I both of them already?"

She accompanied that question with a glance which was meant to be significant, but which, if he noticed it, he ignored.

"Not in the sense which that ring will bring them you. Let me put it on." She suffered him, with a smile. "Isn't it a comfortable ring to wear?"

"Very. And, do you know—perhaps it's my imagination—but it seems to send a thrill right through my finger, and up my arm, and all over my body, positively. Cyril! You darling!"

Quite spontaneously she kissed him. This time he suffered her, without a smile.

"I don't think it enlarges my lady's pretty finger, or deforms her shapely hand."

"Not a bit. It sits much closer than I thought it would, and it fits so well."

"I have not been observing my lady's fingers all this time without making a pretty shrewd guess at the size of the ring which would fit her."

"Cyril!"

She put her arms about his neck, and again she kissed him. This time he laughed in her face, but she did not seem to mind.

It was possibly only a coincidence that from the hour in which she suffered Mr. Wentworth to slip on to her finger that single stone ruby ring a subtle, yet distinctly perceptible, change began to take place in her. No doubt, as she told her father when he taxed her with it, happiness was the motive power. Mr. Bradley was bewildered; he admitted as much to his future son-in-law.

"I don't know what you've done to that girl of mine, Wentworth, but it seems to me that you've worked wonders. She's a different woman, already. She seems to me to have grown younger, both outside and in. I thought to-day, as I happened to glance at her at dinner, that she looked almost pretty. Though I'm her father, I'm perfectly aware that she never was a beauty. But, to-day—well, there! I had to rub my eyes. What's come to her face? It's like a girl's—warm, bright, fresh, eager. And she's skittish, ready for any fun. If she has had a fault, it is that she's always been, well, not exactly severe so much as superior; she's been too apt to look down on everything and every one as beneath her notice. Between ourselves, I've almost suspected, more than once, that she looked down on me. Now she's not only good for any frolic, she's so gentle, so—tender, so careful of wounding people's feelings; she could say nasty things, could Ellen; it's days now since I heard her say one. And, though I find it hard to believe it of my daughter, she's—yes, sir, she's positively spoony. She seems not only fond of hanging about your neck, but, dash it! she hangs about mine! Instead of being one of the snubbiest of daughters, she's become, all at once, the most affectionate. Wentworth, what have you done to her?"

Mr. Wentworth was some moments before he answered. He regarded Mr. Bradley as if that gentleman had propounded to him a problem which was not altogether easy of solution.

"I expect that a change has taken place in me as well as in Miss Bradley."

"I haven't noticed it."

"Perhaps that's because you don't know me as well as you know Ellen; it is not so easy for you to appreciate the difference between what I was and what I am."

"Perhaps so." Mr. Bradley was looking the speaker up and down, as if he were trying to perceive some difference in him there and then, and failing. "I doubt if any man could change as Ellen has changed, or if many women could either. I've seen a few engaged girls in my time, some of them pretty far gone in love, but I never before saw a girl transformed into quite another kind of girl, as it seems to me Ellen is."

"Possibly the transformation may become still more marked when we are married; it is within the limits of the possible that it may even extend to you."

Mr. Bradley shook his head solemnly, as if such a question was too preposterous for serious contemplation.

"I am what I am. I am fixed, sir; I shall never change."

"I wonder."

As he spoke, Mr. Wentworth's finger was in his waistcoat pocket, as if he was feeling something which was in it.

The marriage was to be soon. There was, as Mr. Wentworth pointed out, no reason why it should be delayed; certainly Miss Bradley saw none. She agreed to everything her lover proposed. Had he suggested that they should go off and be married at a registrar's office right away, it is not impossible that she would have gone. She had pointed out, over and over again, in her novels, and out of them, what extremely bad taste it was to flaunt one's affection in public. So far as one could gather, from the law as she laid it down, it was hardly good form for a woman to love a man at all. If one desired—as one ought to desire—to eschew vulgarity between men and women, there ought to be as little of that kind of thing as possible. For nurse-maids and shop-girls—it was impossible to account for people of that sort; but for women of culture, intellect, breeding, position, to associate them with the idea of love in the ordinary sense was an impertinence. Alas for the way in which she "darlinged" "Cyril"! She hardly addressed him without some saccharine diminutive.

They were to live in a fine house overlooking St. James's Park.* Wentworth's idea was to place the entire premises in the hands of a firm who would provide decorations, furniture, everything. For the first time the lady dissented, not brusquely, but as one who craved a boon. She begged to be allowed a voice in the matter; more, she implored him to join himself to her, and let them "make their home" together. He could hardly refuse, the consequence being that she took him from one shop to another—here, there, and everywhere—in search of some particular something which she desired should grace their future home. Anybody but her would have seen that she enjoyed that kind of thing much more than he did. In her normal state she might have seen it also; but, of late, where he was concerned, she seemed to be only capable of seeing what she wished to see. Never the best-tempered of men, the necessity of concealing his ill-temper tried him almost beyond endurance.

"If I thought that there was going to be much more of this, I'd—I'd make her marry me to-morrow, and then—then we'd come to an understanding."

This he said to himself when, one afternoon, they had returned from a fruitless search for an Aubusson carpet of a particular make and pattern. Not only had the hunt itself been galling—he was the kind of man to whom such details are objects of loathing, and to think that he had spent the entire afternoon in looking vainly for a carpet—the thing was maddening. But there had been other matters to cause him annoyance besides the ignobly wasted afternoon.

At that time the newspapers were much occupied with what they called "A Double Disappearance." They had begun with vague announcements that a lady well known in the "smart set" had mysteriously disappeared. Presently they gave her name, and more—she was a Mrs. Van der Gucht, had rooms in Curzon Street, which she quitted one morning, leaving word that she would return that evening, and had not been seen or heard of since. She was still undiscovered when another mysterious disappearance was chronicled. This time it was a gentleman—a Mr. Max Quannell—the peculiar feature in his case being that he had not only disappeared on the same day as the lady, but that, a few minutes after she had gone out, he called at her rooms to inquire for her. It was not denied that they were friends—both the lady and the gentleman had come from South Africa. It was beginning to be hinted that an explanation was contained in one word—"elopement"—when something else transpired which cast a different explanation on the matter altogether.

The lady was found—in an imbecile ward at Hounslow Workhouse. She had been rescued from what was supposed to be an attempt to commit suicide. A ferryman at Isleworth had seen, one morning, a figure on the island in front of Sion House—the figure of a woman. At first he could not make out what she was doing. She was staggering about among the rushes, right at the water's edge, as he put it, "as if she had been having a drop." He shouted at her, but, if she heard, she paid no heed. As she began to get further and further into the stream, he began to get his boat out. When, stepping into a hole, or losing her footing, she suddenly disappeared, he pushed off towards the spot where she had vanished. He got her out, but when they took her ashore they thought that she was dead. It was nearly an hour before signs of life returned. Then they discovered that she was apparently deaf, dumb, blind, paralyzed, and imbecile—a dreadful object.

The question arose as to how she had arrived at her present condition. Was it the result of her immersion? or of injuries inflicted by the ferryman in his attempts to rescue her? The man declared that he had simply waited until she rose to the surface, and had then lifted her out in his arms. There was nothing about her which was in any way inconsistent with his story. On the other hand, while there was no mark about her head or body which pointed to a blow, or violence of any sort, the fact of her having been partially drowned was certainly not sufficient to account for her condition. There was nothing about her to assist identification. On her clothing, which was of excellent quality, there were neither initials nor name.

It was equally difficult to explain how she could have got upon the island. She must have done so during the night, or, at any rate, after it was dark. A dozen persons were prepared to testify that she was not there the previous evening at sunset. She could hardly have swum across. She could not have waded, because, although the tide had been very low in the night, the mud was very deep in places; in the darkness—it had been unusually dark—she would certainly have lost her bearings and stuck fast.

When, after an interval, it was discovered that this dreadful being was none other than the young and lovely Mrs. Van der Gucht, a hubbub arose. She was found, but the gentleman still was missing. Where was he? He had called on her. The manservant who had told him she was out had judged from his manner that he knew where she was to be found, and had immediately gone after her. If so—if he had found her, or if he had not—why did he not now come forward and explain?

A rather curious piece of evidence cropped up in this connection. That night a keeper in Kew Gardens had suffered from neuralgia* to such an extent that, driven nearly frantic, he had risen from his bed in the middle of the night, and gone out into the gardens to try and walk it off. As he was tramping up and down the walk, looking over the river, he all at once became conscious that some one was moving along the river bank. Presently a man and a woman came along, moving towards Richmond, and, incidentally also, towards the island. If they did not see him he saw them—at least, he saw enough to make sure that it was a man and a woman. More, he was struck by the peculiar way in which the man had the woman close to his side, as if he were helping her along.

Was the woman Mrs. Van der Gucht? The thing was at least feasible. If so, in what condition was she? What had happened?

What did happen shortly after? Above all, who was the man? Why did not Max Quannell come forward and explain?

It was on this subject Miss Bradley discoursed on the afternoon on which Mr. Cyril Wentworth was already sufficiently irritated by the fact that he was being "dragged" about in search of what he himself would have described—and afterwards did describe—as a "beastly" carpet.

"You were a great friend of Mrs. Van der Gucht, weren't you, darling?"

They were in the carriage, driving from a shop in Welbeck Street to another in the City. He had previously endeavoured to keep her off the theme, but, for some incomprehensible reason, she seemed exasperatingly pertinacious.

"I certainly knew her."

"Did you think her very pretty?"

"She was not bad-looking—after a fashion."

"Cyril, once I—I was nearly jealous of her."

"Absurd!"

"It does seem absurd now, doesn't it? But I wasn't so sure of you then, darling."

How he hated those continual "darlings"! He would quickly put a stop to them when—when he had a chance.

"I'm sorry for her now, poor woman! I'm sorry for every one who isn't happy, since I am myself so happy. I ought to be. I wonder what happened to her, really. Did you know her husband?"

"Not at all."

"I suppose that man Quannell is at the bottom of it all; a man with a name like that starts with the odds against him. Did you know him?"

"I've seen him."

"What kind of man was he?"

"My knowledge of him was not sufficient to enable me to judge."

"Do you think she cared for him?"

He considered the matter before he answered.

"From what I knew of her I should say that the only person for whom she cared was her husband."

"Cyril! Then in that case she must have been capable of caring very little for any one. If she had cared for him at all she could hardly have been willing to leave him alone, all those thousands of miles away, and come over here all by herself to live the kind of life she did. Do you think I should be willing to leave you all by your lonely little self in London, while I went to have a glorious time in Africa?"

"That would be different."

He smiled grimly.

"I should hope so." She pressed his hand, in the open carriage. He did not venture even to wince. "It seems odd that you should have known them both."

"Why? I have a large and miscellaneous circle of acquaintance. I know all sorts of people; I can't help it, it happens so. Besides, you knew her."

"Yes; but only very slightly, while I suspect you of knowing her much better than you care to admit. I'd have you understand, young gentleman, that I've heard whisperings."

Again she pressed his hand, archly. He would have liked to have pressed hers till she screamed.

"And then you knew him, and I didn't. It's knowing both parties in the matter that seems to me, under the circumstances, to be such an odd coincidence."

"I don't see why. I tell you again that my acquaintance with him was of the slightest. But let's speak of something more interesting. About this precious carpet, lady mine. Tell me—if it's for the five-and-fiftieth time—exactly what kind of carpet it is that your ladyship desires, and why that one we saw just now wouldn't do."

And for the five-and-fiftieth time she told him.

CHAPTER XXV

MR. JOHNSON

IT was after having returned from that fruitless hunt, and having escaped from her society, that, as he was ascending the steps of the Pitt Club,* he told himself that if there was any risk of having to endure much more of the kind of thing he had endured that afternoon, he would force her to marry him to-morrow, and that then—there should be a change. But he was still to suffer; indeed, he had chanced upon a day which, for him, was to be full of pin-pricks.

In the hall he came upon a man named Chandler—Edwin Chandler. Mr. Chandler was in the Colonial Office.* In that part of it whose special subject was South Africa he held, so far as Wentworth was able to understand, a position of some importance. One thing was sure, that he had an irritating knack of knowing things which Wentworth would rather he had not known, and of giving that gentleman the benefit of his knowledge when frequently it was least desired. Whenever Cyril Wentworth saw him he expected to hear something which he did not wish to hear, so that the mere sight of him was enough to put him on his guard. On the present occasion the words with which he greeted him sounded, as it were, a note of warning.

"You're the very man I have been looking for; I've a bit of news to give you, which I think that you may find of interest."

Wentworth put his hands behind his back and looked Mr. Chandler straight in the face, pleasantly, yet with a certain significance.

"Seems to me, Chandler, that all the time you've something interesting to tell me which I'd just as soon not hear, and which doesn't interest me in the least. You don't mind my saying so?"

"Not a bit. I don't mind your saying anything."

There was something in the tone in which he uttered that last sentence which Mr. Wentworth resented, though he showed no signs of it.

"What is it now?"

"It's about that little pal of yours, the Van der Gucht."

"Why do you call Mrs. Van der Gucht a pal of mine?"

"Because she was. Don't play the innocent with me; I know. I'll give you chapter and verse for my knowledge, if you like; though I think that perhaps you'd rather I didn't."

Mr. Wentworth still regarded the other pleasantly, and so showed what a mask the human countenance may be.

"I may tell you, Wentworth, that, knowing what I do know, I am at a loss to understand how it is that you are not more affected by the hideous tragedy in which her life has so suddenly resolved itself."

"It's very good of you, Chandler, to feel like that for me. Pray in what particular manner would you have wished me to be affected?"

"If the tenth part of what has happened to her, poor little thing, had happened to a pal of mine, whether male or female, I'd have made the welkin ring*; I promise you so much. Different men different manners. I've no doubt you have what seem to you sound reasons for your present attitude."

"Thank you, Chandler. Now for the news!"

"Her husband, Van der Gucht, is on his way to England, and should be in London in a very few days."

"As he ought to be, being the lady's husband. If ever a woman stood in need of a husband's tender care—— Is that all, Chandler?"

"Quannell's father, who, I learn, is still a hale and hearty old gentleman, comes with him."

"Does he? He also does well."

"As they will probably—both of them—pay you a visit directly they reach town, I thought you might like to know that they were coming, so that they might not take you unawares."

"I am obliged to you, Chandler, deeply."

Cyril Wentworth sauntered off into the smoking-room, where he had a smoke and a drink. How much he read of the evening paper which he held up in front of him is a query.

That night he gave himself a treat—his notion of a treat. It seemed to him to be so long since he had enjoyed himself, that he stood in need of some relaxation, so he had some. Having gained a night off from Miss Bradley, by means of certain incorrect allegations, he made the most of it; again, his notion of the most. He began with an excellent dinner, not at the club, but at a restaurant in Regent Street. He was very fond of good food and good drink. Then he went to the Empire*; and then—the morning was already far advanced when he returned to his flat in Sloane Street.

A rather curious incident occurred as the hansom in which he was turned the corner into Sloane Street. Some one standing on the pavement, who had apparently been waiting and watching for his approach, hailed him by name.

"Mr. Wentworth! Can I speak to you a moment, sir?"

Mr. Wentworth, leaning over the apron, saw that a man was running along the pavement, keeping pace with the vehicle—a man who, from where he was, seemed shabbily dressed, and a stranger.

"Who are you? And what do you want with me at this hour of the morning?"

"I've something particular which I want to say to you, sir, if you don't mind; I won't keep you half a minute. It's very particular, sir, and I should like to say it to you here."

"Say it to me here? What the devil do you mean?" He stopped the cab; the man came alongside. "Who are you? I don't know your face."

The man touched his billycock hat*; his voice dropped to a confidential whisper.

"Yes, you do, sir; my name's Johnson. I was the porter at the flat."

"The porter at the flat? Then if you have anything to say to me, why can't you choose a more reasonable time, and say it at the flat?"

"Begging your pardon, sir, I said I was the porter, but I—I got the boot."

"Got the boot, did you? That's frank, since I presume you got it for sufficient reasons. Then pray what have you to say to me?"

"Again begging your pardon, sir, I've got something very particular to say, if you don't mind getting down. That driver up there, his ears are wide open."

Mr. Wentworth looked at the speaker in silence, steadily, the man returning him glance for glance. Apparently he saw something in his glances which induced him to accede to his request.

"As I haven't much farther to go, I may as well walk the remainder of the distance as ride it, so I will get down." He descended and paid the cabman. "Now, my man, quick! What is it?"

"Well, sir, if you'll just come for a little stroll round Cadogan Place, we shall be more private there. See this copper coming along? He's had his eyes on me some time. We don't want him putting his nose in. Though you mayn't think it, sir, it might be more awkward for you than for me."

"It might be more awkward for me than for you! Mr. Johnson, you flatter me!" The constable referred to approached, with the usual policeman's measured tread. Mr. Wentworth addressed him. "Good night, officer; fine night!"

The policeman stopped. He thrust his thumbs into his belt, inclining his head towards Mr. Johnson.

"Good night, sir. I don't know who this man is, but he's been hanging about here these two hours and more, ever since I've been on the beat, and my mate told me he was here before I came. I don't know what's his game."

Cyril Wentworth hesitated. Mr. Johnson, during those few moments of his hesitation, came very near to being taken in custody as a suspicious character. Mr. Wentworth would have liked to have seen him marched off then and there, with handcuffs about his wrists; but he refrained. As he spoke, he kept his eyes fixed intently on the ex-porter's face.

"I don't think you need trouble yourself about this man at present, officer; I trust you may never have cause to do so. At the same time you have done quite right in keeping your eyes on him. Good night; and thank you."

"Good night, sir."

The constable marched off, with two half-crowns in the palm of his hand.* When he had gone some little distance Mr. Johnson grinned.

"You were within a pin's point of trying to have me buckled. You'd have been sorry if you had, sorrier than me."

"Should I, indeed? Your manners strike me as very free and easy. No wonder you got the boot. Now, my man, no more nonsense; what tale have you got to pitch? Out with it! And always bear in mind that that constable is still within reach."

"That's what I do bear in mind, and that's what I advise you to bear in mind as well. Since you will have it right here, you shall; you'll soon see which of us two has most cause to shy at a copper. It's about that lady and gentleman who came to see you that morning; you remember."

"Which lady and gentleman do you refer to? My visitors are sufficiently numerous to make it somewhat difficult for me to recognize them by so vague a description as that."

"Oh no, they're not; at the flat, at any rate. You may have plenty of them elsewhere, and I dare say you do, but they don't come here. I could count the visitors you had at your flat all the time I was there pretty nearly on the fingers of my two hands, and I was there getting on for six months."

"You hint at some tolerably close observation."

"Of course I do. That's the principal occupation of a porter in flats—to keep a sharp eye on the tenants, and who comes to see them, and that sort of thing."

"Is it, indeed? We don't seem to be getting much forwarder, since I fear I am not much interested in what you may consider to be the chief excuse for a porter's existence."

"The name of the lady I'm talking about was Mrs. Van der Gucht, and the name of the gentleman was Quannell—Max Quannell. So now you have it."

There was an appreciable interval before Mr. Wentworth spoke again; his tones were still quite smooth.

"I presume they gave you their names as they came in. Is there anything singular in that, that you should shout at me in the street at three o'clock in the morning?"

"There wouldn't have been anything singular if they had, but they didn't. I mightn't never have known what their names were, or anything at all about them, if I had not, by sheer accident, seen their portraits in the newspaper, when all the fuss began about their having disappeared."

"Well? You are some time in coming to the point, Mr. Johnson, if there is a point."

This time it was Mr. Johnson who paused to consider. He was a young man about thirty, with a something about him which betrayed anxiety. He searched the other's face with eyes which were eager, yet nervous. About his whole bearing there was a suggestion of menace, as if, had he dared, he would have played the bully; but, big and burly though he was, he did not dare. There was that about the other which warned him not to go too far. No one could have been more serenely at his ease than Mr. Wentworth seemed to be—his hands in the pockets of his dark dress overcoat; a cigar in his mouth, which he was lazily enjoying; his otherwise impassive features lighted by a faint fixed smile. He was the typical man-about-town returning from a nocturnal jaunt. His eyes were the most singular part of him; possibly it was they who conveyed a warning to Mr. Johnson. Of that faint shade in grey which is almost blue, they had, when their owner chose, a quality of impassivity, almost as if they were two pebbles set in empty sockets. They never flinched. About their continuous stare there was something sinister. They got upon the beholder's nerves, especially when there was cause for nervousness. They were so immobile, so unresting, so callous, so inhuman, that one began to be conscious of a feeling of uneasy doubt as to what the owner might be thinking about, what plan of attack he was formulating, what blow he was making ready to strike.

When Mr. Johnson did speak, it was as if, having taken his courage in both his hands, he had made up his mind to be afraid of no one, and to let Mr. Wentworth know it.

"You remember when I said I hadn't seen them come out, you told me that they'd perhaps gone down the other staircase. I thought that was queer, because I'd been keeping such a sharp look-out that I ought to have seen them even if they had. So when you'd gone I made inquiries, and soon found they'd gone down no other staircase. That started me thinking. If they hadn't gone, why had you said they had? and why had you left them up there all alone by themselves, especially as it was plain that you didn't want any one to know that they were up there. What little game was being played? The parlourmaid in the flat next to yours came down to do a little shopping. I asked her if she heard anything going on next door. She said she had; she'd heard a woman screaming like anything, and she wondered what could be going on. I wondered too. I had noticed, when you went out, that there was a cut on your left check-bone, too high up for a razor, and not that sort. It looked quite recent; I wondered how you'd got that. In fact, when I'd once begun to wonder, the more I had to. I thought I'd go up and make a few investigations on my own account. I went up to your flat and rang the bell; I wasn't satisfied with doing it once, I rang six times, and it did ring, because I heard it. No one answered. I said to myself, this gets queerer and queerer. Either they are in there or they are not. If they're not, where the dickens did they get to when they came out? If they are, why don't they answer the bell when a party keeps on ringing? There's something rum about this job, and it's my business to find out what."

Mr. Johnson moistened his lips with his tongue, then drew the back of his hand across them. Cyril Wentworth took advantage of the pause to make a remark.

"You appear, in some respects, to come up to your own standard of what a porter ought to be."

"You mean so far as keeping my eyes open was concerned. It was my duty to find out if anything shady was going on—it was my duty to my employers."

"No doubt. Of course it was your employers whom you had in view."

The porter grinned. "Well, I might have had, if things had turned out different; but as they did turn out there was something else I had to have in view besides that lot. They didn't treat me so well that I should go out of my way to do them a turn, even if it had been a turn, which, so far as their interests went, I don't say it would have been. Here's that infernal copper coming back again. Hadn't we better stroll? He'll be shoving his silly nose in again."

"I really don't see what this long-winded yarn of yours has to do with me."

"You'll see that clear enough before I've done."

"Shall I? Then, since this early morning air is so fresh and pleasant, I don't mind strolling homewards round Cadogan Place."

They turned the corner before the officer reached it. When he did, he stood and watched them. He ruminated.

"What's up there? Something. Who's the swell? That chap's keener on talking to him than he is on listening—unless I'm wrong."

He was wrong, because, as it happened, just then Mr. Wentworth was listening with a degree of interest which was altogether beyond anything he cared to show.

"You know those iron ladders which are meant to be used as fire-escapes which are at the back of the flats? Presently, when I got a chance, I nipped up them to your flat. As I expected, the blinds were down. I rapped at the windows, all of them, one after the other. No answer. So I opened the window of your sitting-room." The speaker paused, as if to italicize the sidelong glance with which he favoured Mr. Wentworth. Then he added five very simple monosyllables, which, as he uttered them, were disagreeably significant. "You know what I saw!"

He paused again. Mr. Wentworth removed the cigar from between his lips, following it with a thin trail of smoke. Nothing could have been more measured than his manner, with a suavity which was disconcerting.

"How sweet the early morning air is at this time of the year, even in a London street!"

"I'm glad you find it so."

"I do find it so. Don't you?"

Mr. Johnson seemed disposed to be surly, as if he could not make the other out.

"I'm agreeable, if you are."

Mr. Wentworth laughed gently. For some reason his companion started, visibly.

"I'm glad to hear that you are agreeable, Mr. Johnson. What an odd way you have of expressing yourself!"

Throwing back his overcoat, Mr. Wentworth inserted his fingers in his waistcoat pockets. Instantly the other not only stopped, but drew back. His manner changed. With clenched fists, he stood like a man ready to ward off attack.

"Stow that! Don't you try any of your tricks with me! There's a copper within hail!"

Mr. Wentworth stared, apparently both surprised and amused.

"Preserve us! What's the matter with the man?"

"You know what's the matter. Don't you think you can catch me napping. I don't know what it was that you did with those two, but I do know that you played some blasted hankey-pankey trick off on them, and I'll bet you did it before they had so much as a chance of spotting what it was that you were up to. You don't have me that way. You take your hands out of your waistcoat pockets, and let me see what's in them, or, as sure as you're alive, I'll call the copper!"

Mr. Wentworth hesitated, smiled, then held out his hands open in front of him. "Please, what's the matter with them?"

Mr. Johnson criticized them aggressively; then, with the same aggressive air, resumed his scrutiny of their owner.

"Nothing, as it happens, just now, and I don't mean that there shall be. You button up your overcoat, and put back your hands where they were. I don't fancy that there is much in those pockets."

"Some persons might resent both the request and the manner of making it, but I'm in a most obliging mood. There, will that do? Now explain why you've told me that little story of yours at this primitive hour."

"Because I'm on my uppers."*

"Are you? That's sad. So worthy a man!"

"I want money."

"So do we all."

"And I'm going to have some."

"Indeed. You know where money is to be found?"

"I do; it is to be found at your address, Mr. Wentworth."

"Is it? And how much money is to be found at my address, Mr. Johnson?"

"A thousand pounds."

"A thousand pounds? That's a deal."

"I dare say. But I lay you're worth more than that much."

"Do you? You're a sporting man. If you care to stroll the rest of the way, and will come and continue your little conversation in my flat——"

Again Mr. Johnson gave a very obvious start. "Your flat? Me! Why, I wouldn't trust myself alone in your flat with you, not for a single moment, at this time of night, or any other time, not for all the money in the world. I don't want to have the papers talking about another disappearance. Your flat! Why, I dream of it almost every night. If you talk of trying to get me inside your flat—me! I—I may be driven to something for which we'll both of us afterwards be sorry. Listen to me, I'll make myself quite clear. I've got a brother in America who's doing well in the restaurant and boarding-house line; but he tells me that he could do much better if he could find a partner with some capital. You give me a thousand pounds, and I'll go and join my brother, and put the money in his business. It would just suit me, and I'll never trouble you again, or England either. I haven't got a relative here for whom I care a twopenny cuss."

"Do you suppose I carry a thousand pounds about with me!"

"No, I don't. I'll give you an address to which you can send, or bring, the thousand pounds before noon to-morrow, that is, noon to-day; and in the mean time you'll please hand over all the coin you've got about you."

"That amounts to about thirty shillings; I've been making a night of it."

"That'll do to go on with; I'm stony."

"And if I don't send, or bring, the sum you mention by noon?"

"Then I shall tell my story at a police station, and do my best to solve this mystery of the double disappearance which the papers are all talking about. It's worth more than a thousand pounds to you to keep my mouth shut."

"That's a question of opinion, Mr. Johnson. However, have I your permission to unbutton my overcoat to find that thirty shillings?"

"You have, only you take care that you don't find anything else, and when you have found it, you lay the money on the top of those railings. I don't want to touch your hand, not yet come within reach of it. I'm more afraid of you than I ever thought I should be of any man, Mr. Wentworth, and that's frank."

"You flatter me. Pray observe that I follow your instructions to the letter. Here is the money on the railings."

"Now you draw back and I'll take it, and I'll put the address to which you're to send the money in its place."

The exchange was effected. Cyril Wentworth examined the half-sheet of notepaper which the other had laid on the railing.

"'John Smith.' I thought you said your name was Johnson?"

"So it is; but not at that address."

"I see; you're a careful man. 'John Smith, 24, Gunner Road, Wandsworth.' That's odd!"

"What's odd?"

"Nothing."

"What the devil are you looking at me like that for?"

"My good Mr. Johnson, even a cat may look at a king."

"Not like you looked at me just now. No cat that ever lived had eyes like yours. It gives me the fidgets to look at them. What's wrong with the address?"

"Absolutely nothing. 'John Smith, 24, Gunner Road, Wandsworth.' It's a perfectly simple address."*

"You've got something in your head."

"I have, and it is this. It's just as well that we should understand each other before we part. I cannot let you have the money you want by the time you mention."

"Then, if that's the case——"

"Let me finish; but you shall have it within four and twenty hours afterwards, that is, by noon to-morrow, if you, on your part, will give me an undertaking to leave England by the next boat which goes to America."

"That's fair enough; but can I trust you?"

"You can. You shall have a thousand pounds, at the address you have given me, by noon to-morrow. I will keep my word to the letter."

"Then I'll wait. I don't see, if I keep my eyes open, which I shall do, how you're going to spoof me."

"Good. Then, since we have arrived at such a pleasant, mutual understanding, I'll wish you good night."

"I'll wish you good night, Mr. Wentworth. I'd rather you turned your back to me before I turn mine to you, if you don't mind."

Once more Mr. Wentworth laughed. "What a very odd way you have of expressing yourself. But I'm the most agreeable person, I'm always willing to oblige."

Turning, he sauntered off. The other spoke as he went—

"Remember, no tricks; before noon to-morrow."

"Exactly. You have my word, Mr. Johnson."

As Mr. Johnson went, he again encountered that ubiquitous policeman, who unceremoniously addressed him.

"So you've finished your little job, have you?"

"What's it got to do with you what I've finished."

"What were you doing on those railing there? I saw you!"

"Did you? Then perhaps you're happy."

"None of your lip, my lad. Who's your gentleman friend?"

"If you was to ask him perhaps he'd tell you."

Mr. Johnson strode off; the policeman glared after him.

"It's no good following you, but I should like to see where your friend goes. If I was to hurry back into Sloane Street I might get a peep at him."

CHAPTER XXVI

THE MIDDLE FINGER

WHEN Cyril Wentworth admitted himself into his flat, he found in the letter-box a letter. He regarded it askance, being in a suspicious mood; in this case his suspicion proved itself to be, from his point of view, not without justification. It was an official-looking document, and turned out to be written on official paper, being addressed from "Fulham Workhouse,"* and signed "P. Pocock, Medical Officer." According to Dr. Pocock, a patient had been admitted to the imbecile ward of the Fulham Workhouse by the magistrate of the Hammersmith Police Court, who was in a very curious condition. At the time of his reception an examination had been made of his clothing, which was all that he apparently possessed, nothing whatever being found which shed the slightest light on his identity. However, an inner pocket had since been found in his waistcoat. In a corner of this was a scrap of paper, on which was written Cyril Wentworth's name and address. It had therefore been thought possible that Mr. Wentworth might know something of the patient in question, of whom a description followed. Perhaps Mr. Wentworth would be so good as to call, at his earliest convenience, to see the man.

When Mr. Wentworth had finished this communication, he tossed it from him on to the table, with a smile which was scarcely humorous.

"I seem to have struck a vein of bad luck, or rather, perhaps, the vein of my good luck has run a little dry. So that fool Fentiman has drifted into Fulham Workhouse, has he? And he must needs carry about with him, in some beastly place where no one would ever dream of looking, my name and address, after the care I took in relieving him of anything which was in the least likely to give away the show. And the ingenuous Pocock imagines that I will rush round to recognize him—as what? My long-lost brother? Deuce take the man! Why, instead, couldn't he have managed to drift into the river, and so have made an end?"

Mr. Wentworth took off his coat and hat and mixed himself a soda and whisky, while he turned things over in his mind. There were one or two awkward contingencies which he might have to face. The intimation which he had received from the busybody gentleman in the Colonial Office, that Mr. Van der Gucht and old Quannell might shortly be expected to arrive in town, had possibilities which scarcely could be called agreeable. He had met old Quannell; of Van der Gucht he knew something by reputation; neither man was the kind of person with whom one would prefer to have a serious argument. If they came together he might find himself in a distinctly disagreeable situation. One at a time he ought to be able to manage; he had ways and means of his own— but two! He could hardly hope that his magic and spells would prevail against a pair of them.

Besides, was this a matter in which magic and spells would be of use, anyhow? It seemed doubtful. The risk, in any case, would be too great. If these two men came to see him, the fact of their coming would be known to more than one. If he "stopped" them, if he could, he would still have two difficulties to confront; it would be equally dangerous for him if they straightway disappeared, or if they were immediately found. There was Mrs. Van der Gucht with whom to make comparisons; if they once began that game the whole secret would be out. Wentworth devoutly hoped that something might happen to them before they reached London; so far as he could see, it was his best chance, yet he was painfully aware that in such transactions Providence could seldom be relied upon for adequate intervention.

Then there was Mr. Johnson, with his prying eyes and tell-tale tongue. Cyril Wentworth laughed at the notion of the thousand pounds he wanted as if it tickled him.

"He'd invest it in his brother's business, would he? And tell his brother where he got it from, and between them they'd lose it, or drink it, or spend it, inside six months, and then he'd come back for more—perhaps both of them together. I know! With blackmailers I only have one method of treatment, since trying experience taught me that all others were worse than useless—I stop them.

Mr. Johnson is a shy bird; they sometimes are. Under ordinary circumstances I might find it difficult to find myself alone with him in a situation which would render stopping feasible; but, as things are, it mayn't be so difficult as he supposes, poor dear man! I have learned that this is a world of coincidence, people who see little of it have no notion of the extent to which that's true, so I'm not a bit surprised to learn that the address to which 'John Smith' wishes a thousand to be sent is next door to my laboratory. If John Smith is living, even temporarily, at that address I ought to be able to take advantage of the fact to gain access to him in a sense of which he little dreams, although, according to his own statement, he has lately taken to dreaming. And since in dealing with him time is of the essence of the business, I'll——"

He concluded his sentence by producing from his waistcoat pocket the small flat leather case which we have seen before. He carefully examined the tiny syringe of gleaming white metal, which reposed on a velvet bed within, lifting it from its resting-place for the purpose of closer examination.

"I was once more than half disposed to think that I had here a universal panacea for all the evils which might beset a single man; but—I've grown wiser, alas! And woe is to me! The world's such a complicated machine, no man shall ever know it altogether, however wise he be. Indeed, it grows more and more on me that it's doubtful if he shall ever know completely any part of it. One has to think of so many things. No sooner has one provided for one emergency than there's another to be faced. It's wearing; one never knows the sweets of rest." Mr. Wentworth was turning, as he philosophized, the syringe over and over between his fingers as if it were a toy. "This cannot be used for everything and everybody. How matters would be simplified if it only could; but it can't! I wonder if it would not be better to bring this chapter in my life to a close, as I've brought others, and start another, say, in the United States, where, at present, I'm practically not known at all. In that case, the chief point for decision would be whether I should close it as a bachelor or as a married man; if as a married man, then 'twere well done if 'twere done quickly*—indeed, with most common quickness. There's no reason that I know of why I shouldn't have all that the daughter has, and all that the father has as well;

time is the only thing that's wanted. Owing to an unfortunate concatenation of circumstances, over which I can hardly be said to have had control, time is likely, like the importunate creditor, to decline to wait. Van der Gucht and Quannell will require very diplomatic handling if they're to allow me, say, two months quite free. If I could only manage to get two months undisturbed, I believe I might arrange matters with such perfect neatness that no untidy odds and ends should be left lying about to catch the keenest eye. But two months? How am I to get two quiet months when, for all I know, Quannell and Van der Gucht are within a few hours of town? Whatever else I may anticipate, on one thing I may rely, that, when they begin, quietude for me, at least for a space, will cease to exist. Though I strain every nerve, and try all I know—and I know a little—I'll still need to have fortune on my side if I'm to keep them from disturbing my very best laid plans. And then there's Mr. Johnson. As for him——"

Cyril Wentworth made a movement with the syringe which was still between his fingers, as if by way of illustrating the fate which was in store for the too-observant porter. He pressed the piston slightly; but either the pressure was not so slight as he had intended, or he had overlooked a fact which it recalled to his attention. He himself gave the situation voice.

"Damn the thing! I forgot that I was holding it between my finger and thumb."

The consequence of that position being that, when he pressed the end of the piston with the ball of his thumb, the fine point at the other end penetrated the skin of his finger. Both the pressure and the penetration were so slight that the mere spectator would have supposed them to be devoid of the least significance. Plainly, Cyril Wentworth thought otherwise. It was the middle finger which the point had pierced. He surveyed it with an eager keenness which suggested that it was a matter of the first importance. A tiny red spot marked the point of entry. He put the finger to his mouth, and sucked and bit at it, as if he would have bitten a piece clean out. As if dissatisfied with the result, he began to turn out the contents of a drawer in his writing-table, as if in search of something which he wanted very badly, but could not find.

"What did I do with that caustic? I thought I put it in this damned drawer! If I can't find it—it's going right up my finger; I must have injected two or three drops! What the devil am I to do?" He looked at the finger again, even more eagerly than before, the result of his rumination being a degree of dissatisfaction to which no language at his command was capable of doing justice. "It's— it's growing stiff; damn the thing! What the devil am I to do?"

The reiterated inquiry apparently still found him without an adequate answer, or, at least, without one which pleased him. Something was happening to the middle finger. It seemed as if he could not bend it, even when, gripping it with the other hand, he tried main force. He eyed it with obvious uneasiness; with something in his eyes which was almost more than fear.

"Don't let me play the fool! Let me keep my head! Let me think! I can't have touched a vein or—something would have happened before now. And yet it's moving fast enough! If—if I don't take care, if I'm not quick, it'll be a case of queer street! My God! it's beginning to twitch! I can feel it in my hand! It's too late for caustic to be of any use, even if I could find it! I wish I had a handy chopper, or something that would serve as one! I believe I have somewhere, only I mustn't stop to think; it'll have to be a razor. Good God! how it's moving! If I don't look alive, it'll be too late for that!"

He ran out of the sitting-room, across the study, into the bedroom, as if he were running for his life. A case of razors was on the dressing-table; he dragged it open with his left hand. Taking one out, extending the middle finger of his right hand, so that it lay flat on the edge of the table, with the other fingers tucked safely out of the way, he began to hack at it with the blade of the razor. As the steel cut into the flesh, the blood spurted on to the front of his dress-shirt.

CHAPTER XXVII

AGNES CAPPARONI VISITS THE WORKHOUSE

AGNES CAPPARONI was getting into a state of restlessness which affected Miss Mason's nerves, so that young lady asserted.

"What's the matter with you I can't think. You have everything that a reasonable person can desire, and you can be reasonable if you please. You've only just returned from a delightful trip to Germany——"

"We've been back a week."

"Five days, to be accurate, which is not a week. And, though I had no idea that either the country or the people were so charming, still one would think that, after so much travelling, a little rest would be agreeable; but, evidently that's not your opinion, because I don't believe you're still for two seconds together."

"You don't understand."

"I don't—and that's it; because, although you're a dear, you are a Creature of Mystery—in capital letters; and why my uncle should join himself to you in keeping me out of it, when he's perfectly well aware that there's nothing my soul loves like a real, genuine mystery, is beyond me altogether. Please, Agnes, tell me what it's all about. I never have been mixed up in anything frightfully mysterious, and that makes it seem so hard. Only drop a hint—just one—that's all I ask."

"Letty, you're a very nice girl; only——"

"Only you won't tell me anything—I know. No butter; it doesn't make your persistent refusals a bit easier to swallow."

"Only, on certain subjects, Mr. Banner has ordered me to hold my tongue, and I dare not disobey, or, for all I know, he'd send me packing."

"I dare say. As it happens, I believe that sooner than he'd send you, as you call it, 'packing,' he'd send me."

"Letty, you oughtn't to talk like that!"

"I know I oughtn't, that's why I do. My dear Agnes, it really is no good your wearing out your watch by looking at it every five seconds. Uncle's train is due at three-fifty, and nothing will bring it to the station before its proper time. But if your anxiety to see him is getting beyond all bearing, if you choose you can start at once to meet him; and if you like to drive Nancy very slowly—she hates driving slowly, and will probably drag your arms out of their sockets if you try to—you may, by dint of judicious dawdling, get to the station not more than half an hour before the train is due, in which case you'll have the consolation of knowing that you're not too late."

Miss Capparoni was certainly not too late. When John Banner did emerge from the little country station he found an impatient lady awaiting him without, with a pony which was, if anything, almost more impatient than herself. Her greeting was indicative of the mood that she was in.

"I was beginning to think that you were never coming."

He surveyed her with an aggrieved countenance.

"The train's not late. If anything, it's a minute or so in front of time."

"It seems as if it were hours late to me. You never say anything when you write. The feeling of inaction, that you are doing everything, and I nothing, becomes almost more than I can bear. If you only knew how I long for news! Is there any news?" Mr. Banner did not reply so quickly as she desired and expected. "Why don't you speak? I don't want to seem ungrateful—I'm not ungrateful; but if you've nothing to tell me—if we are no forwarder than we were, I must try my hand—I must! My methods are different from yours; I may have better luck."

"I wish your heart were not so set on this wild quest of yours."

"Wild quest! To find my father! What is there wild in wishing to do that?"

"A good deal as things are, especially in the methods you would employ. Moreover, I believe—you mustn't hate me for doing it, but the more I look into the matter the more the belief is forced upon me—that your father is dead."

"What have you learnt that makes you think so?"

"Nothing whatever—fresh. Only the more I put two and two together, the more clearly I find that they make four."

"That's because your twos aren't twos. I don't hate you one little bit for believing anything—quite the other way; but on this special point I don't share your belief, that's all. Have you learnt anything fresh about Jack the Chemist?"

"Odds and ends; nothing that points definitely in the direction you so ardently desire a pointer. I told you I'd gone to a so-called private inquiry office, and set them to shadowing Cyril Wentworth, though I hate myself for doing it. I believe all the people they employ are blackguards—I don't see how they could be anything else—who'd do anything for money; and then I'm ashamed of playing the spy—I don't seem to feel that it makes it any better because it's done by proxy. Then, after all, the results are petty, suggestive of mere impertinence."

"What are the results?"

"Well, for one thing they tell me he's engaged to be married."

"Engaged! Jack the Chemist—to Miss Bradley—the pill-man's daughter?"

"I believe that's the woman's name, though I don't see what it has to do with the search for your father."

"After what I told her! The foolish woman! But, if I can help it, he shan't have her, even yet."

"My dear Miss Capparoni, if you don't take care you may get yourself into serious trouble."

"Am I to allow that woman—any woman—to become the wife of a man like that—think of it; quite alone with him, at his mercy, night and day!—for fear of getting myself into trouble? I wonder that you—of all men—should suggest such a thing!"

Mr. Banner sighed.

"Did I suggest it? It was not my intention. I only wish to point out that she's the kind of woman who knows her own mind; and that I understand she would actively resent any impertinent intrusion, as she would deem it, on the part of an outsider, into her affairs."

"Let her do all the resenting she likes, she'll thank me afterwards. I tell you, if I can help it, he shan't have her; and he shan't! What also have you learnt?"

"It seems—I am sinking lower and lower in my own estimation as I retail this petty scandal, which I have acquired in such a manner."

"Since you have done it for me I esteem you all the more."

Again Mr. Banner sighed. "I hope that's true—really true."

"You know it's really true."

But though he looked very straight at her, she looked away from him at Nancy's head. She had to prompt him to continue, as if the pertinacity of his gaze made her uneasy.

"What were you going to say—it seems what?"

"It seems, if I must re-hash this gossip——"

"You must, if you wish to—please me."

Nancy gave a little start just then, which, perhaps, accounted for the jerk with which Miss Capparoni uttered the last two words.

"If I wish to please you! That settles it. I am beginning to learn what a man can do in his desire to please a woman. It seems that, according to my informant, who is undoubtedly a blackguard, Cyril Wentworth pays periodical visits—sometimes as often as three or four times a week—to a house in a Wandsworth slum, the address of which—I'll be exact—is 23, Gunner Road, Wandsworth. Sometimes he stops for a few minutes only, sometimes for hours. On five distinct occasions my informant, the blackguard spy, has knocked at the door of the house after he has left it, without attracting attention from any one within. As Wentworth always goes in and comes out alone, evidently the house is empty. Indeed, Mr. Spy has made inquiries of the neighbours, after the manner of his kind, and they inform him that the house is empty. It seems that in the neighbourhood Wentworth is understood to be a photographer, and that he uses the house to develop his plates in, and to store them. Some say that he is connected with a company which makes a speciality of films for cinematographic display, and that that explains the secrecy which attends their preparation.* That there is a secret about the house the whole street admits; but as that is a street in which secrets abound, nobody cares, and the matter goes no farther."

"You say that the address is 23, Gunner Road, Wandsworth?"

"So Mr. Spy tells me."

"Then 23, Gunner Road, Wandsworth, is Jack the Chemist's laboratory, where he distils those esoteric elixirs, the secret of whose preparation he learned from Professor Ehrenberg. Before I'm very much older I'll get inside 23, Gunner Road, Wandsworth, and I'll find out, with my own eyes, what's there."

"How do you propose to obtain admission?"

"Somehow; exactly how is but a trifling detail. Where Jack the Chemist is concerned I count burglary as nothing."

"If you will be advised by me—it won't be my fault if you are not; I, also, am capable of applying pressure—you won't do anything which will put you in the wrong. If you do, Cyril Wentworth will pursue his advantage remorselessly; you can hardly expect him not to."

"Let him pursue. I am pursuing him; a little pursuit on his

part won't harm me. I tell you that, where I'm concerned, I care no more what Jack the Chemist does than—that! Now, Nancy, that wasn't meant for you. I give you my word that not the least impertinence was intended towards you, so don't be silly."

Miss Capparoni had flicked her whip in the air by way of rounding off her sentence, an action which Nancy, in the shafts, misunderstood. As she was already spanking along at something like twelve miles an hour, she perhaps thought that a hint to move still faster was uncalled for; but since, as she supposed, such a hint had been given, she was not a pony to ignore it, so that for some minutes Miss Capparoni, who held the reins, was too much occupied to talk. By the time Nancy had been persuaded that she was not required to make a record, they had reached The Croft.

Some few minutes after their arrival Miss Capparoni was looking through the—though it was still but afternoon—reputed evening paper which John Banner had brought with him from town, when her attention was caught by some prominent headlines—

"THE DOUBLE DISAPPEARANCE.

"FRESH DEVELOPMENTS EXPECTED.

"MRS. VAN DER GUCHT'S HUSBAND."

It was the lady's name which caught Miss Capparoni's eye.

"Mrs. Van der Gucht!" she cried. "Why, that's the name of the pretty Boer woman with whom I was told Cyril Wentworth was carrying on a disreputable flirtation. I wonder if there's any connection; it's an uncommon name." She read on. "This is most extraordinary: in the workhouse! Mrs. Van der Gucht! Can it be the same!"

Her excitement seemed to amuse John Banner.

"Surely you know the story! It's been in the papers long enough."

Her manner, as she replied, was scornful.

"In the papers! As if I ever read the papers; when one's in the country, I should like to know who does."

"I do, for one; and I imagined there were others."

"Never mind what you imagined. What's happened to Mrs. Van der Gucht? and what Mrs. Van der Gucht is it?"

He told her the story as it had appeared in the newspapers. As she listened her excitement, instead of diminishing, grew. When he had finished, after she had interrupted him at least a dozen times, snatching up the time-table she began rapidly to turn the leaves.

"What are you looking for?" he asked.

"For the next train up to town, of course."

"I dare say I can give you that information, if you will condescend to ask me, and will let me know what it is you want it for."

"I am going up to town by it, of course."

"You are going up to town by it? What for?"

"My dear Mr. Banner, don't you see that at last I've found what I've been looking for for years?"

"I've no doubt that I am dull, but I'm afraid I don't."

"Cyril Wentworth has been experimenting on Mrs. Van der Gucht. Surely that is plain enough?"

"Is it? I fancy that, in some respects, your sight is clearer than mine. I only hope that the things you see are not merely the creatures of your imagination."

"They're not, at least in this case; trust me for that. That Jack the Chemist is responsible for Mrs. Van der Gucht's being in that Isleworth Workhouse* I feel certain. Since you have told me of his engagement to that pill-man's daughter, I can even guess at the circumstances which prompted him—for his own safety, as he thought—to do to her as he has done."

"But how about the man Quannell—what has become of him? The papers think that he knows more of her than he ought to do, and I confess that I'm of their opinion."

"There's a mystery there. I know nothing about your Mr. Quannell; but I repeat that I'm convinced that Jack the Chemist is responsible for that woman's condition, and, anyhow, I'm going to see her by the very next train."

"But, my dear child, what do you propose to gain by that?"

"Everything! everything! If I'm correct, so soon as I've seen Mrs. Van der Gucht, there's an end of Cyril Wentworth."

"Pray, how?"

"Don't you see? What do you see, my dear Mr. Banner? Then I'll try and tell you. So soon as I get one peep at Mrs. Van der Gucht, I shall know what's the matter with her; at least, I shall know if that particular thing's the matter. If it is, I shall telegraph instantly to Professor Ehrenberg; he said he would come directly he received a wire. He will perform on that poor woman the miracle of healing he told us about; and then—then—I suppose you can see what will happen then?"

"I can see that you seem to be taking a good deal for granted."

"I must take something for granted, mustn't I? But I'm not taking more than I'm entitled to. If I'm right—if the professor carries out his promise, then I say that Mrs. Van der Gucht will be able to tell her story, and, at last, I shall have Cyril Wentworth at my mercy. I shall go to him, and say, 'Give me back my father, at once, or——'"

"Or what?"

The inquiry came from Mr. Banner; the young lady had stopped.

"Or—take the consequences."

The conclusion, after her heat, seemed a little tame.

"Only in the case of his not giving you back your father is he to take the consequences? If he does, is he to go scot-free? That is a point on which the law may have something to say."

"Time enough to discuss points of that sort when they arise. Meanwhile, I'm going to town."

Miss Mason, who throughout the discussion had remained quiescent, at this juncture saw fit to interpose.

"Agnes Capparoni, it's bad enough to have to sit quite still while people are talking in the most mysterious way about the most mysterious things, of whose meaning you have not the dimmest inkling; but when they begin to talk about going up to town without the slightest notice, it becomes more than you can bear. Can't you wait until the morning, please? You know, Dick Sharratt is coming to-night."

John Banner answered for Miss Capparoni.

"Certainly; there will be nothing gained by going up to-night. The next train is a slow one; it stops at every station. By the time it reaches town it would be too late for you to go to Isleworth to-night; you would certainly find the workhouse closed if you got

there. The fast train in the morning will be soon enough; make
your mind easy on that score, Letty."

With that, Miss Capparoni had to be content. Mr. Sharratt
came to dinner, Miss Mason acting as his hostess with her usual
grace. Miss Capparoni and Mr. Banner went up together by the
morning express. They went across London to Isleworth. When
they entered the hall of the great workhouse, the lady stated who
it was they wished to see. Several other persons were in the hall at
the time. So soon as she had announced her errand, one of them,
a gentleman, turned and spoke to her.

"You wished to see Mrs. Van der Gucht? You are a friend of
hers?"

She supposed him to be one of the officials.

"I can hardly call myself a friend of hers, in the ordinary sense;
but if you will let Mr. Banner and me speak to you for a few minutes
in private, we shall be able to give you very sufficient reasons why
you should allow us to see her."

The stranger said, "I am Van der Gucht. I am her husband."

A man who was standing behind him introduced himself.

"My name is Quannell. I am Max Quannell's father."

CHAPTER XXVIII

THE TELEGRAM

THE encounter was unexpected; Miss Capparoni and Mr. Banner
stared at the strangers. The one who said that his name was Van
der Gucht was of medium height, slight, in the thirties, with a thin,
dark, clean-shaven, clever face, and pleasant eyes, though they were
the eyes of a man who allowed no liberties. His companion—who
claimed to be Max Quannell's father—was in striking contrast
to himself. Big and broad, with a slight stoop; unmistakably a
product of the open air. He had a thick grey beard. His skin was
bronzed. His eyes were the quiet eyes of a man who has lived for
the most part at peace with the world and with his fellows. His
huge, ungloved hands were brown, and seamed, and knotted. His
clothes, although in good condition and of good material, were

of rustic cut and easy fitting; one wondered if by any chance they could have been made at home. The whole man was redolent of something which was altogether foreign to his surroundings. One perceived at a glance that Mr. Van der Gucht was out of place; it seemed ludicrous that his companion should be there. It was Miss Capparoni who spoke.

"You are Mrs. Van der Gucht's husband? I am so sorry."

The clever-faced man smiled, a little wearily.

"Why are you sorry? I have always esteemed myself a very fortunate man. You say you are not a friend of hers; what are you then, an acquaintance?"

"I cannot even say that; I have never spoken to her, nor she to me. I merely wish to see her because I believe that if I am allowed to see her I shall be able to say what has happened to her, and——"

The girl stopped; Mr. Van der Gucht drew his own inferences from her unfinished sentence.

"And—who brought her here?"

His companion interposed. "It was not my son; it was not Max Quannell; if any one says it, I will choke the lie in his throat."

Although he spoke quietly, there was a sincerity in his tone which was more significant than bluster would have been. Van der Gucht laid his hand upon his arm with a smile which, this time, transformed his whole countenance and made it beautiful.

"Who says it? Who is so foolish? If any one says it a thousand times, do I not know Max too well to believe? He would die himself rather than that any one should hurt her. I think that the same hand struck both, my wife and your son. Perhaps this lady knows whose hand that was."

Possibly with a view of preventing Miss Capparoni from being guilty of any indiscretion, John Banner answered for her.

"Miss Capparoni—this young lady's name is Capparoni; mine is Banner, John Banner—knows absolutely nothing. Until she saw a paragraph in last night's paper she was not aware that anything had happened to Mrs. Van der Gucht; and even now she is not certain that the Mrs. Van der Gucht in question is the lady she supposes. There may be more than one person of that name."

"I hardly think it—at least in England. But if Miss Capparoni is not a friend, nor even an acquaintance, I do not understand on what grounds she wishes to see my wife. Surely it is not merely out of curiosity?"

This time the lady answered for herself.

"Indeed, it is not. If I can only speak to you in private—here we are so public—I will soon make that clear."

Just then some one came and took Mr. Van der Gucht and his companion away. Presently the same messenger, returning, ushered Miss Capparoni and Mr. Banner into an apartment where they found the pair engaged in conversation with a youngish-looking man, who introduced himself as Dr. Melville, the medical officer in charge of the infirmary. He came shortly to the point.

"Mr. Van der Gucht informs me that although you are not acquainted with his wife, you wish to see her. We do not allow strangers to visit imbecile patients. Is there any reason why that rule should not apply in your case?"

Although the question was addressed to Mr. Banner, it was the lady who replied.

"I understand that you have not been able to arrive at a satisfactory diagnosis of Mrs. Van der Gucht's case."

Dr. Melville smiled benignly, indulgently.

"Have you any medical qualifications, Miss Capparoni?"

"None whatever. For reasons into which I am not prepared at this moment to enter, I believe that I know what has happened to Mrs. Van der Gucht. If you will allow me to see her, I shall be able to tell at once if I am right; if I am, then she can be instantly cured."

Dr. Melville smiled, if anything more indulgently than before, as if he desired to convey the impression that he was conscious that this was a charming young lady, even if she did talk nonsense.

"Instantly cured? I hardly think that this is a case in which one can talk, even lightly, of such things as instantaneous cures. I fancy that it is a much more complicated matter than you have any notion of, especially if you are not medically qualified."

Mr. Van der Gucht interposed.

"Perhaps this young lady has reasons for what she says."

The doctor fastened on the adverb.

"Perhaps? There must be no perhaps, sir, in matters of this sort. This unfortunate lady has already suffered enough, without subjecting her to the risk of empirical treatment."

Miss Capparoni, in her turn, caught at the adjective.

"So far as I am concerned, sir, there will be no question of an empiric. Should my surmise prove correct, I shall send a telegram to Professor Ehrenberg, of Heidelberg University, on receipt of which he will immediately leave for London. On his arrival, in much less than five minutes after seeing Mrs. Van der Gucht, he will have cured her. I take it that you will hardly associate Professor Ehrenberg with empiricism."

Dr. Melville raised his eyebrows.

"Ehrenberg, of Heidelberg? Isn't he a chemist?"

"He is; he is the great chemist."

"I was not aware that he had any medical qualifications, or what pass as such in Germany."

The doctor's tone conveyed a sneer; Miss Capparoni turned to Mr. Van der Gucht.

"I don't wish to hurt this gentleman's feelings, which I fancy are disposed in certain directions to be hyper-sensitive; but I am speaking the literal truth when I say that if Mrs. Van der Gucht can be restored to what she was, there is only one person in the world who can do it, and that is Professor Ehrenberg. May I not see her? Every moment spent in hesitation is a moment wasted."

"I see no reason why you shouldn't. Is there any reason?"

This question was put to the doctor, who shrugged his shoulders.

"As matters stand, that has become a point for your consideration rather than for mine. Speaking for myself, I may say that I know of no reason why Miss Capparoni, or anybody else, should not see Mrs. Van der Gucht, or any other patient, so far as the patient is concerned, in the presence of a medical man. I presume you would wish to see her first?"

"Please. You are sure she will not recognize me?"

There was a wistfulness in the speaker's tone which was pathetic.

"I am afraid not. However, if you will come with me that can very quickly be decided."

The doctor quitted the room with Mr. Van der Gucht and his companion. So soon as they had gone, John Banner favoured Miss Capparoni with a few words of advice and warning, which were not so well received as they perhaps deserved. Indeed, the young lady showed signs of almost feverish impatience.

"You talk to me of being careful what I say, of measuring my words, when I feel—I know that Jack the Chemist has delivered himself into my hands at last, and that my turn has come after all these years of waiting!"

She was still in the middle of some eloquent remarks when Dr. Melville returned, alone. At sight of him she instantly stopped.

"Well? May I come? Now?"

The doctor treated her to what she was beginning to regard as his very exasperating smile.

"Yes, you may come. But you must pardon my observing that I am at a loss to understand for what reason you take such a very peculiar interest in this unfortunate lady."

"Let me see her first; there will be time to enter into the why and wherefore afterwards."

They saw her, she and Mr. Banner together. In a small chamber they found, crouching on the floor, neither sitting nor standing, a woman, or what stood for a woman. She was attired in a single nondescript garment, made of some sort of canvas. Her beautiful hair had been cut; her face had lost all its charm and beauty; her jaw hung open; her unseeing eyes were partly closed; yet it was Mrs. Van der Gucht.

Miss Capparoni glanced at her for a second, then moved forward.

Dr. Melville interposed, "What are you going to do to her?"

"I am going to look at her head."

"At her head? What for?"

"If I am right—and I am—there is a spot just here." She touched her own forehead with the tip of her finger. She and the doctor bent over the crouching woman together. She pointed with her index finger. "You see, I am right! It is there! I will telegraph to Professor Ehrenberg."

CHAPTER XXIX

UNCLE AND NEPHEW

CYRIL WENTWORTH pressed the button of the electric bell, and hammered at the knocker, hammered and hammered.* After what seemed to him to be more than a sufficient interval, the door was opened some three or four inches by a man whose eyes were yet heavy with sleep.

"Who are you? What do you want at this hour of the morning?"

Wentworth unceremoniously thrust the door open with his shoulder, and entered the hall.

"I want to see Mr. Harrison at once."

The man's negative was prompt and churlish.

"Then you can't. Mr. Harrison sees no one except by appointment, and never any one at this time of the morning. It's not yet five. He's still in bed, and will be for another three hours. It would be as much as my place is worth to wake him."

"Hang your place, go and wake him! My name's Wentworth, he'll see me. It's a matter of life and death. Go and fetch him. Damn you, man, don't stand staring at me like that, unless you wish to be hung for murder! Don't you see I'm bleeding to death?"

The man went rushing up the stairs. In a surprisingly short space of time the great surgeon came rushing down in his pyjamas.

"Wentworth!" he exclaimed. "You! What's wrong?"

"I've had an accident—cut off my finger—can't tie the arteries properly with my left hand—they're leaking—I'm nearly done."

In scarcely more than another sixty seconds, Wentworth was in the consulting-room, and the bleeding had been stopped. As he arranged the bandages, the surgeon looked at his patient curiously.

"An accident, you call it; rather a singular sort of accident, wasn't it? It looks to me as if your finger had been jagged off by a razor."

Wentworth's reply was characteristic, even at such a moment. He knew that here was a man with whom a lie would not avail;

he was not prepared to tell the truth, so he declined to tell him anything.

"My dear Harrison, don't you surgeons sometimes encounter cases of cuts, and so on, where they find it desirable to ask no questions? There are three points—and three only—to which I would ask your attention. My finger has got itself cut off—that's point one. Under Providence, I owe my life to you, for which you'll find me eternally grateful—that's point two. And point three is— what's to pay?"

The surgeon continued his bandaging; he did not again glance at his patient's face.

"I never operate under a hundred guineas."

"And cheap at the price. I wouldn't have lost my life just now for that sum several times over. I should have done it if it hadn't been for you. When you've made me look as pretty as you can, I think you'll find that—providentially—I've that amount of money in my letter-case."

After his patient had departed, still walking a little uncertainly, the great surgeon whistled under his breath—a whistle which was eloquent. Then he went upstairs again, with Cyril Wentworth's bank-notes in his hand.

When the woman who, in the mornings, "did" for Mr. Wentworth knocked at his bedroom door, that gentleman was fast asleep in bed, so fast asleep that she had to knock three times before she roused him. When he did awake it was with a sudden start. Sitting up in bed, he stared about him as if he was in doubt where he was. Then he remembered.

"Is that you, Mrs. Morley?"

"Yes, sir; it's past half-past nine, sir. Shall I get your breakfast?"

Mr. Wentworth understood; Mrs. Morley wanted to go, which she could hardly do before she had made his bed and he had had his breakfast.

"Certainly, Mrs. Morley; I shall be ready in a quarter of an hour."

When she had gone he kept looking about him as if his wits were still wool-gathering.

"That dream was infernally real. I dreamt that I'd—lost my finger. My God! so I have! It wasn't a dream! I'd forgotten!" He stared at his dismembered right hand, with its conspicuous bandage, as if it were a thing of horror. Then he consoled himself. "Better to have lost a finger than—something else. The nuisance will be the explanations; every damned fool will want to know all about it, especially—especially my future wife. But I oughtn't to find her difficult to manage."

He ate a capital breakfast, which was apparently not spoilt by an item of news which had the effect of making him think. It was contained in the first newspaper which he picked up; in those headlines which are to some people a royal road to a knowledge of what is doing in the world.

"Messrs. Van der Gucht and Quannell, *père*, arrive at Southampton and go on direct to London."

That was all. To Mr. Wentworth the few words meant much.

"I suppose that, first of all, the affectionate husband will pay a visit to his darling wife. I'm afraid he won't find her quite so charming as when he saw her last. To him, I dare say, she'll seem a good deal changed. Thank goodness she can't talk, or tell— and never will—which is something. Afterwards—pretty soon afterwards, I imagine—the pair of them will come on here; then there'll be trouble for some one. It's just on the cards that some one may be me. But the methods of diplomacy are not yet exhausted; in the hands of a master they should be exhaustless. Let's hope that I shall prove myself a master. I shall have need to be."

As he went on with his breakfast, he read his papers carefully through; it seemed that he had the gift of ceasing to think when he desired. When he had finished, Mrs. Morley cleared away the breakfast things and went; he was left alone. Unlocking the safe in the corner, he took out some account-books—all of which had locks—and began to make a close study of their pages. Their contents seemed to afford him amusement.

"Odd that a man should find himself in a position in which it would be inadvisable to allow any one but himself even to suspect how rich he really is; yet the position has its advantages. In America I'm known to be the owner of this; in England of that; in other places of those. While there are circumstances which would render it extremely inconvenient that it should be known in one country what I possess in another—and sometimes that's a nuisance—still there's this in its favour, that I can leave England to-morrow—I may have to—and go, say, to the Argentine, and be known there as a wealthy man, purely on the strength of my local holdings. That I own a few trifles in other places is a point on which I might desire to dissemble, and, anyhow, wouldn't matter. The mischief is, the world's not larger. Like Dick Swiveller,* I'm stopping up so many streets, and doing it so fast. In a few years, comparatively, if I continue at this rate, they'll all be closed; and then? Then, I suppose, the deluge. Fortunately, I never anticipate evil for myself; for others, that's a different thing. Who's that?" The inquiry was prompted by the fact that the bell rang. "It's queer that I'm getting to associate the sound of that bell with evil, the very thing that I've just been scoffing at. Bah! am I getting superstitious?" He laughed, as if the idea was too absurd. "All the same, it's a nuisance, when I wanted a quiet hour or two to put this and that together." He was gathering up his books and papers, a process in which he found his missing finger a hindrance. "It will be a while before I get used to being a three-fingered man; I keep on thinking the thing is there, and it smarts. All right, whoever you are, I'm coming; but I'm not coming before I've put these things away. Can't you give the bell a rest?" He was hurriedly returning his belongings to the safe, to the accompaniment of an almost continuous ringing. "Who is it? It's not Johnson; I wish it were. It'd save me from a visit to Gunner Road of an unusually delicate kind. But, as he himself admitted, the dear man, he hasn't pluck enough; brutes of his kidney seldom have. Can it be that African pair? It's possible. If so, I shall have to be on my very best behaviour, at my mildest and my sweetest; display, as if I were to the manner born, a cloak of innocence, as if it were the only garb I ever donned—a cloak which won't come off. It should be a pretty interview; a dainty comedy, if neatly handled." He moved towards the outer door. "Now, perchance, the curtain is about to rise."

He was wrong, so far at least as the actors were concerned. He found without, his uncle, Professor Hammond Hurle, of St. Clement's College, Camford, a visitor of whose advent he had never dreamed. His amazement was undisguised.

"Uncle! who on earth would have thought of seeing you!"

The professor's manner, as he replied, was hardly genial.

"Not you, I haven't the slightest doubt. Let me pass." As the nephew drew on one side, the little man bustled past, with an air of obvious impatience. So soon as he was in, without pausing to remove his hat, he commenced to address his relative in a strain which was not at all in keeping with his nephew's recollection of his usual manner. "I've not the slightest doubt that you didn't expect to see me; if you'd known that it was me, you'd have carried out the farce of pretending that you weren't in to the bitter end. As it is, you've kept me waiting as long as you dared. I suppose you never are in if you can help it; you're a man of that sort; your visitors being generally of the kind you would prefer to avoid; people you have swindled. But I took the precaution to inquire of the man in the hall—the porter—if you were in, and he said you were; and if I kept on ringing long enough, you'd be sure to come. Evidently the very servants know your character."

The little man, although he looked very old, and fragile, and weak, and ill, positively shook with rage. His squeaky voice trembled so that it was now and then all but inaudible. He glowered at his nephew as a toy terrier might glower at a bulldog. Whatever Cyril Wentworth felt inwardly, he was all pleasantness. He beamed on his uncle as if he were the one person in England whom he desired to see; indeed, he said as much.

"My dear uncle, what are you talking about? Nothing could give me greater pleasure than to see you. I was trying to overtake some arrears of work, and as I thought it was some bothering man who'd nothing better to do than waste his own time and mine— there are such people—I made up my mind I'd finish what I was doing before I let him in; but if I'd known it was you, I'd have flown to the door. I think you'll find this is the most comfortable chair. Give me your hat and stick, and make yourself cosy. It's awfully good of you to drop in on me like this."

The professor was not to be appeased.

"I dare say. But I don't want your chair, and I won't give you my hat and stick; I want my shares, that is what I want, sir."

"Your shares? What do you mean? You shall have whatever you want, I promise you that. Come, sit down—you're not looking so strong as you ought—and take it easy, and have a rest; then you'll be able to pitch into me all you like. What'll you take? I've some first-rate whisky; a taste of it will do you good."

"Whisky! I never touch it; and in the morning! And I won't sit down! I want you to give me the shares of which you've been robbing me all this time, and then I'll go. This is not a visit of ceremony, sir."

The irate old gentleman punctuated his words by striking the floor with the ferrule of his stick. Mr. Wentworth regarded him with an air of amusement which, possibly, was partly real and partly assumed.

"Your shares? But, uncle, what shares are you talking about?"

Neither his smile, his words, nor his manner calmed the professor. That famous scholar actually shook his stick at him.

"You know perfectly well what shares I'm talking about, you— you—I don't wish to sully my lips by using the only language which can be properly applied to you." Bang came the point of his stick down upon the carpet. "I want my five thousand shares in the Great Harry mine; that is what I want, sir."

"Surely, sir, you have forgotten that you declined to accept them."

"And you declined to take them back again, or return me the money which I had paid you."

"If you will sit down, uncle, I will draw a cheque for the £5000 in question, and hand it to you at once; or, if you prefer it, within half an hour you shall have the cash." Such was the professor's rage that he was reduced to spluttering; his nephew's solicitude was beautiful. "Uncle, calm yourself, I beg; if you don't take care, you will be ill."

"Ill!" screamed the uncle. "You talk of returning my £5000 when I want my five thousand shares! You took it for granted that I was a fool before, and you're taking it for granted that I'm a fool again; you—you rascal! But all people aren't fools, or rogues either. First of all, that girl tried to make me understand——"

"Girl? What girl?"

"Never mind what girl! But I had been reduced to such a condition that I couldn't understand; there wasn't enough life left in my old carcase; your friend Fentiman had nearly killed me——"

"My friend Fentiman?"

"That girl made it plain to me that he was your friend—and your agent. I was an old fool not to have known it all along."

"My dear uncle, I have not a notion to what girl you are alluding, or what you mean by talking about my friend Fentiman."

"Don't interrupt me when I'm speaking! But when John Banner came——"

"John Banner?"

"Don't force me to repeat my words! I said John Banner! When he came, I began to have a dim notion of how I was being swindled. I have been thinking over what he said ever since. Yesterday I saw a stockbroker, who is both an honest and a clever man, with a faculty for elucidation which I never saw excelled; he made it quite clear to me how the matter stands. You're—you're nothing else than an embezzler, sir; and I shouldn't be surprised if you're a forger also! Each of my shares is at present worth sixty-five pounds. Dividends of four, five, and six hundred per cent. have been paid on them again and again; once a thousand per cent. was paid—ten pounds on every pound share. Not one farthing of those dividends has reached me. Your pockets are stuffed with the money of which you have been plundering me; and you talk of returning me—as a final quittance—my five thousand pounds!"

"My dear uncle, your ideas on financial matters always struck me as being somewhat rudimentary——"

"You—you insolent villain!"

"I am not so certain as I should like to be that they are much more advanced now. Would you mind telling me, in as few words as possible, and without any digressions into language of a sort which I am sure you yourself would admit would sound much better in Greek, what it is you desire me to understand, and exactly what you want me to do."

"It is for the purpose I am here; under no other circumstances would I consent to breathe the air which you have contaminated."

"Uncle!"

"You have received, in the aggregate, close on two hundred thousand pounds in dividends which ought to have been paid to me. I want that money—my money, and my shares, within five minutes, or I go to my solicitor, whom I have already seen, and instruct him to have you locked up, which he will do within the half-hour of which you yourself spoke, although you are my sister's son."

Cyril Wentworth reflected, while the professor glared.

It is the unexpected which so often happens that he flattered himself that for the unexpected he was always prepared, but this surpassed the limits of the unexpected. He had counted those shares as his own—long ago. The barest formality, as he regarded it, would have made them so; indeed, had he not had reasons for not wishing to have too many shares standing in his own name, he would have had them formally transferred ages back, which he easily could have done then. But he had taken it for granted that if ever any superficial difficulties did arise he would, as a matter of course, be able to twist the muddle-headed old scholar round his finger, and diddle him precisely as he pleased. He had even gone out of his way to make sure of undisputed succession. There, in fact, was his error; he had been over-careful. Had he been willing to have let well alone, the professor would have been no wiser now than he ever had been. The day after he had learned from Fentiman what had happened at Camford, he ought to have gone down and straightened the affair out on his own lines. It might have been feasible then. Unfortunately, he had not been able to persuade himself that any action on his part was in the slightest degree necessary. Now, apparently, the matter had assumed an entirely different complexion.

But it was no use crying over spilt milk; he never did. The point was, what was he to do—now? To the solution of this problem he applied himself, while he smiled at the quaint little figure, bristling with fury, which stood in front of him; and was almost moved to ask why he wore clothes—even a hat—so much too large for him. As if the old gentleman divined his unspoken criticism, he gave sudden vent to his impatience with a blow of his stick against the floor.

"Well, sir; quick! Which is it to be? My money and my shares, or penal servitude for you?"

Of course, there was the syringe. But at the moment there were reasons why he should not resort to that, if he could help it. Later, probably, as usual, it might serve; but it would be the part of wisdom to postpone its introduction to another time and another place. So he tried to temporize.

"My dear uncle, if you will allow me to explain——"

"I won't; I will have no conversation with you. Your answer, sir; which is it to be?"

"I assure you that the matter is attended with legal complications of which you seem to have no notion. If you are in the hands of a solicitor, who is so ill-equipped for his office as to tender you such advice as you suggest, which, however, I can scarcely credit; for nothing is easier than for the lay mind to misconstrue——"

"Is that your answer? Then I'm off."

The professor moved towards the door.

"My dear uncle, these wretched shares have been a bone of contention between us from the first. Of course you shall have them, and the dividends which have accrued. It has always been my intention that you should have them."

"Has it? Then you've managed to conceal your intention."

"But it is not possible to hand you either the money or the shares at quite such short notice as you mention. I tell you what I'll do, if the proposition meets with your approval. This is Tuesday. On Thursday I will bring both the money and shares down to you at St. Clement's College—at any hour you may appoint."

"Thursday—at St. Clement's? Then I shall expect you to hand me my property at three o'clock on the afternoon of that day, in the presence of my solicitor, and other persons with whom I am acquainted."

Mr. Wentworth's smile was almost on too liberal a scale.

"Is it absolutely necessary that we should have so large an audience—between relations?"

"Relations! It's not my fault that I've a relative who's a thief! Those persons will be present for my protection, sir. From my knowledge of you, I am certain that such protection will be required. You will understand that while I decline to wait, for complete restitution, a moment after three o'clock on Thursday afternoon next, I in no way bind myself to wait so long. My solicitor is waiting for me in the street; he is in a cab at the door."

"Thank goodness," reflected Mr. Wentworth, "that I kept my fingers out of my waistcoat pocket."

"If he advises me not to wait, but, in default of instant

restitution, to proceed against you at once, I shall act on his advice without the slightest hesitation. So you are warned!"

Again the professor moved towards the door; this time his nephew let him. Cyril Wentworth remained as if glued to the particular piece of carpet on which he stood, while Professor Hammond Hurle marched out of the flat with a show of dignity which was, perhaps, intended rather than obvious, and shut the door behind him with a bang. Then his sister's son said things to himself!

CHAPTER XXX

ALMOST WITHIN THE SOUND OF WEDDING BELLS

"THE old griffin! Was ever such an unnatural uncle? I have observed that when a simpleton discovers that you have been practising on his simplicity, he becomes a very dangerous man to tackle—as dangerous an antagonist as the ordinary person could desire, because so pig-headed, so unreasonable. He can only get one idea into his head at a time; if the idea he gets is that he has to be even with you, he gets it badly. Things are shaking themselves down. I am not arranging them, they are being arranged for me. Johnson to deal with between this and to-morrow; my uncle between this and the day after; that African pair to look out for! Things look like humming. Then there's my future wife and her father; something must be done there, at once. Oh, I shall have my hands full during the next few days! Hands? and one of them without a finger!" He held his right hand out in front of him, regarding it with an odd sort of detachment, as if it belonged to some one else. "What an extremely ugly appearance it has! Nature's symmetry destroyed. It isn't only the bandage, though that's not pretty; it's—the deformity. I shall be known for ever as the man with the missing finger. I might have played it off on uncle, only I'd an instinct that his heart was stony, like one of his old Greek marbles, and that even so near and cruel, a loss might fail to unpetrify it. But I will play it off upon the lady."

He played it with an adroitness which was creditable even to one so skilled in feats of legerdemain.

During the early afternoon a brougham* drove up to the door of Mr. Bradley's house in Hyde Park Gardens, from which alighted Mr. Cyril Wentworth, very gingerly, as if abrupt movement would shatter him to pieces. With extreme care he crossed the pavement, ascended the steps, rang the bell. The man who opened the door surveyed him with amazement, so singular a transformation had taken place in him since he had seen him yesterday. Mr. Wentworth wore a long, dark, Inverness cape,* although the sun was broiling. With one hand, the left, he leaned upon a stout Malacca cane— really leaned. The right hand he carried in a sling, hidden beneath the cape. And such suffering on his pallid face. He had become a very sick man since yesterday.

"I hope, sir, you are not ill?" inquired the footman, though the inquiry was superfluous, since it was so obvious he was.

A spasm of pain passed across the visitor's face; his eyes half closed, as if to conceal what he suffered; he spoke with faltering lips.

"Thank you, Partridge. I—I have had rather a bad accident. Is Miss Bradley in?"

Miss Bradley was not only in, she came running out into the hall to greet the welcome guest.

"Cyril! I expected you for lunch, hours ago. What have you been doing?" She saw that there was something wrong, very wrong. Then she turned pale, and trembled. "What—what has happened?"

He smiled bravely, but his courage could not conceal all that he suffered.

"I've had rather a nasty experience, but I'm better now; at least, I hope I'm better. Don't be afraid; it might have been worse."

But though he bade her not to be afraid, she was afraid. While her heart began to beat against her ribs like a sledge-hammer, every pulse in her veins seemed standing still. With shaking limbs she led him into her own sitting-room.

"Cyril! Cyril, tell me—what is it?"

"Let me—let me get into a chair. I shall be able to explain better if I've something to support me."

She conducted him to a chair, guiding him lovingly with her own hands, as if he were some helpless child; and he permitted her. She took his hat and his stick; she propped him up with cushions; she showered on him those various little attentions which, if a sick man loves, a hale man hates. He endured them with a beautiful calmness, as if it were sweet to be ministered to by her. All the time she was growing whiter and whiter—he would not be so quiet if the matter were not serious—till her very lips were white. At last, when he was banked up with cushions as if he were in the last throes of a mortal disease, her anxiety could be restrained no longer.

"Now, Cyril, now; tell me the worst!"

"My darling, I've crushed my finger."

"Crushed your finger!" She had anticipated something much more terrible. She seemed a little puzzled. "Is it very bad?"

"Is what bad?"

"Your finger?"

"My darling, my finger's gone!"

"Gone!"

As she uttered the word it sounded very like a wail.

"Yes, Ellen, it was amputated this morning."

"Amputated—your finger, Cyril!"

"It had to be cut off to save my life."

"My darling!"

Kneeling beside him on the floor, she began to fondle him, while the tears stood in her eyes.

"It is the middle finger of my right hand."

"Darling!"

"So you see, henceforward I shall be known as the man with the missing finger."

"Darling!"

She again interpolated the word, as if to do so did her good, and as if she hoped it would benefit him.

"I came to tell you as soon as I could."

"Darling!" Again the endearing epithet. "If you had let me know I would have come to you."

"How sweet you are!" He stroked her hair with the fingers of his left hand, the only hand, practically, that was left to him, or so it seemed. How she thrilled beneath his touch. How she longed to precipitate herself upon his breast, only she was afraid of hurting him. In his new role of invalid he was so fragile. He went softly purring on. "Will it make any difference to us—to you?"

"Difference? How do you mean?"

"When I won you I was the whole of a man; now I'm only part. You are perfectly entitled to say, 'You are not the man I said I'd marry; you are only what is left of him, and that is not enough for me. So, of course, all ideas of that sort are off.'"

She looked at him with eyes which were not only brimming over with tears, but which were full of something else as well, an agony of reproach. Her lips twitched; she was so hurt that she could hardly speak; it seemed as if it only needed a touch for her to break out into the hysterical grief of a child.

"Cyril, do you—do you think that I'm like that? You don't, do you?"

Apparently he read in her voice, her words, her manner, all that his soul desired.

"Sweetheart, I have been so afraid. I have still one arm; won't you let me put it round you?" She stole within the shelter of his remaining arm. He whispered in her ear—her face was close enough to enable him to do it—"Ellen, will you marry me the day after to-morrow, which is Thursday?"

"The day after to-morrow—marry you! Cyril!"

She drew herself a little away from him, with an uncontrollable start of surprise, her face all red, her whole form trembling afresh.

"You see, sweetheart, I—I've had something of a shock. The doctor thinks that travelling, a sea-voyage, would do me good. I am inclined to be of his opinion if—you'll come with me."

"If I'll come with you, Cyril! I certainly wouldn't let you go alone; but—how can it be managed?"

"Easily; a quiet wedding instead of a function, that's all. We can explain; every one will understand. I'll get a special licence, and we'll just be married on Thursday! I'd love it!"

"Love it!" Her eyes sparkled; all traces of tears had vanished. Her breath came in long respirations; the colour came and went in her cheeks; he told himself that she had become almost good-looking. "Oh, Cyril; if we only could! But—so soon! It—it seems impossible! What about the house—our home?"

"They can go on with that while we're away; it will be ready for us when we return; our home-coming will be all the sweeter because of our absence."

"How long should we be away, and where should we go?"

"A few months only—till the spring; just as long as we liked. We'd go to South America; to the Argentine. I've some property there, and a house already furnished. It would serve us excellently for a honeymoon."

"A honeymoon, Cyril!" She laughed like some excited child. "It—it sounds too good to be true! But father—what about him?"

"If I've your permission to tell him you're agreed, I don't think that he'd object. Besides, he might come with us."

"Come with us?" Her tone was dubious, as if the suggestion was not altogether to her liking. "I don't think that father would be willing to do that." At that moment Mr. Bradley entered, having evidently overheard his daughter's final words.

"What is it that you don't think father would be willing to do? I beg to inform you that I'm here to speak, on all subjects, for myself. Wentworth, I hear you've been in the wars; but, come, it's not so very bad, or that girl of mine wouldn't be laughing, and she wouldn't look like that, with those pink roses in her cheeks."

Cyril Wentworth explained all over again, a little more minutely than at first. It appeared that he had crushed his finger in the hinge of his sitting-room door. Mr. Bradley seemed a little puzzled to make out how he could have done it. But when the subject was broached of the wedding taking place on the day after to-morrow, a little to Mr. Wentworth's surprise the suggestion met with his instant, enthusiastic approbation.

"I call it an excellent idea—excellent. No fuss; no flummery. Just a simple wedding in your own parish church by your own parson. Nothing could be better. After all, you are the two persons who are principally concerned, and what you want to do is to get married. I'll go farther, and say that the sooner this girl of mine is married, the better. She won't be at peace till she is."

"Father, you mustn't say such things."

"Why not? It's perfectly true. As for that Argentine trip of yours, Wentworth, I don't know if you're in earnest, and you really would like me to come with you——"

"I'm entirely in earnest. Nothing would give me greater pleasure. I—I don't want to use big words, but it would be the last drop in the cup of my happiness."

"Cyril!"

This, of course, was the lady, who was very close to him.

"I've a decent property in the Argentine, and not a bad house, though I'll not guarantee that it's furnished in quite the style which this dear lady would prefer."

"As if that matters, so long as there are tables and chairs!"

"I'll undertake to say that there are tables and chairs, and other things; in fact, quite a number of other things. I only wish to state here at once, so as to avoid all risk of future disappointment, that it's not an illustration of the last word in artistic upholstery. That's all."

"Cyril, you're teasing me!"

But, as she went still closer to him, she did not seem to mind, even if he was. Mr. Bradley, who had been fidgeting here and there, suddenly announced that he had achieved a decision.

"I'll be hanged, if I don't come with you!"

"First-rate!" cried Mr. Wentworth.

"I've been feeling for some time that I'd like a change; a real change, not your six weeks on the Continent sort of thing. I never have been to that part of the world, I've always wanted to. I needn't stop as long as you do——"

"Certainly not; you can return at any moment."

"I understand that Dering's not likely to vacate his seat for South Essex till, at any rate, the New Year, especially if I'd rather he didn't. I've no engagements which cannot be performed by proxy. There's no reason why I shouldn't stand myself a good holiday, the first good holiday I've stood myself for years; and I will—that's settled. What steamer shall we go by, and how about berths?"

"The Royal Mail steamer leaves Southampton on Friday; I'll make it my business to see that we have berths in her. You can leave that to me."

So, as Mr. Bradley phrased it, it was settled. On the Thursday there were to be wedding bells; the wedding night was to be spent at Southampton; then—for the honeymoon—there was to be a flight across the seas, towards that far-away land and Cyril Wentworth's "decent property." No soon-to-be bride could have been in a more delicious state of excitement than was Miss Bradley. Mr. Wentworth seemed almost to have forgotten that he had lost his finger. His spirits rose. It was wonderful how far advanced he seemed towards a good recovery before he left the house.

He dismissed his brougham outside a chemist's shop in Oxford Street, telling the coachman that he had no further need of his services. He certainly seemed much better in the shop. No one, except for the arm which he still carried in a sling beneath his cape, would have supposed that he was in the least degree an invalid. From the shop he took a cab to Waterloo Station. As he approached the local line booking-office he saw, just in front of him, the girl whom he had found one night in his study; who had made herself so objectionable to him at Mrs. Tallis's ball; who had interrupted, with such uncomfortable results, Professor Fentiman at Camford. Her back was towards him. She was buying a ticket; she had only eyes for the issuing clerk. He heard her say—

"Wandsworth; first, return."

In another moment the chances were that she would have turned and seen him; as it was, he was able to retreat in time.

"Wandsworth?" he said to himself. "What can she be going to Wandsworth for? It's not a neighbourhood which can offer many attractions to such as she. Can she—can she be going to Gunner Road? If she is!"

He watched her go down the platform and enter a compartment well up in front, towards the engine. He himself chose a seat in one which was right at the back. At Clapham Junction he alighted. He made as much haste as he could to a hansom, asking the driver, as he got in—

"Do you know Gunner Road, Wandsworth?"

"Yes, sir."

"Then drive there for all you're worth. If you do it in record time, I'll give you half a sovereign."

At Wandsworth Station, Agnes Capparoni asked the ticket-collector if he could direct her to Gunner Road. He reflected, then shook his head.

"Don't know it; I've only been here a short time. Perhaps one of the other chaps can tell you. Here!" He called to a porter who was passing. "This young lady wants Gunner Road."

The porter considered in his turn; he did not know it either.

CHAPTER XXXI

THE OPEN DOOR

WHEN at last Miss Capparoni did find herself outside 23, Gunner Road, she surveyed its exterior with eyes which were distinctly critical. The house, as seen from the front, looked so very dirty; so suggestive of neglect and poverty. It was not easy to make out that it was twenty-three, the figures painted on the door had become indecipherable; it was only the fact that the house on one side was numbered twenty-four and on the other twenty-two which made it clear. Before knocking, she crossed over to the other side of the road to favour it with a critical inspection; from that position of vantage she liked the look of it less than ever.

"Horrid-looking place; one can fancy that anything might be concealed behind those dingy blinds. From its appearance I should say it was empty. If there is any one inside they'll have seen me before now, and, possibly, I shall be refused admittance. But I've generally found that there are more ways into a house than one. I may as well commence with an attempt at the orthodox method."

She knocked, or, rather, she intended to knock; directly, however, she raised the knocker the door yielded in front of her. She stared at the inch or two which the door had given way with amused surprise.

"So far from being refused admission, it would seem as if I were going to get in with almost too much ease. It would be more courteous, perhaps, to announce that some one without thought of coming in, before one actually entered." So she did knock. No reply, although the door yielded still more before the assaults of the descending knocker. She pushed the door wider open with her hand. "If there is any one in there, please may I come in?"

Still no answer. Holding the handle, she opened it wide enough to enable her to put her head round the edge and look within.

"Is there any one there?" Ocular proof assured her there was no one. Going farther in, she found herself in a dirty, stuffy, ill-furnished room. "What a very unpromising apartment! It doesn't look as if it had ever been lived in, and certainly it hasn't been swept or dusted for years. I suppose there is some one in the house, or that door would hardly have been left open. If you please!" She raised her voice, endeavouring to attract attention by rapping against the floor with the ferrule of her umbrella and the heel of her shoe. Again not the slightest apparent notice was taken of her proceedings or her presence. "This is odd; almost, one would say, suspicious. I suppose I haven't come to the wrong house, and that that disreputable person who played the spy for Mr. Banner hasn't been deceiving him? I've only his word to show that the place has any connection with Jack the Chemist; if it doesn't, I shall be placing myself in a somewhat invidious position. Yet, to my mind, there's something about the place which isn't—holy; and which, emphatically, isn't sweet. And why doesn't some one come to me? I must have been heard knocking, and calling, and moving about. If you please!" She raised her voice again. "Why doesn't some one come?"

No one did come, although she called several times.

"What am I to do, if the house is empty, as it seems, and I have no actual proof—worth calling proof—who lives here, or lodges here, or is, in any sense, the tenant? I shouldn't think there'd be much harm, anyhow, in just walking through the rooms; at any rate, I shall."

She did. She explored the ground floor without discovering any one, or anything which was in the least degree interesting. Then she paused at the foot of the staircase, calling again—

"Is there any one upstairs?"

Not a sound in return. She ascended the staircase, which was narrow, and more like a ladder than like the staircases with which she was familiar. On the landing she stopped to look round. On this upper floor there were, it seemed, two rooms. The door of the one on her left was shut; that of the other, the front room, stood invitingly open. Through the open door she could see that the room seemed to be decently furnished. She advanced without hesitation, pausing on the threshold to make the usual inquiry—

"Is any one in there?"

Once more silence was the only answer. So she moved forward through the open door into the room, and the moment she was in, the door was shut behind her. Startled by the suddenness of the action, she swung quickly round upon her heels, to find herself confronted by Cyril Wentworth. Utter surprise was the first sensation with which she saw him.

"You! You here, after all!"

If she had been better acquainted with the man's personality, she would have known that the smile, the expression on his face, the something in his eyes, with which he greeted her, meant trouble. But the detestation with which she regarded him so absorbed her whole being, that it never occurred to her to fear him, or to associate him with danger to herself. His voice, as he answered, was soft and pleasant.

"Yes, I! I am here, after all. And may I inquire what you are doing here?"

She glanced round the room and laughed, with, in her laughter, scorn and hatred.

"So the gentleman who's been acting as your shadow was right, after all—this is one of your haunts; and my instinct directed me along the right lines when I guessed that it was your laboratory."

"So you have had me shadowed, have you?"

"I have had you under the closest observation for a long time now. I have been kept posted up in your goings out and your comings in. I know everything you have done, as I am going to prove to you soon, Jack the Chemist."

"You are going to prove that to me, are you, soon? What do you call soon?"

"In a very few hours now. I am going to prove to you that my knowledge of what you have done is even greater than your own."

"Are you? Indeed? Who are you, or what have I ever done to you, that you should go so far out of your way to make yourself objectionable to me—you, such a young, and—if you'll forgive my saying so—such a very pretty girl?"

"Keep your compliments for others. Jack the Chemist. Avoid

that form of impertinence to me—if you are capable of doing anything that a man should do."

"I have no wish to pay you compliments, believe me. I merely wish to know with whom I am—dealing."

Her answer was another question.

"Who is in the next room?"

"You are all curiosity in what concerns me. First of all, satisfy my curiosity in what concerns you, at least in part; then, perhaps, I'll satisfy you."

"Tell me who is in the next room? I hear some one moving. Is it—is it——?"

"Is it—who?"

"Stand away from that door; let me see for myself."

"With pleasure."

He moved on one side so as to give her free access to the door. She made a dash at the handle, only to find that it turned round and round in its socket, and that the door was actually opened and shut by some secret spring. She searched eagerly for something which would tell her how it acted; in vain. She turned angrily towards him.

"Tell me—at once—how this door is opened."

He was leaning with his back against the back of an armchair, the picture of unruffled ease.

"I will tell you nothing unless you tell me something. Answer my questions, and, perhaps, I'll answer yours. I promise you if you don't, I won't."

She was searching with her eyes, not only the door, but the room. There was something on her face which seemed to hint that, for the first time, doubts were beginning to rise within her as to her own personal safety. But her tone was still imperious, her glance, unyielding.

"I ask you again to tell me how this door is opened, or to open it."

"And I ask you again—who are you? What do you want here?" Still her eyes roved round the room with a purpose which he interpreted in a fashion of his own. "You needn't look, you really needn't. There's no pistol, or other toy of that kind, with which you can play hankey-pankey tricks, as you did on the first occasion on which I had the pleasure of meeting you. There's nothing even with which you can defend yourself against me."

Judging from the sudden glance she gave him, it seemed possible that he had read her thoughts aright.

"So you think it's necessary that I should have something with which to defend myself against you, do you?"

"Don't you?"

There was a provocative air about his manner of asking the question which, instead of angering her, seemed to put her on her guard. Her bearing became almost ostentatiously indifferent; her tone matched it.

"I have not the slightest doubt that it is always necessary to be provided with a means of defence against you; so far as I'm concerned I always am."

"Are you? Dear me! Then perhaps you'll be so good as not to go near the window; I assure you that I've no intention of allowing you to find your provision for defence out in the street, in the shape of the neighbours or of the first passer-by."

As she spoke she had moved towards the window, as if carelessly, and not with deliberate intention. He placed himself directly in her way. As their glances met she did not exactly quail, but there came into her face a quality of thoughtfulness, caution, which had not been there when she first came into the room.

"Do you imagine," she asked, "that you can play the bully with me?"

"I not only imagine, I'm sure. You, who pretend to know so much, should be aware that I'm in the habit of playing the bully, especially with women like you."

"Don't indulge in heroics, my man, as if I were an appreciative audience. Did you not hear me tell you to unfasten this door?"

Turning, she took a step or two in the direction of the door. In an instant he was after her, gripping her shoulder with the hand on which had been the missing finger.

"Come here!" he said. "You move about too much, my dear; it fidgets me."

Breaking into fury, she tried to escape his grip; but, though she exerted all the strength at her command, the attempt was unavailing; he held her fast.

"Let me loose!" she cried. "How dare you touch me! You thing! Let me loose!"

"Let you loose!" he laughed. "I'll never let you loose again till you've been a good girl and told me all I want; you may lay your pretty face on that, my dear."

Despite her struggles, putting his two arms about her, he lifted her off the ground as easily as if she were a little child, and deposited her in a huge armchair with her back to the window. While she glared, shaking with the rage which she had become suddenly aware was helpless, he stood in front of her, smiling, shaking his finger at her playfully.

"Now, if you're a wise young lady, you'll answer the questions which I'm about to put to you promptly, without any hesitation, truthfully, and as prettily as you can; if you're not a wise young lady—and one so pretty ought also to be wise too—then you'll be sorry."

"Jack the Chemist!" she replied.

CHAPTER XXXII

MR. BANNER WAITS FOR A LADY, AND DISCOVERS SOMETHING

WHEN John Banner returned to his hotel, he found that Miss Capparoni was not yet in. After the telegram had been despatched to Professor Ehrenberg, they had come up from Hounslow, together with Messrs. Van der Gucht and Quannell. At Waterloo Station they had separated. Mr. Van der Gucht, accompanied by Mr. Quannell, had departed to make arrangements for the reception of his wife on her discharge from the Workhouse Infirmary. It had been agreed that when she was in her fresh quarters, Professor Ehrenberg should, immediately on his arrival, be taken to her, in order that he might try if he could indeed make of her the woman she once had been. When the matter of the lady's quarters had been settled, then the travelling companions were to pay a visit to Cyril Wentworth, and obtain from him certain information of which they both were very much in want. John Banner had conducted Miss Capparoni from the station to the hotel at which they both were stopping, and had then gone off on an errand of his own. It was on his return from that errand that he had found the lady was absent.

He was disappointed. He had hoped to spend the remainder of the afternoon in the lady's company. To find that she had gone out, leaving no message for him, was an unexpected blow. It seemed that after he had left her she had gone up to her bedroom, whence, in a few minutes, she had again descended. At the hotel door she had got into a cab which a porter had called for her. John Banner asked himself, Where could she have gone? His was a wasted afternoon—wasted, it seemed to him, almost in the very worst sense of the word. He spent it in wandering from the public rooms to the hall, and from the hall back to the public rooms. He might have done many things. Had he not been the most abstemious of men, by way of solace and occupation, he might have consumed what some might consider an unnecessary amount of liquid refreshment. He might have gone to his club and had a rubber of bridge, which he played nearly as well as he loved it. He might have paid calls, sauntered about the streets, peeped at the galleries, looked in at a concert; instead of any of which things, he wore out his patience by persistent waiting for a lady who did not come.

As the afternoon became evening, and his impatience began to feel very like anxiety, he did what he might have done at first; he inquired of the porter if he had overheard the directions which, at starting, the lady had given to the driver of her cab. Without the slightest show of hesitation the man replied that the lady had told him to direct the cabman to drive her to Waterloo Station—the local line—which he had done. This information caused Mr. Banner to feel more puzzled than ever. One travelled by the local line from Waterloo to Isleworth. Could the lady have returned to Isleworth Workhouse without vouchsafing him a word of explanation; and, if so, why? As time passed, and still she did not come, he telegraphed to the workhouse, asking if anything had been seen of her, and then fidgeted himself into a state approximating to nervous fever until the answer came—

"Nothing seen or heard of Miss Capparoni since morning.—MELVILLE."

Then what on earth did she go to Waterloo for if she had not gone to Isleworth? There must have been some mistake, some misunderstanding. She must have changed her mind and told the driver to take her somewhere else.

He had not dined, although it was long past dinner-time. He had anticipated a delightful *tête-à-tête* dinner, and perhaps an hour or two at a theatre with her afterwards; the reality was this horrible predicament. He had even gone so far as to order the repast—quite a feast—and named the hour. He kept postponing and postponing it till at last the head waiter came and told him that, if he did not have it now, he could not have it at all, since the hour for serving dinners was already past. So he had it, the feast, all alone; a melancholy feast it was! He gave instructions to omit half the dishes; dined in under fifteen minutes, glancing continually at the doorway, in front of which he had planted himself, in hopes of seeing, at last, a familiar face and form. So soon as he had finished, he tore into the hall to ask if the lady had arrived, and, by misadventure, had not been advised of the fact that he was dining. Not she; nothing had been seen of her.

What was he to do? He must do something. He could hang about that hotel no longer doing nothing. It was after ten. Wherever she had gone she ought to have returned before now, or let him know what was detaining her by wire. He felt sure that she would have done, at any rate, this latter if something had not prevented her; what could it be? He knew his lady; how she was capable of any madness—he esteemed it madness. What wild escapade had she been indulging in? Could she have been so rash as to pay another visit to Cyril Wentworth—to have again bearded the lion in his den? In that case she might have trifled with that extremely wide-awake gentleman once too often.

Staying no longer to think—thought with such a possibility to contemplate was dreadful—hurrying out into the street and into a cab, he told the driver to take him as fast as possible to Sloane Street, to learn on his arrival at Cyril Wentworth's flat that he had come on a useless errand, in common with Mr. Van der Gucht and Mr. Quannell. Those gentlemen were standing in the hall of the mansion as he entered, conferring with the porter. They had been up to interview Mr. Wentworth, to find that he was not there to be interviewed. According to the porter, he had gone out in the morning and had not returned since. No young lady had called to see him; no one had called. Of that the porter was positive. He had been on duty since the morning; no one could have come without his knowing.

With that negative information, Mr. Banner had to be content. However, on his returning to the hotel he found that a telegram awaited him.

"Shall not return to-night.—AGNES CAPPARONI."

It had been despatched from Dover. Dover! What was she doing there? The presumption was that she had gone in order to be the first to greet Professor Ehrenberg on his arrival. If such was the case (and there could scarcely be any other explanation) she might at least have given him a hint of her intention; but—well, it was something, it was a great deal, to know where she was, that she was safe, even if she was all those miles away from him. She might have given him an address to which he could have sent a wire in reply; he would have sent her one which would have made her laugh! However, she had not. Possibly she would reach London with the professor, in triumph, at some very matutinal* hour; then—he could talk to her then.

He went to bed, as soon as he had digested the lady's telegram, so that he might be up early to meet the boat-train. All night he tossed and tumbled, sleepless, tortured, enraptured, anguished, rejoicing—all these things because of a great discovery.

He had discovered why it was that he had suffered so much on her account that afternoon and evening. When a man learns for the first time, suddenly, that the world means to him a woman, and that that woman means to him the whole world, that is apt to be an occasion to him of some disturbance.

CHAPTER XXXIII

23, GUNNER ROAD, WANDSWORTH

PROFESSOR EHRENBERG did not come by the early morning train. They had figured it out that the thing was just within the range of possibility; apparently, it had not been possible for him. Miss Capparoni had not come either. Mr. Banner, who had risen from a bed in which he had had no sleep, returned dejectedly enough to the hotel. There he did what he told himself he ought to have done before. He opened a telegram which had arrived the preceding afternoon addressed to "Agnes Capparoni." As he surmised, it was from the professor, announcing that he would arrive in London that afternoon about five by the Ostend boat-train. Had he opened it before he might have saved himself a useless journey to Charing Cross Station. He told himself that if Miss Capparoni had been there to open it, she would have been of opinion that it would not have been necessary to go down to Dover until to-day. He might have enjoyed her dear society.

Messrs. Van der Gucht and Quannell called to learn if the professor had arrived. Mr. Van der Gucht had found quarters for his wife in a quiet Kensington square; he was going to take her there at once, to await the professor's coming. He and Mr. Quannell had made another matutinal attempt to interview Cyril Wentworth, which had again failed. That gentleman had not returned to his Sloane Street rooms all night.

Professor Ehrenberg arrived at Charing Cross by the afternoon boat-train, as he had said he would. As he alighted, almost ignoring Mr. Banner, who had come to meet him, his eyes wandered in search of a lady; while, on his part, John Banner looked for a lady to follow the professor out of the carriage.

"Miss Capparoni is quite well?" were the first words with which the professor greeted Mr. Banner. John Banner stared in startled surprise.

"I had hoped to have seen her with you."

"With me? Why with me? I give you my word I have seen nothing of her at Heidelberg."

"But at Dover? I supposed, from her telegram, that she had gone to meet the steamer."

The professor shook his head.

"She was not at Dover. I should have seen her if she had been on the wharf; but she was not there."

John Banner changed colour. "Then something has happened!"

That night Mr. Banner and the professor spent for the most part in putting their heads together in endeavours to guess what had become of Miss Capparoni. Nothing further was heard from her, nor from Messrs. Van der Gucht and Quannell. Possibly some hitch had arisen which delayed the transference of Mrs. Van der Gucht from Isleworth to Kensington; but on that point the professor was not troubled.

"With that lady I will easily deal. What concerns me now is what has become of your young friend—of Miss Capparoni. After I have come so far, in such haste, it troubles me to find that she is not here, and that you do not know where she is."

Their ignorance was to continue till the morning.

Mr. Van der Gucht and his inseparable companion appeared while they were at breakfast. Mrs. Van der Gucht was at Kensington; she had been brought there late last night. As the professor was preparing to go to her, a waiter advanced with a piece of paper in his hand; a chambermaid had found it on the mantelshelf of Miss Capparoni's room. Since it had become a matter of common knowledge in the hotel that there was something mysterious about that young lady's continued absence, the girl had thought it better to call attention to the scrap of paper, though in itself it seemed wholly unimportant. It was merely the back of an old envelope, on which was scribbled, in pencil, in the bold writing which John Banner knew very well was Agnes Capparoni's—"23, Gunner Road, Wandsworth, S.W." Mr. Banner eyed it, read it, and was about to throw it carelessly away, as being without the least significance, when he suddenly remembered what it was and what it meant. He recalled her demeanour as he had told her of how the private detective had shadowed Wentworth; her exclamation that she would see what was inside 23, Gunner Road for herself.

"That's where she's gone!" he cried. "And if she has; if she went there yesterday—Mr. Van der Gucht, you must excuse Professor Ehrenberg a little longer. Ehrenberg, you must come with me, if you don't mind. I think I can take you to Miss Capparoni."

The four men went together. Outside one of the houses in Gunner Road a little crowd was gathered. John Banner observed it with a sinking heart. It proved, however, to be outside No. 24.

"What's the matter?" he inquired, as he jumped out of his cab. One of the bystanders explained, a trifle vaguely—

"A chap went mad in the night."

"Went mad in the night?"

"Lodges in this house. A chap of the name of Smith. He's only been here a day or two. Went mad in the night, he did. They're taking him away to the asylum."

As the man spoke they brought an individual—presumably the "chap of the name of Smith"—out into the street. A pitiful sight he looked. The crowd gathered closer to see him consigned to the ambulance. The herculean Professor Ehrenberg pushed his way through the people as if they were not there, crying, as he went—

"He is not mad; not at all. I know what is the matter with him! I cure him in one moment! I show you!"

An official-looking person endeavoured to interpose.

"What do you think you're up to? Who are you? Now, out of the way; we don't want none of your foreigner's tricks here!"*

The professor paid no attention; or, at least, he did not get out of the way as requested.

"I play no tricks! I tell you I will cure him, and in one second! See, he is cured!"

Certainly something surprising had happened to the "chap of the name of Smith," between the front door and the ambulance. Apparently the professor had just touched his forehead with a tiny gleaming something which he held in his right hand. A shudder went all over the supposed madman—shudder after shudder. Then he stood up straight, and looked about him—in his right mind, confusion on his face, anger in his voice.

"What am I doing out here, rigged out like this? What game are you blokes up to? You wait a bit! I'll mark you!"

"John Smith" was Mr. Johnson, late porter at the mansions in which Mr. Cyril Wentworth had his flat. The professor turned to Mr. Banner.

"We are on the track of your Cyril Wentworth. It is he who has left his mark upon our friend here!"

Johnson caught part of what the professor said.

"Cyril Wentworth! who's talking about Cyril Wentworth? I've got a word to say to him!"

While the people, disposed to talk all at once, were gathering round Johnson, John Banner was knocking at the door of No. 23. Some one in the crowd called out to him—

"It ain't no use your a-knocking, governor. There ain't no one in that 'ouse; it's empty."

"In whose occupation is it? Does any one know?"

The same voice replied, "It's a bloke as only comes there every now and again, a regular toff. In the photographic line, I've heard he is."

John Banner said to Professor Ehrenberg, "That's Wentworth; my informant was right, and the probabilities are that Agnes Capparoni came here yesterday and found him. I'm going to get inside if I have to break the door down."

Old Quannell showed sudden resource, if not much respect for the rights of property.

"One need not break down the door while there is a window."

He thrust the palm of his hand against the pane, shivering it to splinters. Some persons in the crowd cheered, others laughed. One of the officials in charge of the ambulance demanded, as an official ought to—

"Here! What are you people doing? You can't go breaking into houses just anyhow. We ought to have a policeman here if you're going on like this. What authority have you got for breaking that window, and effecting a forcible entry into that house? That's what I should like to know, and that's what somebody will have to know!"

While the official talked, Mr. Quannell had inserted his arm through the broken pane, slipped the latch, raised the sash, and climbed over the window-sill into the house. He was followed by Banner, the professor, and Mr. Van der Gucht. When various members of the crowd showed a disposition to follow them that official intervened.

"I don't know what title those gentlemen have to behave as they are doing; they may have lawful business inside the house for all I can tell; but I'm quite sure none of you chaps have, so, if you take my advice, you'll stop where you are."

The four men found Agnes Capparoni crouching on the floor in the front room upstairs. As Cyril Wentworth would have phrased it, she had been "stopped." The professor did with her as he had done with Johnson, he "unstopped" her. In the adjoining room were Max Quannell and Wentworth's whilom partner, Pietro Capparoni. The miracle-worker worked the same miracles with them—he restored them to their manhood. They were strange meetings, that between the father and the son, and that between the father and the daughter. In the continuity of Capparoni's life there was a breach of years; like Rip Van Winkle, he had been awoke from a lengthy sleep.* It was some time before he was brought to anything like a clear understanding of how matters really stood.

CHAPTER XXXIV

OUTSIDE THE CHURCH

THEY never caught Jack the Chemist—he escaped them. Within a few minutes of the discovery of what had been hidden in that Wandsworth house, the whole police of England was on the look-out for him. His whereabouts were easily and quickly ascertained. They learned that he had gone to church to be married; in church they found him. At that dramatic moment in the marriage service, when the ring was about to be adjusted on the bride's finger, some one was heard to enter the building with somewhat unusual haste. The bridegroom looked round. He saw who was coming. Agnes Capparoni was one, Professor Ehrenberg was another; behind were Van der Gucht, the two Quannells—father and son—and Mr. Johnson; while in front strode certain men who, in spite of their civilian costume, were obviously policemen. He waited for them to come no further—he understood. Without a word of warning to Miss Bradley, who a moment before had been one of the happiest women in the world, slipping away from her side, he darted into the vestry, thence into the open air beyond, to find himself confronted by two more constables in uniform.

"It's no good, Mr. Wentworth," said one of them; "we've got you."

He smiled at them. "Pardon me," he replied, in his soft, pleasant voice and inevitable air of being completely at his ease, "I assure you you are wrong; you haven't."

As he spoke he reeled, and fell—dead.* Between the altar-rail and that outer door he had slipped a capsule into his mouth, the contents of which had taken him beyond their reach.

Fortunately for Miss Bradley, she was still unmarried. In a very few more minutes she would have been a widow—of such a man. As it is, she remains a spinster. It is common knowledge that, in her writings, her criticisms of married life, and of all things which appertain thereto, have become more pungent even than before. Mrs. Van der Gucht—the subject of another of the professor's miracles—has returned to Pretoria, where she at present resides with her husband. One can but hope that she is a wiser, if not a happier, woman. Professor Fentiman has also been restored to the possession of his senses, which, in his case, is a doubtful gain to society. Lettice Mason is Mrs. Dick Sharratt; she inherited her uncle's five thousand shares in the Great Harry mine. Dr. Hurle died very soon after his nephew. Greek scholarship lost one of its finest ornaments, of a certain kind. His niece promptly turned his shares into cash.

Agnes Capparoni has, of course, become Mrs. John Banner. Her father died soon after his restoration to her—and to reason. Indeed, since he never again really enjoyed good health, and his thoughts were always with his departed wife, death came to him as a happy release. But Mr. and Mrs. Banner are as contented a couple as you could wish to meet. Professor Ehrenberg sometimes comes to see them. He is the only living person who has it in his power to become, in his turn, a spoiler of men. It is a power which he certainly will never exercise, nor will he ever again impart the secret of it to another. He says that if he had met Agnes Capparoni earlier he should have married her himself. John Banner only laughs.

THE END

NOTES

5   Opals were believed to be unlucky during the Victorian period.

8   *I may be your bravo*: This is a hired assassin.

9   The unusual facial physiognomy of Fentiman marks him as being of a criminal type according to contemporary criminology. Possibly influenced by the Italian criminologist Cesare Lombroso, Marsh often gives his villains physical traits that Lombroso describes as inherently criminal. Interestingly, the novel's main villain does not show such physical characteristics.

9   *a sort of St. Vitus' dance*: St. Vitus' Dance is a disorder that causes involuntary, spastic movement. The quick and sudden movements symptomatic of the disorder can remind the observer of a dance.

17   *Camford*: This is an amalgamation of Cambridge and Oxford, neither of which houses a college named "St. Clements". Robert Aickman, Marsh's grandson, claims in *The Attempted Rescue* (1966), that Marsh attended Oxford but was expelled due to an indiscretion involving women. However, as Minna Vuohelainen observes in her introduction to the Valancourt edition of *The Beetle*, it is likely that Marsh never did attend this university but was educated at his father's boarding school. See Minna Vuohelainen, "Introduction" in *The Beetle: A Mystery*, Kansas City: Valancourt Books, 2008, viii.

24   *The position for which he was fitted was cox*: The cox or coxswain directs the rowers of a racing boat.

30   *Every Man His Own Lawyer*: A number of books with this title were published in Britain during the eighteenth and nineteenth centuries. The intention was to help the layman with matters concerning contracts, wills, etc.

37   *one of the ills which modern flesh is heir to*: Marsh is quoting Shakespeare here, a passage from Hamlet's famous soliloquy beginning "To be or not to be".

37   *But she belonged to that genus of latter-day women which does not
     marry*: This is a description of the New Woman as she appeared
     to many during the period. The characterization of Ellen
     Bradley alludes to a number of texts and characters of late
     Victorian society, but perhaps most directly to Grant Allen's
     novel *The Woman Who Did* from 1895 (featuring a heroine who
     does not marry) and to Annie Sophie Cory's *The Woman Who
     Didn't* (1895), written in reply to Allen's book. Like Bradley in
     A Spoiler of Men, Cory was a writer who never married.

37   *A prominent Boer who had thrown in his lot with the English*:
     Great Britain fought two wars against the Dutch immigrant
     Boer population in South Africa. The war alluded to here is
     probably the second Boer war (1899-1902), an extended, costly
     and bloody conflict that made many people in Britain question
     the ability of the British Empire to keep its dominions in
     check.

42   *screwing himself to the sticking-point*: Marsh is quoting
     Shakespeare's *Macbeth* here, adapting the original passage to
     the situation.

44   Sloane Street is located in Chelsea. In the late 1890s, as today,
     this was a wealthy part of the city. The class divisions of
     London were painstakingly recorded by the sociologist and
     philanthropist Charles Booth. As a part of his ongoing project
     Inquiry into Life and Labour in London that he undertook between
     1886 and 1903, Booth produced a map of the capital that
     assigned virtually all London neighbourhoods with a colour-
     coded status, ranging from black which signified the lowest
     class, (the "vicious, semi-criminal" class) to yellow describing
     the wealthy upper-middle and upper classes. On Booth's map,
     most of Sloane Street is coloured yellow, indicating an upper-
     class population.

51   *turning the corner on his motor-car*: At this point in time, motor
     cars were still relatively unusual. Banner owning one suggests
     that he is wealthy and in tune with the times.

56   *the tale of the West Australian gold*: The Australian Gold Rush
     helped settle the continent for the British. It began as early as
     1851, and gained additional momentum with the discovery of
     new fields during the 1860s and 1870s. The Lake Darlot region

in Western Australia does exist and gold was discovered there in 1894. This discovery started a gold mining boom in the region, lasting until 1910 and there were frequent reports in the papers regarding the progress of gold mining in Australia during this period.

59 *sere and yellow*: Again, Marsh makes use of an expression that originates from Shakespeare's *Macbeth*.

69 *He still had those snapshots*: Identification through photography was still something of a novelty at the time, although Scotland Yard is known to have used professional photographers to document criminals as early as 1862.

79 At this point in time, most of the world colonized by the British could be reached through the telegraph, including South Africa.

88 *he recognized a victoria which was coming up the drive*: The Victoria is an elegant carriage drawn by one or two horses. It was named after then Princess Victoria in the 1830s and has forward facing seats for two passengers, a convertible top and an elevated coachman controlling the horses.

91 *The Bradleys lived in Hyde Park Gardens*: Situated on the northern border of Hyde Park, Hyde Park Gardens was an elegant and wealthy neighbourhood.

94 *I might have stood for South Essex*: Mr. Bradley has apparently decided to put his name up as the MP for South Essex. South Essex was indeed one of the Parliamentary constituencies of Great Britain but had actually been discontinued in 1885 to be replaced by, among others, South East Essex.

98 Wentworth here proves himself to be a part of a completely different stratum of London society. Wentworth has travelled from the affluence of Hyde Park to the poverty of South Eastern Central London. While the houses lining York Street were not poor as such according to Booth's maps, there were indeed pockets of what he referred to as the lowest class. This suggests that Marsh knew London very well.

100 *something that once had been a man*: The description of Agnes Capparoni's father as "dead", yet alive, on these pages brings a number of contemporary stories and phenomena to mind. The most famous living dead of the period was Stoker's

Dracula, of course, but Capparoni is evidently no vampire. His behaviour is more reminiscent of those hypnotised or even of the Haitian zombie which had received some attention in the papers. In addition to this, Wentworth compares Capparoni's state to that of a seed, suggesting that the state may not be terminal. See the introduction for more information regarding this.

106 *to have played the Ancient Mariner*: This refers to Coleridge's famous poem "The Rime of the Ancient Mariner." The ancient mariner carries a great burden of guilt on his shoulders and shares his story with the narrator of the poem.

108 *any reference to be made to King Charles's head*: This is a reference to Dickens's novel *David Copperfield* in which the gentle lunatic Dick is obsessed by the lost head. By 1905, the term had become a stock phrase and here it simply means that nobody is to allude to what has previously been discussed.

110 *bundled off to Germany*: Wentworth was a student at Heidelberg. It may be noted that Wentworth, like Frankenstein—and therefore in good, gothic tradition—has left his home country for a German university to study alchemy and chemistry.

114 *attended the meetings of his old corps*: This is a routine reference to the German as a being by nature a martial creature. Unlike Britain, Germany had a conscript army where one served for a period of seven years. From this perspective, it is not strange that British fiction at the time often projected an image of the German as at the core a willing soldier. At the same time, especially since Ehrenberg must visit them incognito, it is quite possible that the professor partook in the Palatinate-Baden rebellion of 1849 during which Heidelberg was the centre of resistance against Prussian forces.

117 *though he was of almost Falstaffian proportions*: Falstaff is a comical and cowardly knight appearing in three Shakespeare plays. He is a glutton and usually pictured as fat, which suggests that the German Professor is large around the waist.

122 *there is in America a man whose name, I think, is Burbank*: This refers to the American botanist and horticulturalist Luther Burbank (1849-1926) who was famous for crossbreeding plants.

135 *a fine house overlooking St. James's Park*: The St. James' park is a

Westminster neighbourhood which housed primarily wealthy people.

137 *That night a keeper in Kew Gardens had suffered from neuralgia*: Neuralgia is a nerve disorder that causes significant pain. Believed to be sometimes psychosomatic, this ailment was often treated by mesmerists or hypnotists with some success.

139 *ascending the steps of the Pitt Club*: The Pitt Club is short for The University Pitt Club. This socially exclusive and invitation-only club for male Cambridge students was well known at the time.

140 *Mr. Chandler was in the Colonial Office*: Beside the India Office and the Foreign Office, the Colonial Office was a British government agency designed to oversee and administer Britain's colonial empire. Established as early as 1768, the office's main responsibility was the colonies of North America, but as the empire expanded, and due to the American Revolution, the Office was redesigned to oversee all colonies. In 1801, the Office merged with the War Office, forming the War and Colonial Office only to be divided in 1854 into the Colonial Office and the India Office.

141 *I'd have made the welkin ring*: This an archaic term for the vault of heaven derived from the Middle English "welken" meaning cloud. Here, it essentially means to make a lot of fuss.

141 The Empire was an infamous variety theatre and meeting place in the West End, frequented mostly by the upper class. It was briefly closed down in 1894 in attempt to curb prostitution in the area. The mention of this site and the unfinished sentence strongly suggest that Wentworth is treating himself to a prostitute.

142 *The man touched his billycock hat*: A billycock hat is the same as a bowler hat.

143 *with two half-crowns in the palm of his hand*: The half crown equalled one-eighth of a pound, so that the policeman is thus given the equivalent of 25 pence. This coin was demonetised in 1970.

148 *Because I'm on my uppers*: The uppers are the bits that cover the upper part of a boot or shoe. The suggestion is that the soles have worn completely down and now consists only of the useless upper part.

149 *John Smith, 24, Gunner Road, Wandsworth*: Gunner's Road is apparently the location of Wentworth's laboratory. However, no London street is named Gunner Road.

151 *Fulham Workhouse*: Fulham is located in Northern London and a workhouse was erected there in 1848-49. At the time, a workhouse housed primarily poor people but would also function as both a hospital and insane asylum.

153 *'twere well done if 'twere done quickly*: Wentworth is misquoting Shakespeare's *Macbeth* here. The actual line goes: "If it were done when 'tis done, then 'twere well / It were done quickly" (I.vii.1-2). In the scene in question, Macbeth contemplates the murder of Duncan.

159 The French Lumière brothers, generally considered as the fathers of the cinema, took their show to London for the first time in 1892. In 1889, the British inventor William Friese Green began experimenting with the development of celluloid film, and by 1900 films were produced and shown with some regularity in London.

161 *being in that Isleworth Workhouse*: Isleworth is located in West London. There was an Isleworth workhouse there at the time.

168 *Cyril Wentworth pressed the button of the electric bell:* The electric bell was still a novelty in 1905 and suggests a wealthy owner of the house. Evidently, Wentworth does not feel that it is likely to make sufficient noise to wake the owner in question and therefore also makes use of the knocker.

171 *Like Dick Swiveller, I'm stopping up so many streets*: Dick Swiveller is a character in Dickens's *The Old Curiosity Shop* (1840-41).

178 *During the early afternoon a brougham drove up*: The brougham was a closed, horse driven carriage more stately than the victoria or the hansom.

178 *Mr. Wentworth wore a long, dark, Inverness cape*: An Inverness cape is a multilayered coat from Scotland useful in bad weather, or, apparently, when dissembling an illness.

192 *at some very matutinal hour*: Matutinal means taking place in the morning.

195 *we don't want none of your foreigner's tricks here*: The late nineteenth and early twentieth centuries were marked by xenophobia as much of the fiction from the period makes

evident. To many British, foreigners were people who resorted to tricks, and when the Ripper murders were perpetrated in 1888, Queen Victoria suggested that foreign ships in the Thames should be searched for evidence (Tropp, 112-113).

197 *like Rip Van Winkle, he had been awoke from a lengthy sleep*: Rip van Winkle is a lazy but likeable farmer who sleeps for twenty years in a story by American writer Washington Irving.

198 *As he spoke he reeled, and fell—dead*: Marsh's villains tend to escape due process of law by suddenly dying or disappearing. This is a pattern repeated in several of his crime novels and gothic tales.

www.ingramcontent.com/pod-product-compliance
Lightning Source LLC
Chambersburg PA
CBHW011354010726
47494CB00008B/2306

9 781934 555071